Endorsements

I've read June's first two books, *The Estate Sale*, and *Legacy's Path*, beautifully written. It's my privilege to endorse June. Her Southern charm and open-hearted friendship ring true every day, and I love her writing.

Sylvia Stewart, Author, *Sweet Romances Series.*

I was drawn to the promise of finding treasures in June's first book in this series, *The Estate Sale*. She weaves the story of strangers drawn together through the Estate sale. Her second book, *Legacy's Path*, is a mix of friendship, adventure, love, forgiveness, and healing. This series has touched the deep places in my heart and speaks to my soul.

Joyce Ainsworth, Author, *Food, Fitness, and Freedom.*

Whether June Chapko is writing fiction or non-fiction, she has a way of connecting with readers. Her novels and devotional book feel like we're invited to tea and conversation with someone who cares. Not only is this author a talented writer, she has the gift of hospitality through words.

Joy Pater DeKok, Author and Blogger

Reading June Chapko's, *The Estate Sale*, is all the proof I needed to read the third in her Legacy Series. She has the uncanny ability to be lighthearted where needed, to keep the mystery and action lively and enticing, and yet, to chisel out a nugget of serious and common-sense truth that keeps you glued to the very end. *Legacy's Truth* will put the bow on the top when giving this trio as a gift for a dear friend (or perhaps, a treat for yourself).

Judy Sheer Watters, Author, Writer, and Editor

Legacy's Truth

The Legacy Series: Book Three

Legacy's Truth

The Legacy Series: Book Three

JUNE CHAPKO

Chapko, June
Legacy's Truth
The Legacy Series: Book THREE
First Edition

Publishing services provided by 40 Day Publishing
www.40DayPublishing.com

Contact the author at Amazon.com/author/junechapko
www.facebook.com/teatimewithjune
junesteacuptreasures.com

Front and back book covers by Thompson Printing Solutions

This book was printed in the United States of America.

Acknowledgements

I am grateful to you, the reader, because otherwise, there would be no reason to write.

Heartfelt thanks to Hal Carson, for your eagle eye and dedication in pulling it all together.

I'm grateful for the support I've received from my daughters, Kathleen Garcia and Susan Smith.

To my Pastor, Aaron Treanor, and my church family at Brookhill, for always pushing me *to get the next book finished.*

Thanks to Betty Woehlert for sharing your memories. I will always appreciate Janie Hughes, for bringing me soup and candy. I'm indebted to my friend-I-haven't-met-yet, Sylvia Stewart, for your valued suggestions and continued prayer.

I appreciate my husband, Nick, for his love, patience, and belief in me.

Also to my precious Shih Tzu, Chai, for taking naps when I sit down at the computer.

I'm in awe at how God, without whom I would have no message to write, gave me what He wanted me to write.

Chapter 1

7 A.M.

As Director of Mt. Laurel Assisted Living Center, Kenneth Cavanaugh was the first one alerted to the news of a fire at the center. He now raced to get there and help staff get the residents to safety.

"How could this have happened?" he shouted as he zipped down the highway, pounding his fist against the steering wheel. "We just had an inspection two weeks ago and everything was fine," he insisted, screaming to the empty car.

He saw smoke before he rounded the corner. *"Please, God, let all the residents be okay and protect the firemen as they work to put out the fire,"* Kenneth prayed as he pulled up to the curb, keeping a good distance from the fire trucks. He slammed on his brakes, shut off the engine, and jumped out of the car.

Kenneth couldn't believe the scene he stared at. The kitchen and dining hall windows were gaping holes and the surrounding red brick, now blackened soot.

"Nooo!"

"You must move back, sir!" A fireman spread his palm over Kenneth's chest and forced him back.

"I'm the Director here," Kenneth bellowed. "I need to do something—to help!"

"Please, sir. Move back. We need room to work.

"But the residents—I need to help them."

"They are fine," said a voice from the crowd of firemen monitoring hot spots. The Fire Marshal, Louis Allen, overhearing

Kenneth's pleas, made his way quickly over to him. "Don't worry, the nurses reacted quickly when the fire alarm sounded. They moved the residents out into the vehicles here and transported them to your event building on the next property."

Kenneth's knees shook. *"Thank You, Lord,"* he offered as he looked upward.

"I have EMS over there checking each one for any smoke inhalation or problems," the fire marshal assured the director, "but since the resident building wasn't affected, I'm sure they are all fine. Things are under control here for now, but we will stay on top of it until we're sure there are no flare-ups."

"Thank you, sir," Kenneth said, extending his hand.

"Would you have any reason to suspect foul play?" the fire marshal asked.

"No! Definitely not!" Kenneth answered without hesitation, "Why would you ask that? Did you find anything to make you think it was deliberate?"

"No, it's a routine question. I'll be conducting an investigation to determine the cause."

"We just had our regular inspection two weeks ago and passed with flying colors. I don't understand how this could happen."

"We'll find out. You know, you're very fortunate that the fire was in the west wing. The resident's rooms being in a separate structure kept them from harm. There isn't any damage to that area at all. The damage seems to be contained to the section housing the kitchen and dining areas."

"Thanks again. If it's okay, I'm going to run over to the event building and check on everyone and see what I can do there."

"You go ahead. Oh, here's my card. I'll be here for quite a while though."

"Great, once I see the residents are okay, I'll be back," Kenneth said, hurrying to his car. He slid into the seat and immediately called Jewel. "Honey," he said when she answered, "meet me at the event center. The nurses moved everyone over there and I'm headed that way."

"I've been waiting to hear from you. I'll take off now and see you shortly."

***

"Are you warm enough, Clarence?" Greta asked her husband, pulling the quilt close around his shoulders. Thankfully she thought quick enough to grab it when the fire alarm sounded, and the nurses rushed everyone out. Greta was concerned about Clarence since he had only been released from the hospital a few weeks ago. Developing cellulitis in his mid-nineties almost took his life. "Your prosthetic is still in our room, but we're not going to worry about it."

Clarence sat quietly in his wheelchair and took hold of Greta's hand. "I'm fine. Get a chair and come sit by me. I'm sure we'll be okay and back in our own bed before we know it."

Greta managed a chuckle. "You're always the optimist." She spotted a folding chair and slid it over next to Clarence's wheelchair, just as Nurse Josie approached wearing her usual smile.

"Here are two cups of hot chocolate," Josie said, handing one to each of them.

"Just what we needed, thank you, Josie," Greta said.

"If you need anything just wave at me."

"We'll be fine," Clarence said before taking a sip from the cup. "Aah, this is perfect."

"Have you heard anything from the director?" Greta asked.

"He's on his way and should be here any time," Josie reassured the couple.

***

"Of course, I will," Betty told Jewel over the phone. "I have plenty of blankets and I'll make sure we get breakfast over there. I can call around and we will all pitch in. Tell Kenneth we are on our way."

"Thanks, Betty, I knew I could count on you. I'm on my way to the event center now to get coffee going for everyone. I'll see you in a bit," Jewel said before ending the call. She wondered how bad the damage was.

Driving through traffic delayed her but before long she saw the assisted living building on her left. Tears sprung from her eyes as she saw the damage and smoke. She drove by slowly and turned at the corner to reach the event center. Jewel drove to the entrance and parked.

Getting out, she spotted her husband's car and the EMS vehicle. Her stomach churned a bit, not knowing what was happening inside. She rushed in and came face-to-face with Kenneth.

"Hi, Honey," he said, giving her a quick hug. "All the residents have been checked out and are doing great. God was really watching over us."

"He sure did," Jewel said, looking around at the residents. They walked together toward the kitchen. "What started the fire?" she asked. Jewel began prepping the large coffee urn, pouring water into the stainless-steel coffee maker.

"The fire marshal said they would let me know, but since the fire was contained to the kitchen and dining hall, he believes it was electrical."

"I saw the building when I passed by, and it looks devastating."

Kenneth removed the coffee canister from the cupboard and handed it to Jewel. "It looks worse than it was. I'm going back over there now to see what they found."

"I spoke to Betty and she's arranging for food to be brought over so the residents can have breakfast. Be careful and let me know something as soon as you get answers."

Kenneth gave his wife a quick kiss on the cheek as she put the lid on the urn and switched it on. "Great, I'll see you later."

***

One of the firemen, Ryan, greeted Kenneth with a helmet as he entered the burned building and escorted him to check the damage. "You can see for yourself what happened," Ryan said. "Be careful when walking in the kitchen, that's where the worse damage is."

The fire marshal turned and called Kenneth over to where the dishwasher was located. "We believe this is the culprit," he told Kenneth. "The fire originated here."

Kenneth's jaw fell. That dishwasher is only six months old, and the warranty is still good. I already called my insurance company."

"We took a lot of photos, so you can have copies if needed." Louis said. "I'm sure the insurance adjuster will take some of his own photos as well."

"Thanks, I would like to go to the resident's building and see for myself that it wasn't damaged."

"Ryan, take Mr. Cavanaugh to the resident's area so he can observe for himself there was no damage."

"I'd be happy to."

***

Betty Hills hung up the phone. It was the last call to order meals for Mt. Laurel Assisted Living Center. She arranged for breakfast to be sent out as soon as possible and made sure the lunch order was placed. Betty sat still for a moment, still trying to comprehend what happened. She and Kat had prayed when Jewel called earlier to ask for her assistance with meals, thanking God no one was injured in the fire. *Poor Clarence and Greta, they must be rattled. I need to get over there and see how I can help.*

"Kat, would you check with Rita and Ron to see if they would be available to help at the center?"

"Sure, Mum. Do you want me to call anyone else? Our estate sale group is always ready to pitch in, you know."

"Great idea. Ask Ron if he would help contact the others." Betty thought for a moment. "Maybe not Emily and Seth though. They have enough going on with Emily's doctor appointment coming up this week."

"They might be hurt if we don't let them know."

"You're right. Just tell them what's going on, but leave it to them if they want to help."

"I'm on it," Kat said, taking out her phone. "I'll be there when I'm done."

The ringtone on Betty's phone alerted her to Brian's call. "Hi, Honey," she answered. "Anything new at the center? I'm about to leave and head over since I've taken care of the meals."

"No," Brian said, "the investigators are still working to find the cause. I've been helping Kenneth get things set up for the residents to stay in the event building for the night just in case they won't be allowed back in their rooms."

"Do you really think that might happen?"

"It's a precaution. We want to be ready."

"How are Clarence and Greta holding up?"

"Clarence has been a trooper. He said this is a piece of cake compared to how he braved the elements during the war."

"And Greta?"

Brian laughed. "The last time I saw her she was helping Jewel and Kenneth with coffee."

Betty chuckled "Those two were meant for each other."

"I gotta go, break is over," Brian said. "We're putting up dividers for a little privacy."

"Okay, Kat and I will be there in half an hour and breakfast should arrive soon too. Love you."

She hung up and grabbed her handbag along with a box of snacks she had in the pantry. *The workers may need something to nibble on.* After locking the door she hurried out to join the others at the center.

***

Rita Crawford couldn't believe the news she received from Kat Hills. The assisted living center caught on fire, displacing residents at least temporarily. She called Ron and they agreed to drop everything and make themselves available. Thankfully, no one was injured, and the fire seemed to be contained to the kitchen.

Kat said breakfast was being provided by a local restaurant known for its generosity and lunch would come from a neighboring eatery. It was amazing how people came together to help in times of need. *I wonder what we can do to help out.*

The sound of Ron's car out front caught her ear. She locked up quickly and headed out.

Sliding into the passenger seat, she gave him a swift kiss before they backed out and headed for the center.

"Thanks for picking me up. Are you ready to dig in and lend a hand?"

"How do you think we can help?" Ron asked.

"I was wondering the same thing, but they wouldn't have called if we weren't needed."

"It's possible some residents may need transportation to appointments. Maybe we can help out there."

"Ron, that's a great idea. We can check with Mr. Cavanaugh or the nurses."

"Will the others in the estate sale group be show up?"

"I think most of them, except Emily and Seth. She is seeing a doctor this week, but I'm not sure what day."

"Yeah, I've been praying it all comes back negative."

"We all have," Rita whispered.

***

"Hi, everyone," Kenneth said, welcoming the small group of people he had come to know through Betty Hills. She was the creative woman who brought light and joy into the lives of two of his residents, Greta and Clarence, by featuring them in a documentary film about the elderly. Betty, along with her husband, Brian, and his daughter, Kat, had responded quickly when they heard about the fire and relocation of the residents at Mt. Laurel Assisted Living.

Others, he came to know as The Estate Sale group jumped in and began helping Jewel with food and refreshments, making sure those who needed rides to doctor appointments were transported there and back, and keeping spirits up while Kenneth dealt with the insurance investigator and fire marshal.

12:00 Noon

"Kenneth," Brian called from across the hall, "I've secured the back rooms with partitions, so all we need to do is bring in beds if and when necessary."

The director approached Brian and shook his hand fervently. "Thanks, Brian, you're one handy man in the biggest sense of the word."

"No thanks needed. Glad I could help. The partitions are temporary so if we get the all-clear to move people back to the main building, these folding walls will come down quickly."

"You're a genius. I appreciate all the hard work. Let's take a break and get some coffee and some of that spaghetti I smelled when I was passing by the kitchen."

Brian rubbed his growling stomach and laughed. "Right on cue." Together they headed down the hallway following the aroma of spaghetti sauce and hot French bread.

***

4:00 P.M.

Easing her tired body onto a chair in the dining area of the event center, Kat gazed around the room, catching a glimpse of people helping people. *Our estate sale group has generous hearts and hands.* It didn't matter how much or what type of job needed to be done, everyone pitched in and made things happen. Even the assisted living residents who were able did what they could to help those less agile.

Kat smiled seeing Greta take paper towels to a table where someone had spilled a glass of tea. *She was in her nineties and serving others.* Kat remembered their first meeting when Betty and the film crew went to interview Greta. What a feisty and needy woman she was. The transformation in her from then to the film debut over the holidays was beyond belief. Greta came to trust the Lord and then accepted Clarence's marriage proposal. She stood by him during his sudden illness, and everyone rejoiced at his recovery and their hospital-bed wedding. Now, here she is helping others during this crisis.

"Excuse me," a fireman interrupted Kat's thoughts, "may I join you?" he indicated by pointing to the chair next to her.

Kat looked up into the most beautiful brown eyes she thought she'd ever seen. She remembered seeing him from a distance earlier when he was checking smoke alarms in the building. He could reach them without a ladder. He was about thirty with arms strong enough, she thought, to carry several people at one time from a burning building.

"Oh," she finally responded, hoping she didn't act like a teen with a crush, "no, I don't mind. Please have a seat." She noticed he had a bottle of water half gone. "Would you like another bottle?" Kat nodded toward the one he held in a large hand. "Maybe a snack or a coffee?"

He smiled, revealing even teeth and a deep dimple in each cheek. "I'm fine, just thought I'd introduce myself. I'm Ryan Ladderman. I noticed you when I was doing inspections and...."

"Ladderman?" Kat produced a small laugh, not wanting to insult him or giggle foolishly. "Ladderman is really your name?"

Ryan let loose a hearty laugh to put her at ease. "I get that reaction a lot. It's definitely my real name. My parents used to tease me growing up that I would one day become a firefighter. Birthdays and Christmas I'd always get fire trucks and action figures related to firemen."

Kat relaxed a bit and laughed. She felt at ease with him. "I'm sure they're proud of you. Were you born in Texas?"

"No, I'm from Crofton, Maryland originally. I joined the Air Force and came to Texas. When I finished the service, I applied to the fire department and here I am."

"It's nice to meet you, Ryan. I'm Kathy Hills. My family and friends call me Kat."

"May I call you Kat?"

"I'd like that very much," she answered softly.

Ryan looked around the room and then turned back to Kat. "I'm not positive, but I think the chief may give the okay for everyone to move back to their rooms tonight."

Kat's eyebrows arched quickly. "Really? Did he tell you that?"

"Not directly, so I guess I shouldn't get your hopes up. I overheard him talking to the insurance guy, and he said he felt the cause involved a faulty part in the dishwasher. But since it was only the kitchen area affected, he didn't see any reason to keep these folks from their rooms."

Kat was excited and hoped it was true. These people had been through so much.

"How did you get involved in helping out here? Are you related to someone here?" Ryan asked.

"It's kind of a long story, but no, I'm not related to any of the residents."

"I like long stories. Maybe we could go get a bite to eat later and you could fill me in?"

Kat looked straight at his inviting smile. "Oh yes, I'd love to.' She blinked to bring herself to the present. "I'd have to see if I'm needed here first. Even if the residents get to move back tonight, I'd want to be on hand to help."

"I finish my shift tomorrow morning and then I have four days off. Maybe we could get together for breakfast, lunch or dinner on one of those days."

Kat felt a little embarrassed thinking he meant tonight. She lowered her head hoping not to blush. Finally composed, she looked up to see that beautiful smile. "I can give you my number, and we can touch base when you've rested."

He rose from the chair. "Sounds great, we think alike. I'll be back for it before I head out. Right now, I better check with the chief and see where we are as far as inspection goes."

Kat's heart pounded as she watched him stride away. She couldn't take her eyes off of him. Suddenly tiredness left her, and she went to find Betty and her dad. On the way, she jotted her phone number on a scrap piece of paper she found on the counter and tucked it into her jeans.

***

Brian joined Betty in the kitchen just as she finished tying the last of the trash bags. "I'll take them to the dumpster, Honey."

Betty looked up to see her husband sprint over and take command of the refuse. "My knight to the rescue," she said, offering her cheek for the kiss he planted with great enthusiasm. "Any word about the building? Will we be moving residents back to their rooms?"

"I'm not sure but I saw the fire chief talking to Kenneth about a half hour ago. It would be great to see it happen."

At the sound of Kat's voice in the doorway, Brian turned to greet his daughter. "Where have you been camping out?"

"Just catching my breath, a little. I visited with each of the residents and tried to encourage them a bit. Then I plopped down and rested for a few minutes. Why? Do you need me to do something?" Kat caught sight of the trash bags. "I'm sorry; I should have checked in with you, Mum."

Betty smiled at the endearing sound of Kat addressing her as Mum. "Not a problem, sweetie, I just finished, and your dad offered to take them out. We're hoping to hear something good from the fire chief soon."

"Oh, I was talking to Ryan, one of the firemen working inspections..."

"You were, huh?" Brian asked, narrowing his eyes humorously.

"Well, he sat with me while I was resting. He's a nice guy. His last name is Ladderman and he's from Maryland."

"Seems you learned a lot in a short rest break," Betty joked.

"Ladderman?" Brian chided. "Are you serious? That's his name?"

"Yes, it is, and I think it's a great name," Kat said defensively. "Do you want to know what he said or not?" she teased.

"Of course, we do," Betty agreed, "don't we, Brian?"

"Certainly," he managed to say while containing a grin.

"Ryan said he thought he heard the chief telling Mr. Cavanaugh that the residents might get to move back to their rooms tonight."

"Oh, that would be wonderful," Betty said, softly clapping. "Why don't we try to find him, and if that's true we can begin helping everyone get moved."

Brian agreed and the trio headed to the main event room to find Kenneth. Brian kept pace with his daughter and hooked his arm around her shoulders. "So, Kat, does Mr. Ladderman have any family around here?"

Kat looked up at her dad to see if he meant the question to tease about her interest in Ryan or if he really wanted to know. His quirky grin would give him away in a flash. There it was the curve in the corner of his mouth. She quickly faked an elbow punch to his rib. "Dad, you're impossible," she said, barely making her words heard.

Instantly she spotted Ryan standing with the fire chief and the facility director. Heat warmed her cheeks. Now her face was probably red. She shot her dad a squinty-eyed look of warning.

Brian couldn't help himself when it came to teasing Kat. He knew, however, when enough was enough, so he winked at her and stepped over to speak to the men and see what was on the schedule.

Betty hugged Kat as they held back a bit to give the guys time to discuss the plan of action for the residents.

"Excuse me," Kat said softly to Betty. "I'll be right back."

Betty watched as Kat moved quietly toward the men, reached in her jeans pocket and handed a slip of paper to Ryan. They smiled and Ryan mouthed a thank you before Kat moved back.

Betty grinned as Kat looked at her.

"What?" Kat asked.

"Nothing, I didn't see a thing."

Kat laughed a bit. "He just wants to have coffee sometime."

Betty raised her eyebrows and rolled her eyes a little for emphasis. "Sounds like a date to me."

"Not you too, I hope. First Dad and now…."

Betty hugged her stepdaughter warmly. "I think it's wonderful, but I thought you and Clay were, oh, I don't know, in some kind of relationship?"

Kat moved away from Betty just a little and her face tightened. "Clay and I aren't serious. We're more like friends. I thought maybe our relationship would grow or change, but it hasn't."

"Did you tell him how you feel?"

"Yes, on several occasions. He thinks we need more time and who knows, maybe he's right. I'm not sure I want to invest more time when I know in my heart I'm not attracted to him like that. I've prayed and don't feel he is who God has for me."

Their conversation was broken as Kenneth gave out a hearty "Amen!" All heads turned toward the men who were shaking hands. After the men dispersed, Brian almost bounded to where Betty and Kat stood.

"We are good to go," he sang out. "The residents will be permitted back to their rooms, and we can get things rolling now."

"So, they found the cause?" Betty and Kat quizzed almost in unison.

"Sure did! It was the dishwasher. A faulty part was to blame."

"Didn't I hear that the dishwasher was pretty new and under warranty?" Betty asked.

"Exactly," Brian reassured her. "The insurance company will handle everything. Since none of the other areas were affected, they have deemed it safe to return."

Betty placed both hands on her chest and exhaled. "I'm ecstatic for the residents and for Kenneth. It must be a huge load off his shoulders."

Brian nodded. "For the kitchen workers, too. They were nervous and concerned they might have been at fault."

Kat smiled broadly as Ryan waved from the doorway. She waved back. "Okay, can we get started moving people back to their rooms now?"

"Kenneth is working out the plan, so let's go get our marching orders," Brian said.

Chapter 2

The sterile atmosphere of the imaging room at the medical center was just a memory as Emily entered her home. She inhaled and allowed her breath to leave slowly as she sighed and welcomed the warmth of the home she shared with Seth. All she wanted right now was a cup of tea and her recliner.

"Honey," Seth spoke quietly. "I'll put water on for tea if you'll get comfortable and relax."

She turned and touched his face gently, letting her fingers glide down his cheek. The look Emily saw on his face assured her of his protection and care no matter what lay ahead. "Thank you," she whispered, "there's chamomile in the cupboard."

Seth watched his wife make her way slowly out of the kitchen. His heart was heavy when it should be shouting with joy, knowing their first baby was on the way. God chose this time in their lives to knit together a precious child, and yet He also allowed a lump to form in her breast.

He filled the kettle with cold water and set it on the stove. He managed to find her favorite tea cup and the tea. Now he understood why she found brewing tea contemplative. It takes time and offers a space of grace to sort out thoughts privately. *You can't rush tea,* Emily explained once. *It's ready at the proper time.* He stood there with his jumbled thoughts, listening as the water rushed around inside the kettle. His thoughts did the same. *Tell me something, God.* Suddenly the kettle whistled, and Seth jumped. *It's the proper time.*

He pulled a tray from the cabinet and set everything in place, adding a crescent roll and jam in case she was hungry. Seth put on a smile and prepared to remind his bride of his promise that together they would get through this.

Emily relaxed into the white leather recliner, allowing the foot rest to support her feet. Her stomach was upset, and she suspected it came from the uncertainty of the test results. She had expected to hear "It's just a benign cyst." But instead words like suspicious, irregular lines, biopsy, filtered through her ears. *Why now, Lord? Just when I find happiness.* Emily was thankful Seth was with her because she wouldn't have been able to drive home. Her mind was jumbled, and she couldn't focus. Instinctively her hands folded over her stomach. *Our baby.*

Seth placed the tea tray on the coffee table, handed Emily her cup, and sat in his chair next to his wife. "I hope I made your tea the way you like it," he said softly.

"It's perfect, just like you."

"I love you, Emily," Seth spoke quickly while he could still speak without tearing up. His heart was heavy, knowing there was nothing he could do to make the lump in Emily's breast go away.

"I love you more," she said after sipping the steaming mug of tea. She set it down on the side table between their chairs and turned to look straight at her husband. "I don't want to do anything that will endanger our baby. I'm in only my first trimester, and I won't agree to any treatment or drug if there's the slightest possibility of our baby being harmed by it."

Seth nodded his head. "Let's not borrow trouble. After you get the biopsy done next week, and we know the results, we can deal with whatever is ahead. Right now, we're going to trust God and believe for the best."

It was Emily's turn to nod in agreement. "I know, but it's just this sickening in the pit of my stomach."

Seth rose from his chair and knelt by his wife, taking her hands in his. "Whatever lies ahead, we'll face it together. We have each other and God." He felt Emily tremble. Releasing her hands, he gathered her to his chest, holding tight as she began to sob. His heart wrenched and soon the outpouring of his tears melded with hers.

***

Jake Davis surveyed the childhood residence he never thought he would live in again. Boxes stacked in the living room brought home the sharp reality of his mom's death. The decision to move back came with reservations, mostly about memories. How would he be able to move forward with his life when living here chained him to his past? Not that his past was bad, he enjoyed his childhood and was blessed to have had loving parents. With his mom passing just a few months' prior, Jake was caught in a tangle of knowing she wasn't suffering, yet wanting to have her back. *Purely selfish.*

A sound on the porch startled him. Jake jumped a little at the intrusion to his thoughts and turned to the front door. He came eye to eye with Annie.

"Hi, Jake," Annie almost sang the greeting.

"What a surprise," he stammered. Opening the door, he gave her a slight hug. "What brings you this way on a Saturday?"

"I remembered you telling me you'd be moving back here, so I brought lunch." Annie held up a large Cracker Barrel bag. She smiled and handed it to Jake. "I hope I didn't intrude."

Jake felt remorseful at his behavior. Retrieving the bag from Annie, he welcomed her with a genuine hug. "Come on, let's put this in the kitchen and dig in. This is great because I didn't feel like going out for lunch, and I'm sure not in the mood to cook."

Annie relaxed. "Good. I brought chicken pot pies, hope you like them."

"Sure do. My mom made the best ones...."

Quiet settled in the room until Annie began unpacking the dishes from the bag. "I'm sure these won't measure up to Lillian's, but they'll fill our belly and give us nutrition," she teased to keep the mood light. "And no dishes to wash."

They sat at the kitchen table and Jake apologized. "This moving back took a toll on me this morning. I don't know if it was the right thing to do or not."

Annie broke open the crust on her pot pie and allowed the steam to escape. "The way I see it, Jake, you are taking charge of a situation and I admire your courage."

He stared at his pie and followed suit by slicing a line across the top. "Courage?"

"Yes. Facing memories in your childhood home but with the intent to move forward and make it a home to adult in. That's not an easy task."

Jake puffed on a spoonful of the chicken mixture to ward off a burned mouth. "I like the sound of that, a home to adult in. I really do. I can change things by redesigning and repurposing what's here."

Annie dotted her mouth with the paper napkin in between bites. "I'd like to help if you'll let me."

He gazed at her and smiled. "Help is what I'll need. Did you see the mountain of boxes stacked in the living room? There are more in the back of the house, too."

Annie laughed out loud, a good-natured, loving laugh. "I'm great at creating space and organizing, but you'll have to make the big decisions about where to put your belongings."

"It's a deal," Jake agreed. "Are you off all weekend?"

"I work the late shift tomorrow night, but I'm at your service till then."

***

Rita stood, hunched over her worktable in the new studio Ron had purchased as an early wedding present. She paused from scribbling out a design onto draft paper. *My own studio.* She couldn't imagine a more perfect gift. He had given Mr. Roddis a check for the down payment the very day he brought her to look it over. She would hold sculpture classes for the inner-city kids, work on her own art pieces, and have showings all in one place. It was air conditioned, had ample parking, and even a stage out front. There were renovations Rita wanted to work on in the studio, ideas to put her personal touch on the place. She smiled, thinking about the kids' classes which wouldn't begin until summer. *The kids will be so surprised when they walk into the new studio.*

Her eyes scanned the rough sketch in front of her, following the never-ending curves of the cross. Rita wanted to give Ron something special for a wedding present and decided to sculpt a unique infinity cross for the garden in the home they would purchase soon. It would be a promise, a symbol of their love for each other and God. The design needed work, but Rita would begin gathering materials, keeping everything under wraps until April.

The vibration of her phone in her pocket made her jump. She dug it out and saw Ron's number on the screen. "Hello, how's my favorite man?"

"Tired," Ron's voice returned. "What a week. With the fire at the center, building walls, moving residents...tired sums it up."

"Aww, Honey, I'm sorry. I know the day I was helping was exhausting. Sorry I wasn't able to stay and do more."

"No, you were a big help. We had a lot more show up, too, but things are good. The residents have resumed their lives and insurance has damages covered. The kitchen will be back in business by Friday, complete with a spanking new dishwasher."

"I'm happy to hear that. Why don't you come over for dinner tonight? I can throw something together or we can order in."

"I'd love to. Ordering in seems the easiest, and we'd have time to just enjoy the evening instead of you cooking."

"Okay, I'll see you later then. Love ya."

Rita felt Peko brushing against her leg. She reached down and cradled the orange ball of fur in her arms. He purred his approval. She was glad she brought him with her to the studio. He enjoyed roaming around but loved the cozy hideaway Rita had arranged in her office behind the desk. Apparently, it was lunchtime or close to it. She glanced at the clock and decided they would leave now and be home in time to whirr open his favorite seafood.

Setting him down with a pat on the head, Rita began locking up before putting him in the carrier. She gathered her keys and kitten and headed out the door. Tonight, Ron would be over, and she needed to decide what to have for dinner, too. She loved to cook, especially for him. He always showed his appreciation no matter what she served. Rita loved that about him.

Talking to Peko as they walked the short distance to the trolley, Rita asked if he wanted chicken for lunch. "Chicken for a king," she stated. "OOOH, that's what I'll fix for Ron tonight!" she shouted. "King Ranch Chicken! He'll love it and it won't be a fussy meal." She mentally pictured her tiny pantry and refrigerator, assessing if she had everything she needed. *It will be so nice to have a large kitchen, a big refrigerator and a deep freeze.* The sound of the trolley brought her back to the moment. Rita waited at the stop while the trolley halted in front of her. She stepped in, carefully holding Peko's carrier so not to bump him. Looking up, she came eye to eye with Blanca, the lady who was part of the estate sale group.

"Hi, there," Blanca said, revealing genuine warmth in her smile. "How have you been?"

"I'm doing fantastic," Rita answered, returning her smile. "I haven't seen you in forever. I thought you retired."

"I put in my paperwork, and I'm working only part-time until it's finalized."

Rita slid onto the seat by the door, placing Peko between her and the window. A meow echoed displeasure when the carrier bumped the pole. "Oops, sorry," Rita said softly, reassuring her pet.

"You still in the same place, Rita?"

The trolley moved forward. "Yes, but not much longer. Ron and I will have a house soon and once we're married, we'll get settled in. He bought a building for me close by here to have for my own studio to teach inner-city kids about sculpting. It's exciting to know I can expand now and help more children. Speaking of, how's your daughter, Bree. Isn't that her name? Is she still working with Missions in Mexico?"

Blanca, being an astute driver, kept her eyes on the road, but enjoyed hearing about Bree's success in teaching kids in a remote village of Mexico. She also told Rita about Rosie moving out to go live near her son on the east coast and now how empty her place felt.

"Do you have plans for after you're officially retired?" Rita quizzed.

The trolley slowed as two passengers from the back approached the front to exit. Blanca opened the door after making a complete stop and wished the riders a blessed day. They waved as they stepped off. The doors closed and Blanca continued her route.

Rita waited, wondering if she should ask Blanca the question again, but finally she spoke.

"Not exactly. I toyed with the idea of doing mission work but at my age, I don't know where I'd fit in or how much I could do. I've also thought about traveling. Maybe go visit Rosie for a start."

"You definitely have options and travel can be fun," Rita suggested. Then as a food-for-thought comment, she added, "Have you asked God what He wants you to do?"

Blanca was quiet but seemed contemplative. "No, I have to confess I really haven't, other than thinking about the missions idea. Thanks, I'll work on that."

Rita smiled. "Here's our stop," she said, standing and gripping tight to the pole with one hand while picking Peko's carrier up with the other.

The trolley came to a stop and Rita let go of the pole and gave Blanca a quick hug before descending the two steps to the sidewalk. "It was great seeing you again," she called as she approached the crosswalk toward her apartment.

Blanca watched the young woman as she padded with her pet across to her residence. *She's right, I need to see what God wants me to be doing with my life.* She closed the doors and pressed the pedal, moving on to the end of the line. Blanca would spend time doing just that.

***

Rita set the pet carrier down beside the couch and freed Peko. He found his water dish and indulged deeply before he went on the hunt for his mouse toy and retreated to the corner play area. Knowing Ron would be over tonight spurred her to check out the pantry and get things lined up to make her King Ranch Chicken later. "You're on your own, Peko," she laughed as she headed for the kitchen.

Her thoughts roamed to the work going on at the assisted living place, and she wondered if she should make extra to deliver for tomorrow. Her recipe was easy to triple. Yes, she would.

Chapter 3

Greta sat at the easel and contemplated the canvas. It was taking shape, but she had so much to learn. Taking up painting seemed simple enough when the teacher had presented it to the residents last month. The instructor commented that even at her age, Greta seemed to have a bent for it. Of course, Greta had no idea there would be so many decisions to make regarding the type of paint, brushes, and even canvas. Thankfully, Cora, her instructor, guided Greta along to eventually choose to work in acrylics. She went so far as to help her pick the correct brushes, set up the canvas, and discuss topics.

When Greta was younger, lighthouses always fascinated her. The idea of a structure built at the edge of water and rocks to guide ships in and prevent them from crashing both amazed and comforted her. They reminded her of her dad until he left. There was no one around to protect and comfort Greta or her mother after that.

When Betty and her film crew appeared on Greta's doorstep last year, there was no way Greta could have imagined how things in her life would change; providing her with a lighthouse of such power and love, Greta would never be the same. Jesus had become her lighthouse. After all, He had been searching her out for a long time. Greta smiled as she gazed on the canvas sketch. It was primitive and yet the scraggly etched shoreline was a beginning. The shadow of a tall building loomed over the water's edge, waiting for Greta to bring it to life and switch on the light.

"Greta?" The familiar voice called from the other part of their living quarters.

Her thoughts, now broken, responded quickly. "I'm in here, Clarence. Do you need me?"

When no answer came, Greta set her brush down and carefully moved toward the doorway. As she approached their shared room, she smiled at her husband. He sat on the bench he used when trying to attach his prosthetic leg. Greta took in the scene. The artificial limb had slid out of his reach and was beyond the wheelchair as well.

"I'm sorry to bother you," Clarence said. "I tried to do it myself but lost my footing." He began laughing out loud. "Lost my footing...that's a good one," he chuckled.

Greta shook her head, laughing along with him. She was used to his sense of humor. Reaching down, she retrieved the leg, maneuvering the wheelchair around as well. "Good thing I was here, or you'd be stuck on that bench all afternoon." She handed him the limb and set the brake on the wheelchair. "You need to keep the chair close by, my love." With that, she leaned in and kissed his cheek.

Clarence laughed again and pointed to a spot on her temple. "What's this?"

Greta straightened up and looked in the mirror on the wall. "Paint!" She used the corner of her apron to wipe the smudge away. "I was fiddling with my lighthouse painting. I want to get more done on it before Cora comes tomorrow."

"I can't wait to see it," Clarence said excitedly.

"There's not much to see right now, but I think it will take shape soon. I've decided how to do the paintings."

"Paintings? Plural?"

"Yes," Greta continued. "There'll be a story attached to them. Lighthouses fall into disrepair and aren't useful that way. People can find themselves in the same situation, don't you think, Clarence?"

Her husband glanced down at his limb, now attached. "I think so, Greta," he said, his eyes meeting hers. "I believe you're right."

***

Kenneth Cavanaugh made his rounds among the assisted living residents, trying to assess the success or failure of moving them back to their rooms. He loved talking with each person and hoped the trauma of the fire hadn't upset them unduly. So far, Mrs. Green seemed to be the only one to voice concern. Her emotional state wasn't stable before the fire, so Kenneth halfway expected she would react more deeply. He assured her all was well and explained that he'd ordered a nurse to stay with her for the remainder of the week. She was agreeable to the plan.

Now he needed to go to his office and make a few calls. This whole fire issue could have been a tragic event. As it was, no one was hurt and the cause had eliminated wrongdoing by anyone. The insurance company assessed the damages and work was complete. The contractor assured Kenneth that the roofs would be done by Monday. A faulty part on the dishwasher proved to be the reason and the manufacturer made good on everything. Still, Kenneth wanted to put other steps in place to be able to weather any type of similar event.

"Hello, Mr. Knox, this is Kenneth Cavanaugh. I'm the director at Mt. Laurel, I called earlier and left a message. I'd like to have you come out and look at our event building and give me an estimate on a remodel."

"I'd be happy to; Mr. Cavanaugh. Would nine in the morning work for you?"

"It works fine with my schedule. I'll see you then."

Kenneth checked that item from his to-do list. Remodeling the structure wouldn't be easy or cheap, but Kenneth believed it was a long-term solution. Getting several bids would be a step in the right direction and allow him to feel he was doing something positive. It wouldn't cost him anything to find out what price range he would be in.

***

Kat waited for Rita to answer her phone. She hoped her friend was home and would be available to talk. She had no idea what to do in the predicament she was dealing with, and Rita always seemed to know the right questions to ask and advice to give. She counted the rings one ... two, three....

"Hello, Kat, it's nice to hear from you," Rita said cheerfully. "What's going on in your life?"

"I'm good. I was afraid you weren't home." Kat shifted nervously in her rocking chair. "I need to discuss something, and you're the only person I feel can help."

"Aww, Kat. I was cooking and putting a King Ranch Chicken dish in the oven. Ron is coming over tonight. I have time now to talk if you want."

"Well, I'd rather talk in person. Do you have plans for tomorrow?"

"No, we could do lunch if you want. Want to give me a clue as to what's bothering you?"

Kat sighed. "It's complicated."

"Okay," Rita said, "Why don't you come here tomorrow at noonish, and I'll heat up leftover King Ranch Chicken, if you don't mind leftovers. In the meantime, try to do something fun."

"Thanks, and I love leftovers. I hope you and Ron have a nice evening."

Rita hung up the phone and wondered what Kat had on her mind that she seemed so desperate to discuss. After the chaos last year with Jared cleared up, it couldn't be that.

Peko purred and meowed simultaneously, catching Rita's attention. She reached down and scratched behind his ears. "Ah, you smell the chicken don't you, pussycat? Sorry, it's not your kind of food. Besides, you just ate, so go find a sunny spot to catnap."

Peko seemed to understand and padded his way to his favorite napping place by the window.

***

Brian relaxed on the sofa, listening to Betty's activity in the kitchen. Dishes clicking and flatware tinging as she unloaded and put away the clean load. He felt a tad guilty for not helping, but he was worn out. It had been a long week helping at the assisted living residence after they received the go-ahead to move everyone back in. *That's not fair, Betty helped just as much.* He swung his feet to the floor and found Betty loading a new batch of dishes. He gently ushered her away. "I'll load these, you go rest a while."

Betty gave her husband a kiss on the cheek. "Thank you, but I think I'll go take a long soak in the tub first."

He smiled. "You deserve it. I'll finish up in here and maybe we can watch a movie later."

Betty was halfway up the stairs and called down, "Sounds like a plan."

Brian glanced at the wall clock. Eight thirty. *Wonder why Kat isn't home yet?* She was going to meet with Clay briefly before heading home. Maybe they decided to grab something to eat. Since Kat met the firefighter at the assisted living place, she hadn't gone out with Clay, so that didn't seem likely. *I hope this doesn't interfere with the filming Betty has planned.* "Young love," he whispered, "how complicated."

Betty and Brian shared the sofa as *Citizen Kane* started. They both shared a love for classic movies, and this one was dubbed 'best film ever made'. It didn't matter if you saw it before, it was still the greatest. She always pretended to be surprised to find out what "Rosebud" meant.

Kat arrived home about nine-thirty and after quick hugs announced she was going to bed early. She didn't wish to get into a discussion about Clay with her dad or Betty right now. Her meeting with him this evening was strained, and she knew that he wasn't happy with the way their relationship had turned. Kat's biggest concern was how it would affect the film company. He was a great videographer, and she told him as much. Betty loved his work and was looking forward to seeing how he dealt with their next project. Kat hoped Clay would honor her trust in him regardless of their relationship.

She showered and got comfy, stretching out on the bed. Kat looked forward to a good night's sleep and her lunch date with Rita tomorrow. Maybe her friend would offer wise counsel. Her thoughts turned to Ryan. He was working the rest of the week but would have the weekend off. They had plans to do something. Kat liked his spontaneity. Of course, as a firefighter, he could not easily plan things in his life on a schedule. She snuggled into her pillow and closed her eyes, still seeing him in full firefighter gear riding on the truck, ready to rescue. She loved how her name sounded when he spoke it in his deep voice, like he was protecting it...or her.

***

A satisfied sigh sounded from Betty as the last of the Citizen Kane credits rolled over the screen. "I love this film," she told her husband.

"You love films, period," Brian said, hugging his wife, now snuggled against him on the sofa.

"Only *well-made* films," she said firmly.

"Speaking of," Brian brought up, "how's your new project coming along? You haven't said much about it. Have you and your crew met and made any decisions?"

Betty sat up straight and arched her back into a slight stretch. "Not exactly."

"What does that mean?"

"The last meeting I had with Clay and Kat was a bit strained, so we covered only a few basics. Neither of them seemed to have put his or her heart into it, and I'm a little concerned about their commitment."

"I don't think Kat would give you any less than her best. Remember, she's getting ready to finish her degree, so she may be preoccupied."

Betty looked at her husband thoughtfully. "No, it's not that. We talked recently about how excited she is to finally be done with college. Kat doesn't have any qualms about grades or anything. It's definitely something else."

Brian nodded. "I have to agree about her excitement over finishing college. Do you think there's a conflict between her and Clay? I know she's been seeing that firefighter lately, but I'm not sure where Kat and Clay stand. I try not to get involved in her relationships unless she comes to me first."

"You're right. She needs to ask if she wants advice. I just need to know where they both stand concerning our film company. If one or both want to do something else, I'll have to get busy and find replacements."

Brian turned off the television as Betty headed toward the stairs, shutting the light off as he followed. The nightlight on the stairway guided them.

"All of that is discussion for another day," Brian whispered, putting his arm around his wife's waist.

"I know. I'm praying it will all be resolved by divine intervention."

"That's entirely possible," Brian assured her.

***

"Rita, that's the best King Ranch Chicken I've ever eaten," Ron declared, "even measured against my mom's."

"Wow, that's a real compliment." Rita stood to clear the plates from the table and bent to give her fiancé a kiss on the cheek. "I'm glad you enjoyed it."

Ron rose and gathered a few dishes, following her into the small kitchen. "You realize the plates are spotless already. Neither of us left a smidgen behind, so there's no need to scrape them." He placed what he carried carefully into the sink.

Rita laughed. "There's just enough left for tomorrow when Kat comes over for lunch. It's a good thing you didn't want a third helping."

Ron put his arms around her small waist and kissed her neck. "Kat's coming over tomorrow? Special occasion?" he asked, releasing her from his hug.

"I don't know really. She called and wants to talk, so I invited her for lunch."

"While you ladies have your soiree tomorrow, I'll be over at the art studio finishing up the details of the traveling art show."

"I wish I had gotten in on that but the pieces I hoped to enter weren't ready by the cutoff date. Maybe you can arrange to have another one later in the year?"

Ron dried his hands on the dish towel and headed toward the living room. "I'm not sure. We'll see how successful this one is first."

"Want some coffee or tea?" Rita called out.

Ron plopped himself on the sofa. "I'll take some iced tea if you have any."

"Coming right up. Regular or peach?"

"Regular please."

They sat quietly and sipped their tea before Rita spoke.

"Have you spoken to the pastor at your mom's church about coming here to perform our wedding?"

"I did call but his secretary said he was out for the week, and she'd have him call me back when he returned."

Rita sighed slightly. "Isn't that the second time you've tried to contact him?"

Ron knew this was coming. Rita wanted everything buttoned down well in advance and she probably thought he was stalling.

"Yes, but in fairness the first time was after the holidays, and he was playing catch-up."

"Maybe we should drive to Mesquite and talk to him in person."

"We still need an appointment. Don't worry. I'll connect with him, and we'll get it all arranged."

Rita wondered if that were true. Ron always looked at things as if they couldn't possibly fail. While she loved that trait when he was encouraging her in her sculpturing, she was a bit apprehensive about it when it came to their wedding plans.

"Okay, Love, this is your one part of the planning besides the honeymoon, so I'm trusting you to make it happen. And, speaking of our honeymoon, have...."

Ron stopped her. "Don't ask. Remember, I want to surprise you."

"I shouldn't have agreed to the surprise part. But you are working on it, right?"

"Yes, my Dear, I'm working on it." He leaned in and kissed her gently. "Don't fret."

***

Kat pulled her VW into the parking space near Rita's studio apartment, shut off the engine, hopped out and locked the door. Her stomach lurched. Kat suspected her body's reacting to nervousness about talking to Rita was causing distress. She approached the small porch and rang the bell. Almost immediately Rita appeared and opened the screen door.

"Hi, Kat, it's great to see you again! Seems like a long time. Come in."

"Thanks," Kat said. As she stepped inside she was greeted by fragrant food and Peko's meow.

"Hello my fur-buddy," she said lovingly "You look well-fed and happy." She reached down and stroked his back, causing Peko to stretch under her hand. Turning to Rita, she commented on the aroma filling the air.

"Lunch smells heavenly."

"Well, I hope we have enough. Ron ate two large helpings last night, and I almost matched his appetite. I made an avocado salad to go with it."

"That sounds delicious."

"By the way, I made another batch to take to the assisted living center, if you think Betty would be okay with dropping it off."

Kat helped Rita put everything on the table and poured the tea. "She wouldn't mind a bit, and I know the residents would enjoy it. I'll be happy to take it home with me."

"I froze it and wrote out the directions for preparing it."

"Great, I'll make sure to give it to her."

After they were seated, Rita joined hands with Kat's to pray before digging in.

"Lord, thank You for providing for us and watching over our comings and goings. May You bless this food and cause our bodies to be strengthened that we might serve You better. Amen."

"Amen," Kat said in agreement.

"So," Rita began, "what's on your mind that brings us together to discuss?"

Kat hesitated by taking a bite of the King Ranch Chicken and chewing thoroughly before setting her fork down. "I find myself in an awkward situation, and I'm not sure how to handle it."

Rita took a bite of the salad and waited for Kat to continue. When she didn't, Rita drank some tea and asked, "What kind of situation?"

"You know that Clay has been part of the filming for Betty's documentaries, and also a good friend to me."

"Yes, y'all are dating, aren't you?"

"Not exactly. For a long time I considered him as I would an older brother. We went out to eat a few times, and he assumed it would lead to something."

"But it hasn't?"

"I tried to give it a chance, which was all he asked at one point. But I just don't feel attracted to him from my heart. He's a good friend and does fantastic with filming, but I can't act like I'm interested in a relationship when my feelings say something different."

"Apparently you haven't told him all this or you wouldn't be wanting my advice."

"You're right. I met with him yesterday to see how he felt about the filming. He's sensed my feelings, I think, and now he's acting like he doesn't want to continue working with Betty. That concerns me because it's not fair to her. I feel it would be my fault if he quits."

"Have you discussed this with Betty?"

"No, not yet. But there's a little more to my dilemma."

"Oh?"

While I was helping out at the assisted living center, I met this guy, a firefighter named Ryan."

"Ah, now the pieces are coming together. You are attracted to Ryan and don't know how to tell Clay...or Betty."

"I think Betty knows. She was there the day I met Ryan. But, yes, I don't know how to tell Clay and still keep our friendship and work relationship. Remember, I'm part of the filming crew, too."

Rita continued eating while she mulled Kat's words around in her head. Finally, she asked, "How long have you known Ryan?"

Kat looked quickly at her friend. "Not very long, just since a couple weeks ago. Why?"

"Well, I'm just thinking that you may or may not develop a romantic relationship with him. Suppose it doesn't happen. Would you then turn to Clay?"

Kat was surprised at the comment and question. "My possible relationship with Ryan doesn't have anything to do with Clay. My feelings toward Clay have nothing to do with Ryan. I've known for some time that I'm not attracted to him, so to answer your question, no."

Rita winced at Kat's reaction and thought she might have hurt her feelings. "I didn't mean to offend you; I just wanted to see if there was a connection. Did you plan to tell Clay about this firefighter?"

"I thought about it but now that you mention it, I probably shouldn't. Maybe I'll just reemphasize that I want us to be only friends."

"That's what I think, too. Then no matter where you and Ryan go in a relationship, it won't affect your work with Clay and Betty."

Kat smiled. "Thanks. I knew I could count on you to guide me in the right direction."

Rita drank the last of her tea and seeing Kat's glass near empty, rose to refill them both. She headed into the kitchen and noticed Kat bringing dishes to the kitchen as well.

"Don't bother with the dishes, Kat. I'll put things away later. Let's just talk and enjoy our tea. I have some things I'd like your opinion on."

"If it's about marriage, you ought to talk to Betty," she said, laughing.

Rita chuckled. "No, but it is about the wedding."

"Great, I love talking wedding stuff. I know you're getting excited. It's only four months away."

"I am excited. Ron has only two things to be responsible for. One is the honeymoon to who knows where, since he wants to surprise me. The other is to secure the services of his mom's pastor to come here and perform the wedding. It seems he still hasn't even made contact with him. I've been halfway tempted to contact his brother, Jake, and see if he can get us an appointment with the pastor."

"Ouch, that stings. Do you think Ron would feel hurt if you went that route?"

Rita led the two of them back to the living room and took a seat, indicating for Kat to do so as well. "He may not be so much hurt as upset. I just think we need to move faster to get that done."

"I don't know much, but my mom always gave Dad the benefit of the doubt and even when he messed up, she let him take ownership of it."

"Hmmm, you're right. Ron is usually responsible and if I can't trust him to secure the person to perform the wedding ceremony, I won't be able to trust him with the marriage. Thanks, you've helped me solve my own dilemma."

Kat laughed. "Well, we're even then." She glanced at her watch. "I really need to go. I want to get back and call Clay."

Kat picked up her purse and gave Rita a hug. On cue, Peko rubbed against her leg. Kat picked up the orange ball of fur and gave him a hug, too. "See you soon, Peko." He jumped down and went looking for his mouse toy. "Okay, I'm gone...thanks again for lunch and advice."

Rita walked her to the door.

"Oh, wait. I almost forgot the dish for Betty. Let me get it." Rita disappeared into the kitchen and returned with the foil-covered pan.

"Thanks again," Kat said, taking the pan carefully after slinging her purse strap over her shoulder.

"Want me to carry it out?"

"I can handle it," Kat assured her.

They waved goodbye as Rita watched her friend head for her car.

Alone now, Rita ran their conversation through her mind again. She decided that Kat had more wisdom than the girl realized. "Thank You, Lord, for godly friends."

***

Clay Young picked up his phone and saw Kat's name. He almost decided not to answer; After all, they just had a meeting last night and it didn't end the way he hoped it would. In the end, curiosity took over and he punched talk.

"Hey, Kat, what's going on? I thought we covered everything last night," he said curtly.

"Hi, Clay, I know we talked about some things, but today I realized that I left out something very important."

"What might that be?"

"We've known each other a good while and you've been there for me when I needed a friend. I believe God caused us to be friends, and I don't want anything to destroy that. When we've had previous conversations about our relationship, there was always a remnant of thought that it would turn into a romantic one."

"I actually thought it was at one point," Clay interrupted.

"You asked me if I would give it a chance, if I remember correctly. I did try. We went out to dinner, movies, and hung out a lot. The thing is, Clay, I enjoy our friendship without the pressure of romance. I like who you are and that you love the Lord. You're fun to be around and work with. I would like it to stay that way."

Silence.

"Clay?"

"I'm here. I just don't have a response to that. I need time to think about it."

"Do you think we can at least work together on the filming?"

"Is that what you're concerned about?"

"Not just that. I mainly want us to be friends but we both committed to the upcoming film project, and you're the main part of the film crew. It wouldn't be a success if we didn't give it our best."

"I wouldn't let Mrs. Hills down. She's treated me well and I respect her. Of course, I'll do my part."

Kat let out a soft sigh. "Thank you, Clay. I really do consider you a good friend."

Clay smiled to himself even though he wanted to give a retort. "I'm glad, and I want you as a friend, too."

"Thanks," she said, meaning it deeply. "I think Betty wants to get going in a week or so, and she'll let us know when she has a date and subject."

"Great, I'll be ready. Will it be someone from the same assisted living place?"

"I don't think so, but who knows. Remember, this documentary will be different."

"Oh, that's right. Well, we'll find out soon."

"Clay?"

"Yeah?"

"Nothing, I'm just glad we talked again."

"I am too, see you soon."

Kat hung up her phone, feeling much more at peace about things between her and Clay. The best part is that she really did consider him a good friend and didn't want to lose him. Rita was right, regardless of what happened with Ryan, the friendship with Clay was not connected, and she didn't want to destroy a friendship.

She reached the staircase and caught a hint of Betty's soup wafting up the stairs. Kat loved homemade soup, and Betty had several great recipes. This had to be the vegetable and sausage. Hurrying downstairs to the kitchen, she found her stepmom stirring the large soup pot.

"Hi, Mum, smells like vegetable soup today."

Betty turned around and smiled at the loving name Kat gave her last year. "Mum" was endearing and brought them close together.

"Hi, Sweetie, you smelled correctly. The official name is Janie's Friendship Soup."

"How did you come to name it that?"

Betty replaced the lid and set the large spoon on the spoon rest, then took a seat at the breakfast bar. She patted the bar. "Come join me and I'll tell you the story behind the soup."

Kat slipped onto the stool and sat wide-eyed. "It sounds intriguing."

"Years ago, after my father died from a heart attack and my mother died a week later, quietly in her sleep, I had funerals to plan. My church family surrounded me with love, and they all pitched in. They brought so much food, and I kept thinking it would go to waste. Then one sweet lady, her name was Janie, brought a large pot of soup." Betty paused and pointed to the pot on the stove. "She pulled me aside and told me she shared her soup with many people who lost loved ones, were dealing with illnesses, going through hard times, and many other occasions."

"So she gave you the recipe?" Kat asked.

"There's more to the story than the recipe. Anyway, what she told me I've never forgotten. She said that she prayed over every ingredient that it would meet not only nourishment needs, but spiritual needs as well. I do, too, now. That's why I named it Janie's Friendship Soup."

Kat looked into tear-filled eyes as Betty seemed to be remembering. "That's such an expression of love and friendship. Thank you for sharing it with me. I just had a phone conversation with Clay today. It was about the importance of friendship." Now Kat's eyes watered.

Betty reached across the bar and patted Kat's hand. "Friendships are to be treasured. They are a reward for unselfish giving."

Kat nodded because the lump in her throat wouldn't let words pass.

Brian called out as he entered the house. "Must be someone home. I smell soup!"

"We're in the kitchen," Betty answered. "Come join us."

"Ah, my two favorite girls. What time do we eat?" he asked, kissing each on the cheek before taking a seat.

"How was your day? Did you have a nice drive back from the writer's cabin?" Betty inquired.

"Sure did and managed to make a lot of progress on the book. I wanted to include Greta in the last section, since they were married last year."

Betty laughed. "That was generous of you."

"Well, the book is about Clarence after all. But his story wouldn't be complete without her."

"Indeed, whether in life or in the book. They belong together and at their age, it's a God thing that they met and married."

Betty rose to begin setting the table. Kat stood and offered to help.

"What can I do?" Kat asked.

"The oven is preheated so if you'll put the artisan bread on a sheet pan and warm it, I'll get the bowls and utensils."

"I'll sit here and wait for the soup ladle, and then I'll dish it up," Brian offered.

Kat and Betty rolled their eyes at the same time.

Chapter 4

Emily and Seth waited in the Obstetrician's exam room. They held hands, each consumed with their personal thoughts of what the doctor would reveal to them since getting the biopsy report. Emily glanced down at their hands entwined.

"No matter what the doctor says," Emily whispered, "God will not allow anything to harm our baby or come between us."

Seth squeezed her hand and with his free one, wiped an escaping tear from his eye.

"I believe that, and I know we'll get through this. God brought us together and we will be stronger through this challenge." He let go of her hand and took her in his arms. He could feel her body tremble a bit, and then relax.

A slight knock on the exam room door separated the couple as they said, "Come in."

"Hi, I'm Doctor Rebecca Sanders." She smiled and extended her hand. "How are you both doing today?"

Seth stood and shook the doctor's hand while Emily nodded.

"We're a bit anxious but want to know what's going on."

"Of course," the doctor acknowledged as she pulled up a stool in front of the computer screen and tapped a few keys to bring up the images and information. "I have the results from all the tests thus far, including the biopsy." Rebecca Sanders was focused on the screen and yet well aware of the young woman sitting silent. She'd seen it so many times and it always tugged at her heart. As a doctor, she must remain calm and provide the facts without emotion. This time, the patient was in her first trimester of pregnancy, so the stakes were high.

"I've been in touch with your oncologist and your primary doctor, so we are all on the same page. She turned and looked directly at the concerned young couple.

Emily spoke for the first time. "Dr. Sanders, I want to tell you something."

"Certainly, what is it?"

"My husband and I have made a decision."

Doctor Sanders was puzzled. "You have? What kind of decision?"

Emily looked at Seth and he nodded.

"No matter what you tell us, we will not allow any treatment no matter how slight, which could endanger our baby."

Rebecca gave a deep sigh. "Of course, and I would never suggest a treatment which would put your baby at risk." She turned to the computer screen. "In the first trimester of pregnancy, *if* a lump is malignant there are some things we can't do, but there are still other options which will protect a baby and the mother. We can also delay some treatments until after the third trimester."

Emily sat up straight. Her throat closed for a moment. She managed to swallow before speaking. "You're telling me that my lump is malignant?" Emily began to cry uncontrollably.

Seth wrapped his arms around her but kept his eyes on the doctor. He silently begged for denial from her.

Rebecca quickly responded with a gentle smile as she reached her hand out to pat Emily's arm. "No, my dear. The biopsy shows a benign cyst, which is not malignant."

Emily exhaled and wiped a tear of relief from her eye.

"However," the doctor continued, "in the process of looking at the cyst there was something else discovered that we need to talk about."

Seth put an arm around his wife and squeezed her a bit. "It's okay, Hon, it's okay."

Rebecca looked into her patient's eyes. "They did find something that you probably would not have known about without having the biopsy. It's called Stage 0 LCIS, or Lobular Carcinoma in Situ. It's generally not considered cancer."

"Then what is it?" Seth asked.

"It's a growth of abnormal but non-invasive cells forming in the lobules." She took out a drawing and showed the couple where it was located.

"What does this mean for me?" Emily asked.

"We will monitor you closely because you may have an increased risk of developing breast cancer. No surgery is required, but we'll do exams and mammograms every six months and maybe look at hormone therapy."

Emily pulled a tissue from her purse and dried her eyes.

The obstetrician spoke with compassion as she rose from her seat. "No matter what, your baby is safe. Even if it were cancer, those cells would not spread to or harm your baby. We shall not worry or stress about this, it's not good for you or the precious cargo you're carrying. My assistant will get you set up on a six-month schedule for tests, but we already have you scheduled for your next OB appointment."

Seth thanked the doctor before she left the room. He turned to Emily. "Why don't we go to Olive Garden and celebrate. You love their grilled salmon."

Emily tossed her tissue in the waste basket and leaned against her husband for a moment. "I think I'd rather go home. I'm drained. We have salmon in the freezer if you feel like grilling."

"I can do that," he assured her. "Whatever you want to do, we'll do it."

"You know," Emily said, "me finding that lump was a blessing. Otherwise I might not have known about the other, whatever she called it, until it became cancer."

He put his arm around Emily and held her close. "I think she said it was Lobular Carcinoma, and I agree, God is definitely looking out for us, but especially for this baby. We're going to be okay."

They clasped hands and headed out, both realizing how fortunate they were.

***

Betty hung up the phone and began preparing a pot of tea. After getting the kettle going she chose a teapot, cup and saucer decorated with snowmen. They smiled at her and she almost didn't pour hot water in the pot for fear of melting them. She chuckled, and with good reason. Her conversation with Emily put her in a good mood. No cancer! The baby was safe. That's the best news ever.

Brian popped into the kitchen. He opted to brew a cup of Southern Pecan coffee. "Hi, Sweets! You're in a jovial mood," he said as he set a K-Cup in the Keurig and hit start.

The kettle whistled. Betty emptied the hot water from the pot, measured the tea leaves, adding them to the snowmen's home, and poured the boiling water over them. "Brian I just received the best news from Emily."

He turned quickly to see his wife's expression. "No cancer?" he asked.

She bobbed her head up and down. "It's a benign cyst, although there was something else they found, but it's not cancer either. She said the doctor wants to monitor it every six months to make sure it doesn't turn into cancer. But she and the baby are fine."

"I can just imagine how relieved they both are. Seth was extremely concerned for his wife."

"I know," Betty said, moving the teapot, cup and saucer to the breakfast bar. "Emily said that now they want to pour their energy into getting the bed & breakfast on the fast track."

"I'll call Seth and see how I can be of help," Brian suggested.

"I'm sure he will appreciate any help he can get. "

Brian retrieved his coffee from the machine and sat next to his wife. "You know what would make this coffee perfect? A slice of cinnamon streusel cake"

"It goes great with tea also. How about cutting two slices?" Betty nudged him, laughing.

***

Sheila Jennings relished her time playing with Mary Dee. Even though it had been just a few months since the two-year-old had come into their lives, both Sheila and Lane couldn't imagine their lives without her. It's a shame tragedy had to strike twice for it to happen, but God had a plan even when they couldn't find their way after their son, David, died from cancer almost four years ago and their marriage suffered. It was a journey moving through the grief and heartbreak to a place of comfort and peace, made possible only by God.

The second tragedy was when Mary Dee's parents were killed in a horrific car accident, leaving the toddler without family to raise her. When she and Lane applied to become foster parents last year with the hope of adopting, they had no idea what God would do in their lives or Mary Dee's. The adoption is planned for next month and this precious child will be theirs forever.

Sheila smiled as she watched Mary Dee sniff the pansies and garden pinks planted along the path near the side fence. The toddler seemed to love flowers; which was exciting for Sheila. *How fun it will be to teach her to garden.* She could see them digging in the dirt, side by side, laughing and having mother/daughter fun. Sheila laughed out loud, causing the baby to turn to look at her, boasting a huge grin.

"Are you having fun?" Sheila asked in her higher-pitched mommy voice.

Mary Dee clapped her chubby hands together and then pressed them against her nose.

"Me fmell," she responded.

"Yes, sweetie, you smell the flowers."

Sheila heard Lane's car pull in the driveway and rose from her Adirondack chair to scoop Mary Dee into her arms.

"Let's go find daddy, he's home."

"Da Dee," she repeated, and clapped her hands before pressing them against her lips. "Me kiss."

Sheila laughed and hugged her cargo gently. "Yes, daddy will give you big kisses."

Before they made it into the house Lane greeted his two girls on the porch, pouring his attention on Mary Dee first. Kisses were exchanged and the toddler wrapped her arms around his neck. He gave her his modified bear hug before setting her on the floor.

"Okay, mommy's turn for kisses," he promised as he pulled Sheila into his arms and kissed her gently. "How was your morning?"

"We had fun and I think we have a budding gardener in our midst."

"Oh really?" He squinted down at Mary Dee.

"She fancies the garden pinks best, I think. They tickle her nose when she smells them."

"I've got some exciting news for you," Lane said, looking his wife in the eyes.

"What?"

"I talked with Seth today and they saw Emily's doctor. The lump isn't cancer."

"Thank God!" Sheila almost shouted. "Then she's home free?"

"Well, there is a little something they found."

"Nothing serious, right?"

Lane escorted Sheila to the living room and settled Mary Dee with her giraffe before explaining what Seth told him about Emily. Since he wasn't proficient in medical terms, he did his best. "Bottom line is that the doctor will do an exam and mammogram every six months and monitor her to make sure cancer hasn't developed. They are both happy, especially with her being so early in the pregnancy."

"That is exciting news. I'm so relieved for Emily; I know she was anxious about it. I'll give her a call this week and see how she's doing."

Lane scratched his head. "You may see her before then. They'll be at the future B & B in a couple days to discuss a few renovations with the crew."

"Oh good," Sheila said clapping her hands together, "it's one of the benefits of having the Bed and Breakfast next door.

Mary Dee, seeing her mommy clap, put her hands together and mimicked the action.

Lane and Sheila laughed simultaneously. "Monkey see…"

Chapter 5

Blanca Moreno curled up in her new recliner, a Christmas gift to herself last month. Now that she was retired and didn't have a clue what to do with her life, at least she'd have a chair for contemplating things. She watched as the marshmallows in her cup of hot cocoa melted on one side. *Too hot to drink just yet.* Placing the mug down carefully on the end table, Blanca leaned back after using the remote to start the heat in the chair. Thinking about the rare cold day in San Antonio, she wondered how Rosie was faring on the east coast with her son.

Blanca had hoped Rosie would stay with her and Bree on a more permanent basis. It seemed like they just began settling in when Rosie announced she was moving to Connecticut to be near her son, Roland. Not that Blanca held it against Rosie; after all, Bree lived here. Well, at least she did until she went into the mission field and ended up in Mexico. Now Blanca was alone and retired with time on her hands.

She reached for her cocoa and sipped gingerly, making sure it had cooled enough. The sweetness from the melted marshmallows made it rich and creamy. She returned the mug to the table and leaned back into the warmth of the recliner, closing her eyes for just a bit. Memories of her years with Carlos before Bree was born, before he left her to look for work up north, flooded her mind. *If only I had stopped him from leaving. If only I had gone with him.* Blanca knew that Carlos would never have agreed to her leaving their home to travel over two thousand miles to Michigan with his not having a definite job or place to live. She was pregnant with Bree at the time, so traveling was out of the question. *He should have returned instead of hiding the fact that he couldn't find enough work.* She sighed deeply. It was unchangeable now so there's no point in thinking of what could have, should have, been done. Carlos was dead and Blanca had survived raising Bree on her own. His life in Waxahachie, Texas was still a question though. He did find decent work, even though it was years later. He met Rosie there, but Carlos had become a Christian by then and it was through sharing the story of salvation that they came to know each other.

Blanca liked Rosie and found some sort of connection with her… most likely because of Carlos. He helped Rosie find Christ and that one thing meant everything. If only she hadn't chosen to move, perhaps they could have found something meaningful to do together. Rosie was a great cook, so maybe they could have opened a restaurant. A thought struck Blanca. *I'll give her a call and see how she's doing.*

"Hello," Rosie answered the phone after seeing Blanca's name on the caller ID. Her voice carried a smile over the distance, "It's good to hear from you. How are things in Texas?"

"To tell you the truth, Rosie, I'm lonely. Since I retired and Bree is in Mexico, this house is too quiet. I really miss having you here."

"Aww, bless your heart. I miss you too."

"How are things going with your son?"

"Well, honestly, I don't see him much. He met a young lady and spends mucho time with her at Cape Cod."

"Have you met her?"

"Yes, and she's nice enough, but she seems clingy. She is always hanging on him."

Blanca laughed. "Young love most likely."

"You're probably right but it was his idea for me to move up here and now I'm stuck in this apartment wondering what to do. I don't really know anyone so I rarely venture out except to the store once in a while."

"I understand that feeling. Say, why not fly down here for a visit? We could have lunch, do some sightseeing that you missed when you were here, and even check out the Bed & Breakfast that Seth and Emily will soon be opening."

"Hmm, sounds like fun. Besides, you still have some of my things stored there. I could check them out and see what I might need. Let me think about it and I'll call you in a day or so."

"Great," Blanca almost shouted, "we'll have so much fun. By the way, remember I told you about Emily's finding a lump?"

"Yes, how is she doing?"

"The lump isn't cancer after all. I can't recall what it is but they are just going to keep checking her every six months. It is answered prayer."

"I'm very happy for her. God is good."

"Yes, He is, Rosie. I'm really excited that you might make the trip down here. I'll be praying you decide quickly."

Rosie chuckled. "It would surely be more enjoyable than sitting alone in this tiny apartment. I'll call you tomorrow and let you know."

"Okay, I'll be close to my phone, waiting. Bye till then."

Rosie put her phone down, but couldn't get the conversation with Blanca out of her mind. *That woman has such a big heart.* She remembered the compassion Blanca showed after Carlos died in a tragic car accident. The money she gave Rosie was a life changer and to think it was because of Carlos. He had shared what Jesus did to transform him into a new man and wanted to have the same thing happen in Rosie's life. *It did, Carlos, in more ways than one.* If that wasn't enough, Blanca and Bree invited Rosie to move in with them. Guilt surged through Rosie, remembering how she told them she was moving to be near her son, Ro. Looking at it now, Rosie wondered if she made the right decision. The first couple weeks during Christmas were a blessing. She tried to share with Ro the Gospel as Carlos had done with her, but Ro had a closed mind. He was more interested in rituals and religion than a relationship with Jesus. It saddened her. Then he met Monica and was seldom around anymore. Now she was stuck in this tiny apartment and had to battle freezing weather if she wanted to go anywhere. San Antonio's warm climate sounded better and better. But Ro did invite her to move up here and she wanted to be part of his life now that he was out of the Air Force. Of course, since Monica entered Ro's life, Rosie seemed to be put on the back burner. *Moving back to Texas would open up opportunities that I don't have here.* She decided to pray deeply and then call Blanca tomorrow with her decision.

***

Ryan Ladderman removed his fireman's hat, pulled a handkerchief from his back pocket, turned a metal bucket upside down in the yard, and took a seat. He wiped the sweat from his ash-covered face and gazed at what was left of the small wood-framed home. He had finished putting out a few hot spots in the front, but a small section of the front porch seemed untouched by the fire which raced through the structure during what seemed like just moments ago. In truth, Ryan and the other firemen from Fire Station #20 had been battling the inferno for over an hour. It looked like creosote in the chimney was the cause, but the inspector hadn't rendered his final cause yet. The cold snap this week begged for homeowners who had chimneys to build a nice fire. Unfortunately, many of them ignored the plea to have their chimney inspected. It was sad that in this case, no one survived. They found the remains of two people—the elderly couple who had lived here for several decades.

A sudden commotion caused Ryan to jump up, knocking the metal pail from under him. He put his long legs into motion and raced around to the back to find out what was wrong. He prayed it wasn't another fatality. Rounding the corner and entering the back yard, he spotted three firemen huddled to the ground. Ryan approached cautiously only to discover a small dog was lying helplessly on the ground and one fireman giving him oxygen. His heart plummeted. *Please, Lord, breathe life into this little guy,* he prayed as he went to his knees. Ryan didn't want to add another body to the count. Silence filled the damp smoky air as it seemed as though everyone at the scene held his breath. Then there was movement in the little dog's front paws, and all the firemen exhaled collectively. A huge shout went out as they all exclaimed "Yay, good work, Piper."

Alex Piper removed the oxygen from the quiet furry bundle. "It wasn't me, it was the good Lord," he said wiping his brow on his heavy jacket sleeve. "I was just the tool He used."

"Amens" were heard all around. Ryan noticed a gathering of people by the back fence and they were applauding, some even crying.

Piper turned to Ryan. "A neighbor grabbed me when we were checking everything and said the couple who lived here owned a dog. We all started looking quickly and found him behind the door." Piper carefully picked the dog up and wrapped him in a towel someone found, and then handed the pooch to Ryan. "Can you watch him for a bit? I need to go to the truck."

Ryan took him tenderly into his muscled arms. "Sure, I'm a huge dog lover." The furry pet looked up at Ryan and his droopy eyes then closed. Ryan felt his heartbeat; though it was not very strong, it was regular.

"Go to sleep little guy, you're safe now," he whispered as he nestled his face next to the pup. *He's an orphan, unless the deceased couple had relatives who might take him in.*

***

Betty sat at her dining room table, silently shifting her gaze from Kat to Clay, sensing their discomfort. She called this meeting in her home to keep it informal and yet conduct some semblance of business. The two young adults avoided looking at each other and either stared at the papers Betty placed before them, or looked anxiously at her, their eyes darting invisible words, "let's get this over with."

"Okay," Betty uttered a bit too loudly, "let's clear the air so we can accomplish something in the hour ahead of us. I hope you both can be professional and work together with Brian and me as we try to create a documentary that will benefit women facing a traumatic event in their lives. What do you think?"

Kat spoke first and put a smile on her face. "I certainly can and will." Her head turned toward Clay as she reaffirmed her decision. "Our personal and professional lives are totally separate and my commitment to Betty and this project remains in force."

"I think I can say the same," Clay responded without looking at Kat.

"You think you can?" Betty asked, holding his gaze, hoping for a bit more enthusiasm. "For us to move forward as a cohesive team we each must give it all we have. So, Clay, if you don't feel you can do that wholeheartedly, tell me now."

Clay didn't blink. "Yes, Mrs. Hills, I will work with the team and do my best to produce the best film I'm capable of."

Betty's firm expression softened into a gentle smile. "Thank you, that's all I ask. Before we begin I have some fantastic news to share." Betty watched as they both came alive with expectation. They leaned in waiting as they both asked in unison, "What?"

Betty laughed. "That's better, now we're really a team again. I received a phone call from a sponsor who viewed our first documentary about Clarence and Greta. He was so moved by it and told some of his sources about what we're working on now. Turns out that two of them would like to co-sponsor our work."

Kat and Clay sat with mouths open in astonishment.

"There's more," Betty added. "Because of their generosity I'll be able to pay both of you a small salary."

"That's awesome, Mum."

"Great, Mrs. Hills, I can use it in my photojournalism."

"You both deserve to be paid. You do wonderful work. And, Clay, please call me Betty. We are a team."

Clay lowered his eyes, a bit embarrassed. "Sorry, I know you told me that before. It's just that ..."

"I know, you were brought up to regard your elders with respect in how you address them. You have had good training, but, we are all working together."

"Thank you," Clay responded, offering a genuine smile, "Betty."

Betty chuckled inwardly. "Good, let's start with our star. Her name is Penny Evans and she's a 64-year-old widow. She's estranged from her only son and works at a local Walmart at minimum wage. She recently received a call from her doctor's office about an abnormal mammogram and she is scheduled to have a second one done this week."

"How did you make contact with her?" Kat asked.

"Her doctor had seen the public service notice you created, Kat. He provided Penny with my contact information."

Kat beamed. "Then my marketing skills are helping, along with Clay's filming."

"You're both doing a great job. We have a responsibility now, to bring attention to the plight of women in Penny's situation, but even more, to help her spiritually as God leads us."

"Betty," Clay spoke up, "In the paperwork you've given us you want to do several interviews and follow her as she goes through tests. Will I be filming or is it going to just be verbal?"

"Good question, Clay. When we meet with her the first time we'll know more on how to proceed. She seemed open to filming but that depends on what they find. We pray it's nothing serious, but in the event it should be more involved, well, we'll see. In either case, her story could possibly help other women in her circumstances. Let's finish going over the plan I've written out and then pray for Penny and ask God to guide us in how to help her."

Brian waved as he passed by Betty and her team at the dining table and headed to answer the doorbell. Opening the door, he was a bit startled to see a fireman cuddling a small dog in the crook of his arm. Their eyes met and Brian greeted the young man. "Hello, Ryan, what brings you and your friend this way?"

Ryan, still wearing his uniform, stroked the dog softly. "I'm hoping Kat's home. We rescued this little guy today and he needs a home for a while, at least until we locate his extended family, if he has one."

"Sure, she's here. They're in a meeting at the moment, but please, come in and make yourselves comfortable. Can I get you both something to drink?"

Ryan stepped inside, following Brian to the kitchen and suggested the dog might need some water. He sat on the stool, holding the furry fellow, who by now was awake and licking his paws. "Do you think Kat would like to foster him?"

"Well, I can't answer for her, but she has a tender heart so there's a strong possibility she would." Brian wondered what would happen when Kat and Clay emerge from the meeting and find themselves face-to-face with Ryan, Kat's new love interest.

"That would be great. I can't take him because of the hours I work."

Brian set a plastic bowl on the floor next to the table. He gently took the dog from Ryan and placed him in front of it, watching as he lapped water, splashing some onto the floor.

"He sure was thirsty," Brian observed. "I don't have any dog food, but if Kat wants to keep him, I'm sure she'll pick up some."

"Not a problem, said Ryan, "I stopped at a convenience store on my way here. I have a couple cans in the car."

Voices in the hall signaled the film crew meeting had ended. Brian hurried to tell Kat about her visitor before she was blindsided. Too late. Kat came around the corner and halted in step.

"Ryan," Kat finally uttered, "what are you doing here?" She thought she heard Clay make a comment but Ryan's cheerful voice overtook the sound.

"Hey there, I brought you something and I'm hoping you'll want to keep him if necessary." He reached down and produced the black and white fluffy bundle. "Ta-da!" he said.

Kat rushed to take the dog in her arms, forgetting Clay was still present. "He's adorable. Where did you find him?"

"We had a house fire early today and sadly, his owners both perished. We haven't found any relatives yet so I'm hoping you might foster him."

"I'd love to," Kat said, rubbing her cheek against his fur." She noticed he had a tag on his collar. "His name is Crackers," she declared. "I love it! I wonder why they chose that name for you," Kat said lovingly as she stroked his whiskers. She turned to show her dad and Betty, who by now had gathered close. Then she noticed Clay still at the doorway.

"Clay, isn't he the cutest?" she quizzed, trying to dispel any awkwardness having him and Ryan in the same room.

"Yeah, real cute. I need to get going. I can see myself out."

"No, let me walk you to the door," she offered, clutching Crackers. "Thanks for being here and agreeing to working on the film project. When we know more I'll call so we can get started."

Clay didn't respond except with a head nod as he stepped outside, but then felt guilty for acting jealous, so he turned and gave a small smile. "I'm looking forward to this project."

Kat smiled back, then held Crackers' paw and waved. "See you soon."

Clay left without waving. *I might as well forget about any future relationship with Kat. I can't compete with a furry, homeless dog and a fireman in uniform.*

Kat returned to the kitchen and her family staring, waiting to see her reaction. She stood, petting Crackers. "Okay, so what does this little guy eat?"

Betty had made hot chocolate for them and was setting out mugs. Brian had found a basket and brought it in for their new resident canine.

Ryan approached Kat and gave her a hug and a kiss on the cheek. "You're just as your dad said. I brought some food for Crackers, I'll be right back."

She watched him disappear out the door, and then turned to her dad. "May I ask what you said to him?" she asked in a skeptic tone.

"He asked if I thought you would take the dog in and I said I couldn't speak for you but that you have a tender heart."

Kat leaned in and kissed her dad on the forehead. "I get it from you."

Chapter 6

Driving to work, Sarah Witte was smiling. Today was a big day. She had waitressed for Tim at the Blanco diner almost two years and it was time for her to move forward in her life. She was 22 and wanted more in her future than waiting tables. Not that she regretted her decision to take the job two summers ago, and the money she earned was in her savings account. Living at home afforded her the opportunity to save some money and explore her options. Then she met Jared Orlov. He seemed to be a complicated young man, mysterious and yet attractive. Sarah's dad cautioned her about him at first, but after Thanksgiving and having him join the family for dinner, he backed off a bit. "He seems nice enough I suppose," was the way her dad put it. Sarah thought so too, especially since Jared allowed the Lord to lead him. After he shared with her about his past trouble in San Antonio, along with how he made amends with the girl called, Kat, and her family, Sarah's heart softened and was able to see a different, Jared. It takes a big person to admit to their wrongs and then make them right by facing those hurt by it. Jared admitted that he couldn't have done it before George shared Scriptures with him about what real love is.

Sarah pulled her Toyota truck into the parking lot and shut the motor off. She slung her messenger bag across her shoulder and clicked the key fob, locking the doors. Inside, she greeted Tim as she stashed her bag in the drawer and retrieved her apron. "Good morning, Tim, isn't it a beautiful day?"

Tim grunted a rough hello.

Sarah knew he was going to play the hurtful act about her quitting, so she hugged his arm. "Tim, when the new lady, Leila

Farmington comes in on Monday, I'll start training her. After the interview the other day, I think she'll do really well. She has a great personality and good references. I love that she's so bubbly. That's not very common with women her age."

"She's not you," he pouted, revealing a scowl across his forehead.

"Come on now, give her a chance. She really needs the job too. Her family is going through a struggle and this job will come in handy."

Tim looked at Sarah. "I know, I'm sure she'll work out just fine. It's just not going to be the same around here without your sweet smile."

"Aww, thank you, Tim," she said, reaching up to smooth down his rebellious hair. Sarah loved how his gray cowlick refused to stay down. It made him look younger than his 70 years. "It's not like I'm moving away, I'll still be around to pop in and tease you a bit."

Laughing, Tim turned his attention to the pot of chili on the stove. "I'm glad of that; my day wouldn't be complete without it."

"My days won't be the same either," Sarah admitted.

"Just what are you planning for this new venture of yours?"

Sarah sighed excitedly as she began filling the condiments on the tables. "Well, remember how I talked about my love of plants and flowers last summer?"

Tim laughed, "Sure do, the diner proved it. There were and still are a lot of your creative potted beauties here."

Sarah stopped filling the ketchup bottle and freed her hands. She seemed to paint a picture of her future job with flowing fingers in the air. "I'm going to college and get a certificate in basic nursery and landscaping. A friend of mine at the garden center was telling me about a nursery where they are opening a new location late next year. They will need a manager and she knows my skills and love for plants."

"And what if you don't get that position?"

"The way I see it, there will be other nurseries and opportunities. I can also take future courses to hone my skills. But, the best part is that I can work in a nursery while going to school."

"Where? What college?"

Sarah stood quietly. "San Antonio. Palo Alto Community College," she said softly. "I can drive back and forth to school, and the part-time job is here, working at the garden center. I'll start next week and work full-time until I start school in the fall."

Tim came around from the kitchen and put his big arm on her shoulders. "I'm happy for you, Sarah. I know you've given this a lot of thought and I really am proud of you. What do your parents think of all this change?"

"My parents are fine with it. They're happy I'll still be at home. I haven't told Jared yet though."

Tim's eyebrows formed a V. "Is that a concern? I didn't know you and Jared were a couple."

Sarah gave Tim a teasing smirk. "Technically we're not a couple, as you put it. We date and do things fun together, but nothing more. I just haven't shared my career change."

Tim patted her on the shoulder as he made his way back to the kitchen to check the chili. "I'd say going from diner waitress to college student to horticulturist is a big change worth sharing, wouldn't you?"

"It'll be a while before the horticulturist happens, but yes, it is. I plan to tell him this weekend. He's taking me to Wildseed Farms in Fredericksburg on Saturday. I'll share my plans with him then."

"Whose idea was that outing?" Tim winked at her.

Sarah laughed. "I might have suggested it."

***

The door opened and in bounced a bright-eyed, silver-haired woman, decked out in turquoise jewelry, khaki skirt, and Old Gringo short boots sporting turquoise stones down each side. She quickly greeted Tim, introducing herself as Leila Farmington, his new right-hand gal. "My name is pronounced Lila but has a silent e, thanks to a clerical error when my birth certificate was recorded," she explained.

"I'm happy to finally meet you, Leila, with a silent e," Tim looked up from chopping onions and responded with a big smile. "Sarah," he said, nodding in her direction, "told me a little about you, but I'd like to know more. Come in and have a cup of coffee and we can talk a bit before I turn you over to Sarah," he said, rinsing and drying his hands before leaving the kitchen counter. He held out his hand and motioned for her to follow him to a nearby booth so they could talk.

Sarah waved and smiled before heading to a table where a couple had taken a seat right after Leila came in. She chuckled to herself, knowing Tim would take an instant liking to Leila's bubbly personality. Sarah purposefully didn't tell him everything last week, because she wanted to surprise him. Mission accomplished.

***

Jared pulled into the driveway at his half-brother's auto repair shop, noticing several cars up on lifts, the helper, Charles, working under the hood on another in the open bay, and Gus walking into the office. Jared gave a quick honk causing Gus to turn around and wave. Jared parked and exited the Charger, meeting his half-brother at the door.

"You're a sight for sore eyes," Gus shouted in a friendly tone. "What brings you back here? Tired of Blanco so soon?" Gus ushered Jared into the office and offered him a seat and coffee.

"Nah," he said, pouring the black caffeine into a dusty mug and plopping down by the window, "just wanted to see you and discuss something. Looks like you're swamped with work. Is Charles able to keep up with it?"

Gus sat behind his desk and retrieved his mug of the now cold coffee. "Yeah, all of a sudden work doubled. Guess I could have worse problems. You looking for a job?"

"In a way, I am, but it would have to be part-time. I'm going back to school."

"You're kidding me, what prompted this?"

Jared stared into his cup and took a sip. "I'm ready to do something with my life. There's this girl in Blanco...."

"Now I understand," Gus said, laughing. "I should have known." He looked at Jared and realized how serious his expression was. "Sorry, I just had to pull your chain a bit. I'm glad you're looking ahead and trying to put down some roots."

"I'm enrolling at San Antonio College and taking a Cybersecurity course to get a degree."

Gus sat up straight and set his mug down. "Jared, that's fantastic. I'm so proud of you."

"Thanks, as you know it's something I've been interested in for a long time. I'll need a job though and thought you might need some help if you can be flexible with my hours."

Gus stood and went around his desk giving Jared a slap on the back. Jared turned and hugged his half-brother. "Thanks for putting up with me through all the bad stuff. I think I finally have my head on straight. I've enrolled in the fall semester, so I'm all yours full-time until then."

"Come on; let's go tell Charles the news." Gus suddenly stopped in his tracks. Jared followed suit. "Will you need a place to live?"

Jared laughed. "That would be helpful. I didn't want to spring that on you too soon. My car is a little cramped with all my stuff in it."

"We'll tell Charles the news, and then go grab some lunch and head over to my place so you can unpack," he promised.

"Great plan, and Gus, thanks again."

"No need for thanks. Truth knows that family helps one another."

***

Blanca secured the two suitcases in the back of her car, closed the trunk, and hurriedly jumped in to move the vehicle from the passenger pickup curb.

"I can't believe you're here, Rosie," she said excitedly, checking her side view mirror before merging into the exit lane at San Antonio Airport. "I'm so happy you decided to visit. We'll have a great time."

"Thank you for inviting me. It's good to get out of the snow and ice, Rosie said, shivering a bit for effect. "I'm not used to that kind of weather."

Blanca laughed as she exited the airport and made her way onto Loop 410. "I know our weather here isn't as bad but it's far from Texas heat that you remember. We've had a rare winter spell this month."

"It's okay, at least there's no ice or snow. How is Bree?"

"She's doing well. I'm not sure but she might make it home for the wedding in April."

"Who's getting married?"

"Do you remember Ron Davis? I think you met him on the Christmas River Cruise."

"Yes, he's a handsome young man. Who is he marrying?"

"Rita, the sweet lady who creates sculptures from junk and recycled things. She teaches inner city kids how to do it too."

"How nice, who knows, maybe I'll be here for the wedding," Rosie said, chuckling a little.

Blanca focused on the traffic backing up ahead of her. "Oh dear, looks like we'll be here a bit, unless I can get in the right lane and take the exit." She mechanically flipped on her right signal light and watched for an opening.

Rosie glanced to her right and noticed a car lingering back and waving them over. "You can move over, that car is waiting," she told Blanca.

They finally reached the exit and Blanca breathed a sigh. "It's good that I was a bus driver all those years," she said proudly. "It helps me to know alternate routes. We'll be home in 10 minutes. I know you're probably tired from traveling, so you can rest while I fix us some lunch."

"Please don't go to a lot of trouble."

"It's not trouble. I'm so happy to have you here and to be able to cook for more than just me. Besides, I prepared part of the casserole last night, so I only need to heat the oven and add some cheese on top. It's all good."

"I love to cook also. When I worked at the restaurant in Waxahachie, I mostly waited on tables, but Alfredo, the owner, loved some of my recipes. He would ask me to prepare them for certain days' specials. The customers loved them too."

Blanca's mind was whirling, thinking of food-related possibilities that would keep her friend in Texas. But she would take it slow and wait for the right time to approach her with the idea.

"Rosie, I know firsthand how good a cook you are. Bree and I loved the meals you made when you were with us last year."

"The best part was sharing them with you and your lovely daughter."

Blanca pulled into her driveway. "Here we are," she uttered happily, "home." She turned to see Rosie wearing a huge smile.

"Yes, home, for a while anyway."

Blanca undid her seatbelt and patted Rosie's arm. "Come on, let's get your luggage and settle you in. We have a lot of catching up to do."

***

Brian loved working with Seth in the soon-to-be Texas Tribute Bed & Breakfast. He was glad Seth pulled Mary's house off the market and decided to transform it. Brian was happy to have a part in the renovations, although his skills were limited in that area. He did know how to negotiate though and managed to get Seth the best contractors at the most reasonable price. Walking through the place now, with most of the interior work completed, Brian was pleased. He knew Seth and Emily were as well. He heard Seth in the back yard, so he headed that way, anxious to know why Seth called him over.

Seth looked up from the stack of lawn edging he had just unloaded, to see Brian Hills come through the house and settle on the porch step. "How ya doin', Brian? Glad you could stop by."

"I'm good but hoping you're not thinking I'm a landscaper." He laughed.

Seth stood and waved Brian to follow him into the house. "No, I'm just getting things ready so when the time is right, Sheila can get started. You know she volunteered to do some landscaping out back, right?"

"No, I didn't, but that's great. I remember her saying that she spent a lot of time out there when Mary's sister, Bertha, was alive. I think they both enjoyed gardening."

"That's true, and I know she'll do a great job. I told her to let me know what she needed, including strong muscles if necessary."

"So, how can I help?" Brian quizzed.

"I want to provide names for the different rooms and emphasize Mary's legacy. I'm not too creative so I figured with you being a writer, perhaps you could come up with suggestions. We have the bedrooms furnished now, so you could do a walk-through. The library is almost done, and the common room will soon be

57

complete. We need 8 names. Once we have them, I'll order name plates."

"Wow, I'm thrilled to be asked to do this. It'll take some thought but I'll come up with names that will be meaningful. Any guidelines I need to know about?"

"I'd like to tie the name to each of the people who attended Mary's Estate Sale. I don't want their names of course, but somehow tie it to who they are, especially after they received their special legacy gift from Mary."

"Let's see, there's myself, Kat, and Betty. Also, Blanca and Bree."

"Yes, and Sheila and Rita."

"What about you and Emily? How about Mary...it was her sale?"

"Don't count me, I wasn't at the sale. Nor was Mary. Emily would make 8."

Brian jotted down the names in his pocket memo book. "Okay, when do you need them?"

"As soon as possible of course." Seth laughed but then gave a serious look. "Sorry to rush you but having name plates made will take time."

"Don't worry, I can handle that part too if you sketch out what you want them to look like."

Seth slapped Brian's back. "Thanks, my friend, I knew you were the right person for the job."

"How's Emily?" Brian asked as they approached the front door.

"She's doing and feeling great. Actually, I heard her humming to herself this morning while making tea."

"Now that's a good sign of recovery."

Seth paused, leaning against the doorpost. Brian turned, wondering what was on Seth's mind. "Is there something you want to talk about, Seth?"

"Let's sit here a minute," he said, crouching down on the step.

Brian followed suit. "Sure, I don't have anywhere I need to be."

After a short silence, Seth began. "I know the cancer scare changed Emily. It changed me too. We've done a lot of thinking and praying during and since we found out it wasn't cancer and the baby is okay."

Brian didn't feel comments were necessary so he remained quiet.

"The truth is, when we sat with the doctor, Emily said she wouldn't agree to any treatment that would harm the baby. Of course, I agreed with her a hundred percent. She was ready to sacrifice herself to make sure our baby was protected."

Brian simply nodded his head in an understanding way.

"I've come to realize that if anything happened to my wife, our baby would be safe. That's the truth of her legacy. Sacrificial love." Seth's voice broke a little so he lowered his head and stopped talking.

"You're right, Seth. Defending what's most precious to me is a rule of life I learned from God. I remember when Kat was in danger from that guy, Jared. I would have gone down to my death to protect her. I also know someone else who demonstrated sacrificial love."

Seth raised his head knowingly. "Yes, Jesus Christ, when he went to the cross and died for us."

"Yep, you're right. He is the Truth of our legacy. He loves us and is always with us."

Seth wiped his eye with the back of his hand as he stood. Brian rose and the two men shook hands and smiled.

"I'll get to work on the room names and when you're happy with them, I'll order the name plates."

"Thanks, Brian. I'll talk to you soon. Give my regards to Betty."

"I will, and you do the same to Emily."

Chapter 7

Ron hung up the phone. "Whew, I'm glad that's done," he said to Harry.

"What's done?" Harry asked absentmindedly while going through the tightly strung keys on his keyring.

"I finally secured the pastor for my wedding."

The key-laden ring fell to the floor, startling Ron, deep in his own thoughts. He had stopped by the office of his friend, Harry Roddis, owner of the building Rita was using for her sculpture classes for inner city kids. Since Ron had purchased a different building for Rita as a wedding present, he needed to sign papers and get the keys.

"Sorry," Harry apologized, picking up the pile of steel. "I know I have your keys on this ring. It's an odd-shaped one and a square. You'd think they would stand out."

Ron laughed. "You need to get a larger ring or have fewer keys."

"I know, but as soon as I throw one out I'll remember what it's for. So, you found someone to tie the knot for you and that gorgeous gal, huh?"

"Not just anyone, Harry, he was my mom's pastor. I thought about our getting married in Mesquite, my mom's hometown, but Rita wanted to have the wedding here where our friends are. The happy compromise was obvious, get Pastor Todd to come here."

"Sounds like the perfect plan."

"Yeah, I've had a hard time reaching him though and I think Rita thought I was shirking my duty."

Harry removed two keys from the ring and shuffled over to Ron at the desk. He plopped them down. "She's a bride-to-be and wants everything organized, planned, and accounted for."

Ron picked up the two keys and nodded his appreciation. "Rita is unique and special. I want to be the best husband I can be. It's just that I run on a different timeline than she does. I fit things in and don't get flustered if at first I don't succeed."

"And Rita does? Get flustered I mean."

"In fairness, I think her background has something to do with it. She needs security and wants to be sure things get done. The honeymoon for instance."

"You do have the honeymoon arrangements made, don't you?" Harry asked, shooting Ron a quick glance.

"Yes...and no, but I can explain."

"You don't need to explain to me, I'm not marrying you."

Ron laughed. "I've been working on a train trip but I'm having trouble deciding between two fantastic ones."

"Run 'em by me and I'll help you make up your mind."

"The first is the Canadian Rockies. We'd go to Seattle, Whistler, Vancouver, plus more. They have great chefs on board and locally-sourced dishes."

"Sounds relaxing and delicious, what's the other one?"

"We would take a vintage train out of Arizona passing through pine forests and dry desert to the Grand Canyon National Park. Once we get there, they have endless activities, like hiking, river rafting, helicopter rides, and hot-air ballooning. Or we can just stay put and enjoy each other."

"Which do you think your bride will enjoy?"

Ron looked at his friend. "She'd be happy no matter where we go or what we do. We'll be together and that's what matters."

"I think you know where to go."

Ron's face split in a wide grin. He got up, collected the keys, and shook Harry's hand. "Thanks, my friend. I'll see you at the wedding."

***

Jake folded himself into the remaining chair left after the yard sale. Last week was so chaotic and rushed, trying to decide what to keep and what to get rid of. As much as he wanted to hang on to his mother's furnishings, Jake knew that if he was going to succeed in moving forward toward a new life, things would have to change.

After Annie helped him unpack and sort everything, it only made sense to have a yard sale. He had donated Lillian's clothes and personal belongings to the women's shelter, thrown out unusable stuff, and kept only the most meaningful mementos. The rest was put out for the sale, which was highly profitable. Not that he did it for the money; after all, he ended up donating the money to the hospital where Annie worked. He added a substantial amount to it in his mother's name.

His new furnishings would arrive in the morning and Jake couldn't be more pleased with his selections. Annie did help a little, but, overall, he chose what pleased him. He stretched out in the well-loved recliner, intending to sleep in it tonight and put it outside in the morning with a *"free"* sign on it. His mom used it a lot those last days at home, but he didn't want to keep it. *It's time to begin a new chapter.* Jake closed his eyes. How would this chapter begin? Where would it lead? Annie's face appeared and faded quickly. He cared about her but would she want to be part of Jake's life makeover? He had been so busy with work and taking care of Lillian he hadn't made time for dating. The few occasions he took a woman out were usually coffee houses or a quick lunch. There hadn't been any serious dates much to his mother's disappointment. He smiled and opened his eyes. The empty room was waiting to see what was coming next. So was Jake. He pulled out his phone and rang Annie's number.

"Annie," he said quickly upon hearing her soft, cheerful voice. "If you don't have any plans for right now, would you like to go out to dinner?"

"Hello, Jake," she returned, in answer to his surprising invitation, "you get right to the heart of the matter, don't you?" Not giving him a chance to answer, she continued. "I was actually just getting ready to heat up some homemade chicken noodle soup I made yesterday. Would you like to come over and help me finish off the leftovers?"

Jake laughed. "I'm sorry, I guess I was pretty abrupt. I was sitting here in my almost empty living room and was thinking of you. I appreciate all your help getting things organized for the sale the other day and would love to do something special for you."

"You're welcome, but you don't have to pay me back. I had fun and spending time with you was great. I'm sure you're worn out so why don't you bring yourself over here and we'll have soup and crusty bread. We can watch a movie if you'd like."

Jake gave in to her suggestion. "You had me at the crusty bread. Let me shower and change and I'll be there in about an hour."

"Okay, I'll set another bowl out and look forward to seeing you."

Jake hung up the phone, pulled his body from the sunken recliner seat, and whistled his way to the shower. *Maybe Annie will enter this new chapter with me.*

***

Kat's heart ached as she sat, looking into Crackers' sad eyes. He hadn't eaten in the three days after Ryan brought him to her. Even later, he would only accept a little cooked chicken if Kat held it to his mouth. He drank water okay, but his refusal to eat was worrisome. Mum said he was grieving his owners, which was probably true. Kat remembered after she lost her mom she had no appetite for a long time.

She would have to be patient with him and hand-feed the little guy if necessary, until he became comfortable with her. A part of Kat felt guilty for keeping him. Maybe there was someone who was close to his owners who would be better suited to take him in. Someone perhaps whom he knew. She wondered if his human mommy walked him daily, played with him on a regular basis, or just let him cuddle on her lap.

Kat decided to call Ryan and see if he would try to find out more information about Crackers. Not that she wanted to give him up; after all, she was really just his foster mom for now anyway, but he deserved to be where people know him and know what he likes.

She stroked the back of his neck and he seemed to enjoy it. He nuzzled his head against her hand. "Aww, do you like that?" she whispered. He adjusted his position, rolling onto his back within the confines of the basket. His short hind legs protruded straight up while the two front paws folded slightly in the air. Kat remembered reading somewhere that when dogs lie like that, exposed, they feel secure. She hoped it was true.

***

Sarah and Jared walked hand-in-hand down the walking trail at Wildseed Farms. The weather wasn't ideal but neither was it bad. This time of year there were no wildflowers but there was still plenty to see in the country store. She bought some preserves and a few gifts for her mom. Jared insisted on buying her a necklace with a Bluebonnet engraved on the front, saying every Texas girl needed the state flower on a piece of jewelry. They laughed. She enjoyed being with him.

"Let's sit for a while," Sarah suggested as they approached a covered sitting area.

"I'm for that, you've walked my legs off," he laughed.

They sat on the stone bench. In spring it would be surrounded by wildflowers, waterfalls, and fragrant smells.

"I guess we came a bit early," Sarah began, "nothing is really blooming. But I wanted to talk and get away from things."

"I don't mind. I enjoy being with you and the drive was great. So, what do you want to talk about?"

"I've made some decisions. I've given my two weeks' notice to Tim at the diner."

Jared widened his eyes. "Really? What will you do?"

"It's a little complicated. You know how much I love working with plants and gardening, right?"

"Boy, do I. Look where we are today."

Sarah laughed. "Well, I've decided I want to accomplish something in my life and just like the seeds germinating, growing, and blooming, that's what I want my life to do. So, I'm going to start college in the fall. For now though, I'll be working full-time at a local nursery."

Jared stood and faced her. "Wow! I can't believe it. What will you major in?"

"I'll get a certificate in basic nursery and landscaping, to start at least. We'll see where that leads. I'm going to work at a nursery full-time until fall, and then I'll go part-time."

"Where are you going to college?"

"Palo Alto Community College in San Antonio. I'll live at home and drive back and forth."

"You'll be so busy driving, working, and studying, I won't see you much. I had hoped you'd be more a part of my life. You know I care a lot for you."

Sarah patted the stone next to her. "Sit back down. Jared, I care about you too and I'm so happy how you turned your life around. That took courage. But, right now, I need to find out what I want in life and focus on discovering what God has ahead for me. I'd still like to see you and spend time together when we can, but I'm not looking for a serious relationship at this point." She searched his face for reaction, praying he wasn't hurt. Unfortunately, his eyes seemed to dim.

Jared stood and looked down the yet unexplored trail. "I'm not in a position to have a serious relationship anyway," he said with a deep sigh. "I actually decided to make something of my life. I registered at San Antonio Community College to take a Cybersecurity course. I start in the fall too."

Sarah jumped up and flung her arms around his neck and quickly let go, looking at him with a wide smile. "Jared, that's awesome! I'm so excited for you. Cybersecurity is a great field to get into with all that's going on in the world lately."

"Thanks, it'll be a big change for me. I've moved back in with my half-brother, Gus, and he hired me full-time until I start school. Then my schedule will be flexible on an as-needed basis. I'll have to see how it goes." He avoided Sarah's eyes, not wanting her to see the hurt he knew his face would reveal.

"I'm so proud of you, Jared. We'll both be crazy busy but we're doing what we want and we'll have something to build on." Sarah looped her arm around his elbow. "We don't know what our futures hold, but we know who holds them."

Jared felt his heart tug, knowing she was right. "I lived in denial so many years, but after meeting George in your little town, my life was turned around in the right direction. I owe him a lot. He showed me what truth really is."

"George is a godly man and has helped many people whom God sent his way. It's his mission I think." She squeezed Jared's arm. "How about we circle around this trail and make our way to the other side and see what's there."

Jared nodded as they headed off down the trail. "Remember when we pulled onto the street before we turned in to the farm and I mentioned the street sign?"

"Yes, you noticed it was called Legacy Drive."

"I think my legacy will be truth."

"What truth?"

"The one George showed me."

Sarah smiled to herself, feeling content in how Jared had responded. She said a silent prayer, thanking God for guiding her words earlier. "I'm glad we're friends, Jared. You're a very special man."

Jared's neck bristled just a bit. *Friends?* He had hoped for more. He remained silent as they continued their walk, side by side down the unfamiliar path.

***

Blanca and Rosie sat at the kitchen table pouring over several cookbooks from Blanca's collection. Rosie thumbed through one which was from Blanca's childhood, belonging to her mother and containing many handwritten notes, in Spanish, jotted next to favorite dishes.

"My mother's Chili Verde Enchiladas recipe is in that book," Blanca commented. "I've made it for years. It was Carlos' favorite dish when we were together."

Rosie looked up. "You truly loved him didn't you?"

Blanca smiled. "Yes, even after he left I never stopped. Sometimes you have to let someone you love go. If they return then it was meant to be." Her smile faded.

"I know he loved you," Rosie said softly. "He talked about you with such devotion and never took his wedding band off."

Blanca quickly caught an image of his ring, now safely tucked into her small jewelry pouch next to her own. There, they would be together. Her lips forced a little grin. "Okay, let's look through some of the other cookbooks. I have so many. Bree always teases me that when she is officially moved out, I will turn her room into a cookbook library."

Rosie laughed and recognized it was time to steer away from the subject of Carlos. "So, tell me more about the idea you have concerning the cooking at the Bed & Breakfast your friends are opening this spring."

"Yes," Blanca agreed and brightened up at the mention of Seth and Emily's Texas Tribute B&B. "I casually asked Seth one day who would be doing the cooking when they open and he said Emily was in charge of that decision. I suggested he mention to her that you and I are great cooks and we know how to create southwestern recipes, as well as traditional ones. He said when tourists come to San Antonio they often want food that doesn't come from a chain. He's going to talk to Emily and then we'll discuss it more. In the meantime, I thought we could come up with some basic recipes and shape them into a one-of-a-kind unforgettable dish."

"You're assuming I plan to move back here of course."

Blanca blinked and smiled, nodding her head sheepishly.

Leaning back in the chair, Rosie let out a quick startling laugh. "You have provided a purpose for my life. If your friends decide to hire us, I'm all in. If they don't, maybe we could start our own restaurant and...."

"Hold on there, my friend," Blanca interrupted. "Let's not get ahead of ourselves. Blanca laughed at the serious look on Rosie's face. Not wanting to discourage her, Blanca continued. "We could start our own place but then we'd be arguing about whose name to use, Blanca's Hacienda or Rosie's Cantina," she said, breaking into a huge grin.

"You're so funny," Rosie said, slapping Blanca playfully on the wrist. "We are good together. No arguing between us. We could always name it after Carlos."

They both laughed.

***

Seth pulled back from the table and patted his midsection. "Great meal, Honey. You are such a good cook."

"You're just saying that because you love me," she teased as she hugged his neck from behind and kissed his cheek.

"You're right, and I love you because you put up with me. But, speaking about good cooks, I was thinking...."

"Oh no, I am not hiring on as a cook at our B&B." She stood up straight and faced her husband, patting her tummy. "I'm carrying your son, remember? I love cooking for you but...."

Seth made a school guard hand gesture. "STOP. I have no intention of having you cooking for people at the B&B. I do have a possible interview coming up though and they are people we know."

Emily sat down across from him with widened eyes. "Really? Who?"

"Blanca and Rosie."

"Rosie? The name is familiar but I can't place her."

"She was staying with Blanca and Bree, remember? Rosie knew Blanca's husband, Carlos, when they lived in Waxahachie."

Recognition set in. "Yes, didn't she work at a restaurant there?"

Seth nodded. "Blanca mentioned that Rosie is almost certain of moving back in with her and was telling me that she's a great cook. Of course, Blanca added that she, herself, is no slouch in the kitchen. She let me to know that since retiring she wants to do something different and wondered if they would be considered for the B&B job."

Emily was contemplative. "I think the world of Blanca, but she's been a bus driver most her life since Carlos left all those years ago. She is a committed, hard-working woman. It's just that I'm wondering if the type of food she's familiar with would be a fit for the Texas Tribute."

"Why wouldn't it be? San Antonio is known for Tex-Mex foods and tourists usually look for it when they visit. Let's at least talk to them and maybe have them cook a few dishes for us to sample?"

"That's an excellent idea, Seth. We could invite some of the others to join us and get their opinion too."

"Great. I'll call and let her know. We have plenty of time but I'd like to have that part of the hiring finalized at least."

Emily stood and began clearing the dishes from the table.

Seth gathered the cups and followed her to the sink. "You will still be cooking meals for me, right?" he said, jokingly.

She set the plates down on the counter and playfully punched his belly. "Yes, although I might have to subtract some of the calories from them if this gets as large as mine will in the coming months."

"Call it sympathy pounds," Seth joked as he hugged his wife.

Chapter 8

Greta sat opposite Kenneth Cavanaugh, the director of the assisted living residence. His wife, Jewel, occupied the wing back chair by the bookcase. She was dressed casually in blue jeans and tan blouse decorated with peonies. Greta wondered what Mr. Cavanaugh wanted to talk about and why his wife was present. Were they unhappy with Greta over something? Greta kept a slight smile, waiting for what was to come.

"Good morning, Greta," Kenneth began. "We're glad you agreed to meet with us so early."

"It's not early for me," Greta responded. "I'm always up before dawn and have my special coffee, read my Bible, pray, and make my bed." *I'm talking too much.* "What did you want to see me about? Is there a problem?"

Kenneth's face broke into a wide grin. "Heaven's no, Greta, quite the contrary. We want to ask you about your painting."

"My lighthouses? Are they in the way? If so, I can move them somewhere less visible."

Jewel spoke quickly. "No indeed, Greta. Your paintings are beautiful. I had no idea you had such talent."

Greta tilted her head down a bit. "I didn't either. My instructor told me she thought I had natural talent. I've never painted anything before coming here, but everyone seems to like them."

"Yesterday," Kenneth said, "Jewel and I were in the dining area and saw two we really fell in love with. We would like to buy them from you if you would consider selling them."

Greta's head popped up in wide-eyed surprise. "Buy them?" she asked in amazement? "Which pair?"

"The set titled, Transformed. You did an outstanding job of showing how the broken-down structure in the before painting was transformed into a beautiful lighthouse in the after piece. The colors are dramatic, bringing it to life."

"I can't think of anyone I'd rather have own those paintings. You both have helped me and Clarence through rough times. But, I won't sell them to you."

"Jewel's expression almost broke Greta's heart. She could see the disappointment on her face. Looking straight at Kenneth, Greta said softly, "The paintings are my gift to you both.""

Jewel's face lit up brighter than a lighthouse beam as she jumped up and went to Greta, hugging her. "Are you sure? We would gladly pay you a good price for them."

"Mrs. Cavanaugh," Greta started, "I have everything I need right here. At my age money means very little. The truth is, I have love and don't want for anything else. I found love in Jesus Christ. He gave me Clarence, and I'm surrounded by friends I never had before. Please accept the paintings in love."

Kenneth came around from his desk to join his wife. They both hugged Greta. "Thank you. They will enjoy a place of honor in our home. Now, you'll have to get busy and create another masterpiece to replace them in the dining room."

Greta laughed. "I already have a set in progress. Clarence made a suggestion and I'm following up on it so we'll see how it looks on canvas."

"I'm sure it will be beautiful," Jewel said, patting Greta's shoulder. "Thank you again.

"You're welcome. I best be going and make sure Clarence eats his breakfast. His appetite hasn't been too good these past couple days."

"Oh?" Kenneth said, surprised. "Should I have the nurse check him over?"

"I don't think so. He seems fine otherwise, but if I notice any other changes I'll let you know right away." Greta excused herself and made her way down the hall. She smiled as she thought about the Cavanaugh's wanting her paintings. *Thank You, Lord, for allowing me to be useful at my old age to bring joy to others.*

Greta reached the suite as she called it. Mr. Cavanaugh had converted two rooms into a suite last year when Greta and Clarence married. She always appreciated that beautiful gesture of love from the director. She quietly opened the door, assuming Clarence was still asleep. Making her way to the bedroom, she peeked in but he wasn't there. The bathroom door was open but she noticed the wheelchair wasn't in its usual place by the wall. Maybe he went to the sunroom. Greta headed out of the room and down the hall to find her husband. As she turned toward the doorway, her body froze almost refusing to carry her feet over the threshold.

She heard him moan and her feet moved swiftly as she took in the scene. The wheelchair was overturned near the table where the telephone was located. Clarence laid askew, half in and half out of the chair. She bent to her knees and cradled his head in her hands. She noticed blood on his forehead.

"What happened, Clarence, are you okay?"

***

Kenneth and Jewel walked through the foyer toward the dining room. "I'm so thrilled about getting the paintings. That was such a sweet thing for Greta to do, gifting them to us," Jewel said, excitedly.

"It was, indeed," agreed her husband. "I can't believe how quickly her talent has grown. She may have gotten a late start in life but I believe that God instilled that gift of painting when she let him into her heart. She doesn't just paint lighthouses, she paints what you can't see; transformation."

"I know," Jewel added. "I love that she does them in pairs, before the structures are restored and then after. It's like she's painting what takes place in a person's heart when they hear the truth of God."

"You've hit it right," Kenneth agreed, nodding his head.

A shrill sound echoed down the hall. It sounded like a scream and yet Kenneth thought it might be a whistle or siren in the distance. He stopped in his steps, placing his hand on Jewel's arm. "What was that?"

"I'm not sure. Could it be an alarm going off?"

"Alarms don't stop after one shrill. You go on to the dining room. I'm going to check down the hall," he said, spinning on his heel and moving past the office.

His instruction went unheard as she followed after him. He swiftly turned down the hallway, his long stride putting him a great distance ahead. Jewel sensed the urgency not just from the curdling sound, but in the haste Kenneth used. His inner sense of danger was always on target. She prayed in her spirit for this to be an exception to his quickness.

Kenneth stopped in his tracks as he entered the sunroom. Clarence was lying on the floor, half-in and half-out of his overturned wheelchair. Greta's frail body bent over her husband as she called his name, willing him to answer. Kenneth rushed to them and quickly took Clarence's pulse. It was very faint.

"What happened?" he asked.

Greta choked out her words between sobs. "I don't know. I'm not sure how long he's been like this. I came in and found him like this. He told me his chest hurt and he was going to call for help but couldn't reach the phone. I guess he tried standing up to get it and then fell, tipping the chair over. That was all I got before he passed out."

Kenneth helped Greta up and placed her in a nearby chair. He pulled out his phone to call 911 just as Jewel appeared in the room. He gave the address and hung up.

"I'm going to get a blanket," he told Greta. "The ambulance will be here shortly."

He looked at his wife's astonished face and motioned for her to stay close to Greta. "I'll be right back," he said half-running from the room.

Jewel pulled a chair next to Greta. "He'll be okay, my dear. Try not to worry." She put her arm around Greta's shoulder and prayed silently.

Kenneth reappeared with a blanket and covered Clarence. He also brought a pillow to place under his head. "I alerted the nurse and she'll show the paramedics down here as soon as they pull in." The three of them waited. Kenneth checked his pulse again and though very faint, he was able to detect it.

What seemed like eternity was 7 minutes when the two paramedics, rolling a gurney, rushed in, escorted by the head nurse. "What happened?" the older man quizzed. Greta tried to talk but her throat was choked with tears. The man repeated his question. Kenneth encouraged Greta to speak up.

"I...I...don't know except he said his chest hurt and was trying to reach the phone." She couldn't continue.

Kenneth told the men of hearing a scream and he rushed in to find Clarence on the floor. "No one really knows how it actually happened."

Jewel watched as the younger paramedic put oxygen on Clarence. She noticed the older man wore a name badge with the name Samson on it. He took Clarence's vitals, and then asked for personal information on him. They checked to make sure nothing was broken. "He only has one leg?" Sampson asked.

"Yes," Kenneth responded. "He wears a prosthesis."

After getting him onto the gurney, they buckled him in and headed out to the ambulance.

"We'll follow you to Metropolitan," Kenneth said.

The paramedics waved in agreement as they rushed him out the sliding front door and into the back of the ambulance.

"Come on," Kenneth told Greta, you need to be there to provide any information you can think of that might help."

"Jewel, would you stay and make sure the residents aren't upset by all the noise and commotion?"

"Certainly," she said, giving her husband a quick kiss on the cheek. She turned to Greta. "Don't you worry, he's in good hands."

Greta nodded, wiped tears from her eyes, and kept in step with Kenneth as they headed to his car.

***

Kenneth and Greta sat in the ER waiting room watching for the doctor to come out.

"It's been over an hour," Greta said softly, "maybe we should go ask at the desk."

Taking her frail hand, patting it gently, Kenneth tried to reassure her. "Clarence must be holding his own or we would have been notified by now."

Greta adjusted her position in the hard chair, feeling her bones sharp against the blue, plastic-molded seat. "I should be with him."

"They have to focus on treating him and if you were in there you would be a distraction. Why don't we pause and pray?"

Greta nodded.

Kenneth began. "Father in heaven, you're the great physician and we are trusting you to do what's right for Clarence. You know Greta's love for him and his for her. Help the medical team working on my friend right now, and give them wisdom to know what's wrong and how to help him. Provide patience and comfort for Greta and me, as we wait. Amen."

"Amen," Greta whispered, brushing tears away.

Thirty minutes passed and a middle-aged man in scrubs appeared. He addressed Greta. "Mrs. Hartman?"

Greta stood, feeling relief from the uncomfortable chair. "Yes, how is my husband? May I see him now?"

"Please come with me" he said, his face etched with sadness, "so we can talk in private."

"Is he okay?" she pleaded.

The doctor led the couple through the double doors to a small room which had a *consult room* sign on it. "Have a seat, please," he encouraged. Once seated, Dr. Salvas removed his glasses, carefully placing them on the small table. "Mrs. Hartman," he began slowly, "your husband had a heart attack."

Greta inhaled to hold back tears.

Kenneth put his arm around her and asked the doctor, "What's the prognosis?"

"I'm sorry to have to tell you, but Mr. Hartman passed away minutes ago. There was nothing else we could do for him."

Greta sat immobile except for a slight rocking back and forth, her mind racing back over the last few hours before she found Clarence on the floor in the sunroom. They had a nice day planned. She went to visit with the director and was so happy that he and his wife wanted to purchase her paintings. She couldn't wait to tell Clarence about it at breakfast, but...*How did this happen, Lord?*

***

"Are you okay?" Dr. Salvas asked.

"I'll be fine as soon as I see my husband."

Kenneth looked at the doctor and they both remained silent.

Finally, Dr. Salvas stood. "Come, I'll take you to him."

Reaching the doorway where Clarence lay, Greta walked slowly to the side of his bed. She placed her hand softly on top of his and whispered his name. She laid her head on the pillow next to Clarence. "I love you, husband, I'll meet you at the river."

Chapter 9

Brian Hills sat staring at the screen, watching images of Clarence in the documentary Betty had done last year. It had been a month since the funeral and Brian still couldn't believe he was gone. Clarence's never give up attitude was an inspiration, and now he is a memory. Watching him on TV and seeing the moment he asked Greta to be his wife caused Brian to smile. Clarence had a humbleness that few men possessed. It went deep and drew people to him. The humility of truth was woven into his heart and spirit by God and was what Brian hoped to possess as well.

"Honey, I'm back," Betty's voice carried into the living room.

"I'm in here," he responded, clicking off the TV. He rose to greet his wife and planted a kiss on her cheek as they collided in the hallway. He relieved her of one of the two bags of groceries in her arms, as they took them to the kitchen.

"What have you been up to while I was at the store?"

Brian became a bit somber. "I was watching the video of Clarence's documentary."

Betty turned to look at her husband. She gave him a hug and then stood back a little. "We should ride out and visit with Greta this weekend. What do you think?"

Brian began unpacking his sack of groceries. "I think she would like that. I spoke with Kenneth and he said she finally picked up her paint brush again and is back at the easel."

Betty felt anguish in her heart for Greta. To find her true love at such a late age and then lose him after such a short marriage had to be crushing. "I'm glad she's getting back to it, she is such a good artist. I'm sure it'll keep her mind occupied and give her purpose."

"Yeah, but the funny thing is that she won't allow anyone to get a peek at it."

"Well, artists can be a bit mysterious," Betty said as she finished putting up the last of the food and folded the bags. "How about us going on Saturday? Maybe she'd like to have lunch with us. I'll call and invite her."

"Saturday sounds fine with me. Do you think Kat would like to go along?"

Betty squinted her eyes. I'm not sure. I think Ryan is off this weekend, so they might have plans. I'll check with her. Meanwhile, I'm fixing a meatloaf snowball casserole tonight, so make sure you're hungry."

Brian laughed as he headed upstairs, "I'm always hungry."

Betty turned her attention to preparing a cup of Earl Gray and settled herself at the breakfast bar. She mourned Clarence and knew he would always be a sweet memory. He was the first person she interviewed for the documentary she, Kat, and Clay did for Public Television. Clarence had become like family and would be missed greatly. Greta was a huge part of Clarence's last year. Betty's heart swelled with compassion thinking about the short courtship and marriage of the two nonagenarians. Now Greta must carry on without him.

Betty thought about how she had waited to find Mr. Right. God brought her and Brian together at the estate sale that Emily set up for her patient, Mary Ludwig. The legacy of love they received had exceeded anything she could have imagined. Losing Brian would crush her.

She sipped her tea and brushed aside the tear sliding down her cheek.

Crackers, Kat's foster puppy, appeared at her feet. She smiled and reached down whisking him into her arms. "Hi little guy, are you waiting for Kat to get home?" Betty had fallen in love with him since the day Ryan dropped him into Kat's arms. "I'm sorry you lost your human parents, but Kat and the rest of us will love and take care of you." Crackers rewarded her promise with several licks on her cheek. She squeezed him gently, loving his soft fur against her skin. "I need to get busy little one," she whispered as she placed him back onto the floor. "Go find a toy or take a nap. Kat will be back soon to play with you."

She turned her thoughts to the next documentary on the calendar; praying that as she connected with women facing breast cancer alone, she could tell their story and put them in touch with helpful resources. After observing how Emily dealt with finding the lump in her breast and having Seth to support her emotionally, Betty realized how important it was for women to have someone to lean on. Perhaps she could find a support group or mentoring program for those women without family. *Please God, use me in the lives of the women you bring into my life through my filming. Help me to help them find strength and truth.*

Betty finished her tea and rinsed out the cup, setting it near the electric kettle and box of tea. She needed to get some laundry started and then work on the checklist for her meeting with Kat and Clay next week. They would be visiting with Penny Evans on Thursday to find out the results of her biopsy. *Lord, let it be benign, but if it's not, show me how to help her with the truth.*

***

Tim Fairbanks placed the closed sign on the door to his diner. Leila, his new employee was almost done refilling condiments and wiping down tables for tomorrow's breakfast crowd. He missed Sarah, but her replacement was working out great. He liked that he didn't need to tell her repeatedly what to do or how to do it. Maybe her maturity and life experience taught her well.

"Leila," Tim called out, "come sit down and have a cup of coffee with me so we can talk."

Leila turned toward his voice. "Sure Mr. Tim, be right there," she replied. "I'm about done anyway."

"You can drop the Mr." he said, laughing. "I'm Tim to everyone."

They settled at the small table and he placed a cup of coffee down for each of them.

"Have I mentioned that I'm very pleased about how well you do your job here?"

Leila gave a hearty laugh. "Yes, every day. I'm glad you're happy with my work because I really like my job."

Tim nodded his head. "I've had this diner twenty-five years and it has provided a living for me. After my wife died ten years ago, I poured myself into it. The people in the area love hanging out here and I know most everyone. I'd like to know a little more about you."

"My husband, Aaron, passed eight years ago, and I've had a rough go of it. He had no life insurance so I was pretty much on my own in New Mexico."

"I'm sorry to hear that, Leila."

She gave a quick hand wave, her silver bangle bracelets tinkling. "It's okay, I survived. I'm a tough old broad as some have said. I don't let things break me down. I just tell the Good Lord I need help and he provides."

"How did you end up in Texas?"

"After Aaron died and I settled everything in Taos, I came to Texas to stay with my brother, Darrell. He later decided to move to Arizona and told me I could stay in his house for as long as I needed. He's still in Arizona and I'm still in his house."

"I'm going to give you a raise, but along with it, I'd like to make you a manager."

Leila stared in disbelief. "A manager?"

"Yep," Tim said, slapping the table. "You work too hard and you do much more than a waitress would do. I'd like to show you my ordering process and other details of how I run things. That way, if I'm not here you'll have full authority to keep things going."

"You're not planning on dying or moving are you?" she joked.

"Neither," he responded with a laugh. "I think we'd make a good team."

Leila raised her cup toward Tim. "A toast then, to our new relationship."

Tim matched her toast with his cup and winked. "To our new relationship indeed."

***

Blanca and Rosie put the finishing touches on the breakfast dishes they had prepared for Emily and Seth, along with some of their friends from the estate sale group; Betty, Brian, Rita and Ron. After Blanca and Rosie met with Seth to discuss a possible job offer at the B & B, it was decided that they would cook sample dishes to show off their creative flair.

Rosie surveyed the tray of Mexican Fruit Salad. "Blanca, where did you learn to make these beautiful salads? Putting the mangoes, pineapple, papaya and watermelon into the hollow pineapple make it look so elegant, but the seasoning is so flavorful."

"Thank you, it was a combined idea when Bree and I were trying to eat lighter. I made the chili and lime seasoning and she came up with the idea of serving them in the pineapple itself."

"They look beautiful and I think they'll be a hit."

"I hope so. Did you make the sausage casserole when you worked in Waxahachie? It smells delicious."

"Yes, it was a weekend favorite. My boss, Alfredo, loved the dish. For today, I prepared two. One mild and the other with a chili-pepper sausage for an extra kick.

Blanca rounded up the serving carts so they could begin rolling the food into the dining room. "We have way more food than six people can eat," she commented as she added other dishes to the cart."

Rosie laughed, "We might have to take home leftovers." She loaded the top level of one cart with Sopapillas, Pan Dulce, salsa, and a carafe of Orange Atole. "Do you think we should start serving?"

"Yes, I'm excited to see their reaction," Blanca agreed. "It's ShowTime at the Texas Tribute B&B."

***

Seth stretched out his legs, eager to kick back and relax. Today had been a success as they enjoyed the dishes Blanca and Rosie prepared. He was pleased with the taste testing. The duo had proved their creative cooking skills beyond what he thought possible. Emily was doubly satisfied and agreed with him that Blanca and Rosie would head up the kitchen when they opened next month. The pair would work on their recipe lineup and seasonal specialties, while Seth promised to make sure supplies were ordered and everything they needed was on hand.

***

Emily, Betty, and Rita, took advantage of the gathering to discuss plans for a wedding shower for Rita, so Seth returned home alone. He remembered the magical wedding he and Emily had in England, thanks to the generosity of Mary Ludwig and the legacy she left to Emily. He'd been so busy readying Mary's former house, transforming it into a B&B, that the beautiful home in Essex slipped his mind. Emily was in a quandary about what to do with it. They had agreed to live here rather than move across the pond, and the caretakers, Teddy and Ruth, were more than happy to continue in that role. Weddings were held there and the income from that was allocated to a charity, but Emily felt that Mary's legacy wasn't being honored.

He heard a car in the driveway and soon Emily's voice carried a thank you and goodbye to whichever woman dropped her off. He rose to greet her at the door.

"Hi Sweetie," he said, planting a kiss on her rosy cheeks. "You look radiant, did you have a good time?"

"The best time possible," she said in her chirpy voice. "We are planning a great shower for Rita. Betty had a couple fun ideas and Rita was delighted about the whole plan."

"It's going to be a busy spring with the shower, our grand opening, and the wedding. Speaking of weddings, I was reminiscing about ours and what a beautiful bride I have."

"Aww," she answered with a hug around his neck. "It was a fabulous wedding and I was blessed with a handsome groom."

"Betty and Brian came in a close second, don't forget."

Emily smiled. "Yes, I'm glad we made it a double wedding." She released Seth from her hug, and slipped off her shoes. "I'm really tired. I think I ate too much of Blanca and Rosie's food. Maybe I should take a short nap."

Seth swooped her up in his arms. "Your wish is my command. You lay down and I'll work on some papers I need to turn over to my associate at the office."

Emily snuggled her face into the crook of his neck. "Okay," she whispered.

***

Rita exited the bus and crossed the street to the new building Ron purchased for her as an early wedding present. He told her he'd meet her there when she was done with the shower planning with the girls. *I really need to get a car,* she thought as she crossed the street. Rita spotted Ron's car on the side of the building. He waved from the doorway and hurried to walk her to the entrance.

"Hi Hon," he said excitedly. "Did y'all finish your plans?"

"Sure did," she said, slipping into a hug from her fiancé.

"Come on, I want to show you some things and tell you what I've planned."

"Should I be nervous or excited?"

Ron laughed. "Probably a little of each," he said as he took her hand and led her inside.

Once they entered, Ron flipped the lights on and led her to the large table near an office. He proudly pointed out multiple buckets of paint with color splashes across the top of each lid. "They arrived this morning but I wanted to surprise you. I ordered each of the colors you looked at for the different work areas. Do you think your students will be inspired?"

Rita couldn't believe her eyes. She had daydreamed bold, inspiring colors out loud to Ron describing how she wanted to decorate the inside and give her classrooms some pizazz. Now, here they were.

"Ron," she squealed, hugging him tight on the arm as she examined each bucket of paint. "They are exactly what I envisioned, but you didn't have to get them so soon. We don't start until fall."

"There is a lot on the calendar this year, my love. I figured I'd get the paint and we can hire painters when we're ready. Besides, I have more news for you."

Rita calmed herself down to give him her full attention. "What?" she asked excitedly.

"I spoke with Pastor Todd and he will be coming here to perform our wedding ceremony."

Rita threw herself into Ron's arms. "Thank you. Now our friends can be there and not have to travel to see us get married."

Ron pulled back and looked directly at his bride-to-be. "I want you to be the happiest bride ever and I'll do anything to make it happen." He saw tears pool and he gently kissed each eye. "Now, the last surprise for today, although I can't tell you specifics, is that I have made honeymoon arrangements."

"Oh Ron, this day couldn't get any more perfect. I love you so much."

"Every day is perfect for me as long as you are in it," he said folding her against his chest.

***

Brian sat, hunched over his desk, working on developing names for the B & B rooms he promised Seth he would create. Right now, his brain kept remembering the delicious food he enjoyed earlier, prepared by Blanca and Rosie. He made a note to book a room after the B & B opened for business so Betty and he could try other dishes. *Get your mind off of food, Brian, focus on names.* He looked at the list he had written so far.

The name he chose for one of the bedrooms, he picked as a reminder of when he met Betty at the estate sale. He literally bumped into her and when she turned around she was wearing a sassy blue hat she found there. The name, *Blue Chapeau*, seemed to fit perfectly. He knew she would be pleased.

Brian remembered Sheila's gifts from Mary after the sale, a bounty of quilts. There was one in particular that meant a lot to her because of the loss of her son, David. It had denim pockets all over the back filled with notes from hospital people who cared for him. He decided to name a bedroom, *Denim Pockets*.

A name in Rita's honor was easy, considering her love for transforming rustic pieces into art. With her and Ron getting married soon, he chose *Rustic Romantic*, which could serve as the honeymoon suite.

Deciding on a name to represent Kat came easy. She and her mom laughed a lot about daffodils, and Kat nicknamed the flower Laffadill. The name on the door would be *The Laff-A-Dill*. Kat will certainly get lots of laughter from that.

Now to figure out names for the rest. He liked the thought of a jewelry name for Blanca and her daughter, since that was what Mary left to them. There were so many to choose from though. Ah, the thought struck him. *Circle of Love*. The members of the estate sale group made a circle of love. At least that's what Blanca said at the banquet in a roundabout way. That would be perfect.

It seemed more difficult to come up with a name for him. He had received books, first editions, but what name would he create to reflect that?

A name for Emily was easy. He will forever remember his and Betty's fairytale double wedding in England at Emily's inheritance house, *Summer Bride*. It was enchanting.

The only name he thought of for Mary was *The Legacy Room*. She left each of the group a legacy of a lifetime. She would like that.

His was the only one left. He sat back in his chair and looked around at the bookshelves filled with the books he inherited. Each volume contained words written for generations to follow. *The Scribe*. That was it. He put the names in an email and sent it to Seth, praying they sound good to him. He closed that file and opened the manuscript he had in progress; the book about a very special man named Clarence.

***

Jake drove home from work with Annie on his mind. He enjoyed their evening together last week. Her homemade chicken soup leftovers and crusty rolls were better than he ever had at a restaurant. What made the night special was the conversation after the dishes were put away. Annie seemed to enjoy hearing Jake talk about his childhood. For him, the memories were dull but Annie listened intently and hung on every word, asking questions about some of the antics he shared. He even apologized at times because he felt guilty talking so much. Her words touched him when she said, "I see the young boy in your eyes; the playfulness flickers when you tell me things."

He pulled into his driveway, parked the car and went inside. Tossing his keys on the table, he opened the fridge to retrieve a pitcher of tea, and after pouring a glass, settled into a leather theater chair. His living room smelled like a furniture store showroom. He wasn't sure he was pleased about it. Once he removed his mother's old furniture and had the new furnishings in place, the home became a house. That thought struck him hard. It made him realize that his life was in the same condition. The warmth he experienced throughout his life in this home left when his mom died. Getting rid of her things and filling it with new stuff was like sterilizing the place. He had nothing. Even his brother would soon be getting married and starting a family. *What do I have? A frame house with new furnishings and a job at a hotel.*

Jake sipped his tea and picked up the phone. He punched in the number and waited.

"Hello, big brother," said Ron on the other end, "How ya doing? It's been a while since I heard from you."

"I'm okay I guess. I just thought I'd give you a call, I know it's late."

"Don't worry about it. I generally don't turn in till after eleven. Is there something you need to talk about?"

"I was just thinking, wondering actually, if you might have time to drive up here for a couple days."

"Sure, Jake, something serious going on? I could be there tomorrow evening unless it's really important and you need me sooner."

"Tomorrow evening's fine. I just wanted for us to talk in person."

"Done deal. I'll call you when I'm in the city limits."

"Great, thanks Ron."

Jake ended the call and stretched out fully in the recliner. Now he needed to figure out what he wanted to tell Ron. *I'm sorry I moved back to mom's house? I'm envious that you have a life and I don't? I hate my life and want to move away?* Even Jake knew it sounded ridiculous. No matter how he phrased it, the truth is that he needed family in his life to put the warmth back into the house. He closed his eyes. *Lord, show me what I'm missing. Help me see my purpose.* He dozed off before he could say amen.

Chapter 10

"Hey, Gus," Jared called out from the stockroom in his half-brother's auto repair shop; "we need to order more fan belts. I need one for that blue Ford truck." When Gus didn't answer, Jared walked to the office to repeat his request.

Finding the office empty, Jared entered the shop area. "Gus, you out here?" he yelled over the sound of an air compressor.

"Over here," Gus answered loudly, "in bay 3."

Jared maneuvered around mechanical obstacles over to where Gus and Charles were hunched over a Chevy engine. "We need a fan belt. The one on the Ford I'm repairing is shot and we're out of them in the stockroom. I can run to the parts place and pick one up if you don't need me."

Gus jerked his head up from his work and raised his hand, motioning toward the office. "Sure, and while you're at it, take the list on my desk and get the other stuff I need."

Jared nodded. "Got it covered. I'll be back in an hour", he said, making his way to his Charger, parked on the side of the building.

Heading toward the highway, Jared's thoughts turned to Sarah, wondering how she was doing and if she got the job at the nursery. He missed her. Maybe he'd give Sarah a call tonight and see if they could meet up this weekend. Then again, she didn't seem to want to build their relationship now that she was planning to go to college.

Jared couldn't understand his luck, or lack of it, with women. It seemed like whenever he got close to someone it fizzled out or got so complicated there was no future. Granted, a lot of it was his own fault, but since he changed his life, allowing the Lord to lead him, you would think something positive would happen. Jared quickly deleted that thought from his mind. A lot of positive things happened after he prayed, asking Jesus to take control. He reunited with his family, was forgiven by Kat, for how he treated her, got a job, and enrolled in college. That's a lot of positives. *Thank You, Lord. But now I'd like to have someone special in my life. I thought it was Sarah. What's up with that?* No answer boomed from heaven or whispered in his ear.

***

Kat felt happy and content sitting across the table from Ryan as they enjoyed lunch at The Canopy. Today was mild with a slight breeze, making it perfect for outdoor seating. Ryan had two days off and would be back at the firehouse tomorrow. Kat looked forward to this evening at the movies. She found herself thinking more and more about Ryan when they weren't together. He made her feel special just in how he looked at and treated her.

"I found out something about Crackers that you might be interested in knowing," Ryan said, breaking into her reverie.

At the mention of the dog Ryan brought to her after the fire, Kat quickly responded. "What? I don't have to give him up, do I?"

Ryan laughed. "No, don't worry about that. But, I was in the neighborhood the other day and talked with the neighbors of Cracker's owners. I asked if they knew anything about the little guy that would help you care for him better."

By now, Kat was wide-eyed, listening intently. "And?"

"It seems he was a rescue dog and after they had him a while, they found that he loved to eat those little fish-shaped crackers."

"Goldfish?" she offered.

"Yes, Goldfish. So the neighbors told me they decided to name him Crackers."

"How cute. I need to buy some today. Did they tell you anything else?"

"Only that the woman had cancer and Crackers was such a comfort to her."

Kat's eyes pooled. "Poor little guy; I'm sorry he lost them, but I'm thankful you brought him to me. I'll love and take really good care of Crackers."

"You have a good heart," Ryan said, smiling. He reached for her hand and squeezed it lightly. "I'm glad there's room in it for me too."

Greta sat quietly, staring at the half-finished painting on the easel in front of her. The brushes lay on the palette beside her chair and a breeze blew gently through the window of her room. She missed her husband terribly and even found herself calling his name at times. They had only enjoyed only a few months as a married couple and since his death she really hadn't taken time to grieve. Oh sure, she cried at his funeral, but the time to grieve didn't seem to arrive. She closed herself off from people, preferring to spend time with the Lord, and then she turned to her canvas. Perhaps that was her way of grieving.

The canvas seemed to stare back at her. This lighthouse was different. She usually painted them in pairs showing the transformation from rubble to restoration. Greta wanted this one to evoke her grief which would then become gratitude. She had completed the bottom half of the structure illustrating scattered stones and faded colors. Midway up the canvas, clouds encircled the top half of the lighthouse, which she hadn't painted yet. The underside of the clouds appeared dark and destructive, while the top half was lighter and serene. In her mind's eye she saw it completed with the beam from the light shining on the cloud and a shadow of a man ascending out of sight. There would be another addition to the painting at the very end, but for now she focused on the sky above the clouds and the scene she hoped to create.

A knock on her door drew Greta's attention. She quickly covered the canvas and rose to answer the knock. "Who is it?" she called.

"It's Betty Hills."

Greta opened the door. "How nice of you to stop by," she said with a small smile. "Please, come in."

Betty stepped inside and her eyes were drawn immediately to the easel. "Did I interrupt your painting?"

"No, I was doing some mental painting," Greta responded. "Sit down and I'll get us some coffee."

Betty took a seat by the bed. "I'm okay; I can't stay but a minute. I was in the area and wanted to come by and invite you to have lunch on Saturday with Brian and me."

"I don't know," Greta said, sitting back down in front of the easel, stalling so she would have time to decide if she really wanted to go out.

"Please," Betty insisted, "we would love to visit with you over lunch."

"I don't have much of an appetite," Greta said softly. "I usually just eat light about six."

"We could go to La Madeleine and have some quiche."

Greta looked up at Betty's kind smile and saw the compassion of a dear friend. How could she say no.

"Well, I suppose it would do me a bit of good. I haven't gone anywhere since...."

"I know, Greta, and we've missed you. Is two o'clock okay?"

"Two is fine, and thanks for thinking of me."

Betty rose from the chair, leaned in to give Greta a hug, and felt how frail her body seemed. "I'll be going now, and we'll see you Saturday."

***

Sarah sat in her car filling out the application for a job at the Blooms-A-Lot Nursery, her friend, Mason Trevor's place of employment. Mason said she already spoke to her supervisor and put in a good word. Sarah watched as crowds of people streamed toward the front entrance. Excitement rose at the prospect of working here, helping them choose the perfect plant or tree. Her only concern, looking down at the experience section of the application, was her lack of similar work. She had gone to Tim's Diner right out of school, and she had his letter of recommendation, but other than her interest and love for plants, she might not be the best applicant.

Sarah did bring along photographs of her landscaping efforts at home. They highlighted the various shrubs and showstopper plants she created for her parents. She was particularly fond of the waterfall corner and hoped it would impress her interviewer.

She signed the application and gathered her things. Sarah slipped out of the driver's seat and took a deep breath as she locked the car and headed toward the door. She really wanted this job and planned to convey that message during the interview. This position would be her entry into her future at Palo Alto College in the fall. *Please Lord, show me favor for this job. Amen.*

***

Rosie read the letter she received from her son, Ro. "He has boxed up my things and shipped them to arrive next week," she told Blanca, who was sitting quietly across from Rosie. "Listen to this part," she continued, "'I'm sorry you chose to leave but of course that's your privilege. I can't really understand why you and Monica didn't get along. She told me she tried to make you like her.'" Rosie slapped the letter down on the coffee table. "Ha, she *tried* to make me like her???" she said out loud to Blanca, "How did she try? By keeping Ro so busy that he never spent time with me?"

Blanca remained silent, allowing her friend to compose herself. Rosie's hands were shaking and she collapsed back into the sofa cushion. Finally, Blanca spoke in a calm voice. "Rosie, it may be that your son isn't aware of what his girlfriend is doing. She may be presenting things to him in a different way than what you are aware of."

Rosie sniffled a bit. "It doesn't matter because he's in love with her and will stand up for her. He'll believe whatever she tells him no matter what the truth is."

Blanca rose and came around to sit by Rosie, handing her a tissue from the nearby box on the coffee table. "I think we should pray before you respond to him. It's better to respond than to react."

Rosie pulled herself together and nodded her head. "You're right of course. I love him and I see him as being manipulated, but I can't do anything about it."

"Except to continue loving him," Blanca added. "Let's pray. Lord, You alone are able to change people's hearts and we call upon you to reach into Ro's and Monica's hearts and cause them to turn to You. Help Rosie to respond lovingly to her son and keep their relationship strong. Amen."

"Amen," Rosie added.

"Now, let's go have some tea and later, if you decide, you can either call him or write a short letter. Maybe invite him and Monica here for a visit when the B & B opens."

Rosie jerked her head around. "Blanca! That's a great idea. Why didn't I think of that?"

"Because that's why you have a friend," Blanca said, laughing. "Let's go work on more recipes for our chef debut."

The two friends ignored the pages of Ro's letter on the coffee table and headed into the kitchen. "You know, we make a great team, don't we?" Rosie stated rather than asked.

"We sure do," Blanca said, squeezing Rosie's shoulder, "With God on it, we are unbeatable."

***

Greta ate her quiche very purposefully, slowly, a half-bite at a time. She was grateful to Betty and Brian for picking her up and treating her to lunch at La Madeline's. Greta thought this quaint restaurant was perfect and the quiche was delicious. She just wished she were hungry.

"Is your quiche okay?" Betty asked, noticing the slowness of Greta's eating.

Greta looked up. "Yes, it's wonderful, but my appetite isn't what it used to be. Maybe I can take the rest home."

"Certainly, I'll ask for a to-go box. That way you'll have supper tonight."

"I would like more coffee though. Don't tell the director, Mr. Cavanaugh, but it's better than his special coffee," she said cracking a mischievous grin.

Brian guffawed. "You're right, Greta, I have to agree with you there. So how is your painting coming along?"

Greta leaned back in her chair. "It's almost finished. I just need to add a little something to it."

Betty excused herself to go get more coffee and the box for Greta.

Brian looked at Greta intently. "What's next when it's done?"

Greta returned his look and never blinked. "I guess that's up to the good Lord, isn't it?"

"Yes, and I believe He gave you your talent for painting with the intention you would use it for His glory. I can't wait to see your next piece."

Greta didn't respond. Her gaze focused on a plaque near the window. It read, *Live in such a way that those who know you, but don't know God, will come to know God because they know you.*

For an instant, Brian saw a spark ignite in Greta's eyes.

She sat up straight and smiled. "You're right," she said with a sudden passion. "I just received direction from Him."

Betty returned to their table with a small to-go box, setting it next to Greta's plate. "Here you are, this should be just the right size. The young man at the counter is bringing the coffee."

"Thank you, Betty," Greta said cheerfully.

Betty looked at Brian who hunched his shoulders discreetly with his I-don't-have-a-clue, look. When Betty left the table, Greta seemed disconnected from their conversation and now she was back in the game. Again, Betty looked at her husband with a *what-happened* look.

Greta broke the silence. "Thank you, Brian, for helping me see what's next."

Now it was Brian's turn to look perplexed. "I don't know how, but I'm happy to be of service," he said, chuckling.

"Both of you have been dear friends," Greta said, sliding the remaining half of her quiche into the box. "You've helped me more than I can ever explain." She winked at Brian. "I have something more to do, a purpose, and God will be pleased."

"I think God is pleased with your paintings," Betty said.

"It's not only my painting; I want to please Him with my life as well," Greta assured them. She took a sip of coffee and smiled at her two hosts. "I don't have a lot of years left but what years I do have I'll make count."

"That's something we should each be doing," Brian commented.

"Can we take our coffee to-go?" Greta asked, "I'd like to get back if that's okay with you."

Brian scooted his chair back and stood. "Certainly."

Betty gathered the coffees and followed as Brian escorted Greta to the car. *This lady is full of surprises; I hope I'm like her at that age.*

***

Ron steered his car into Jake's driveway, cut the engine, and sat staring at the familiar house—the childhood home in which they both enjoyed growing up. Ron's memories of his parents flooded over him suddenly. His dad was a guiding father who lived what he taught about honesty, generosity, kindness, and love. When he gave his word it meant something. Ron never knew his dad to lie about anything, whether among family members or business associates. Lillian's face appeared in his mind. His mother was the inner strength of the family. Her faith made her strong and she tried to instill that into her two boys from the time they could distinguish right from wrong. She must have succeeded because neither he nor Jake ever got into serious trouble; although they found mischief easily. Their mother was forgiving but made sure her children knew there was a consequence to their choices.

Ron's reminiscing was curtailed by a shout from the porch; his brother motioned for him to come inside.

Entering the front room, Ron was taken back by what he saw. The once homey interior had been replaced with a stern décor yielding only to a soft side by the leather chairs and sofa.

"Wow!" was all Ron could muster at the moment.

"Do you like it?" Jake quizzed.

"It's definitely a change and gives the place a bachelor's look. Did Annie help you pick out furniture?"

"No, she helped with the yard sale, but I chose the new stuff."

Ron kept looking for what wasn't there; something that said, WELCOME. "Did you change the other rooms too?"

"Not the guest room. I haven't gotten that far."

"May I sleep there tonight?"

Jake laughed. "You don't like this, do you?"

"What matters is whether you like it." Ron looked at his brother. "You do like it, right?"

Jake ignored his brother's question. "Throw your bag in the guest room and I'll make some coffee. I really need to talk to you."

Ron sat across from his brother at the new kitchen table. It wasn't actually a table as much as a breakfast bar on casters— moveable if ever it became necessary. "So," he said, after taking a swallow of coffee, "what's going on that you needed me to drive all the way up here so suddenly?"

Jake thought for a moment as he twirled a spoon in his cup, dissolving the overload of sugar he put in. "I was hoping you might help me figure that out. Changing things in the house hasn't helped."

"Helped you?" Ron asked. "I didn't realize something was wrong. You haven't said anything."

"I know. It's hard to explain. I'm really not happy, or maybe that's not the right word. I'm trying to figure out who I am now. With Mom gone, after watching over her so long, I feel lost. Moving in here didn't help. I felt like a young boy at first and then memories multiplied my misery. I thought if I changed how the place looked it would make it mine instead of hers."

"Well, it's definitely not hers," Ron quipped.

"Touché," Jake responded halfheartedly. "It's not really mine either, that's the problem."

Ron got up and walked to the living room, then the bedrooms, before returning to where Jake stood in the hallway.

"Sell it," Ron said firmly.

"But I just bought the stuff."

"Not the furniture, the house,"

Jake stood in shock, speechless.

"I mean it. You're not happy here so why stay? You can probably return the furniture and just sell it unfurnished. I'll be glad to help you find a new house or an apartment."

"I never thought I'd sell our childhood home."

"Jake, we're not kids anymore. Mom and Dad are gone. We can live where we want and I know Mom would want you to live where you feel comfortable."

"You're right. I've felt stuck for a long time. I'm too young to let life just roll past me."

"How are you and Annie getting along?"

Jake smiled for the first time since his brother arrived. "We're good. I was over at her place the other night for dinner and we had a nice evening together."

"Do you think your relationship is headed anywhere?"

Jake headed toward the kitchen with Ron following. "Possibly. I think a lot of her. I know she's a bit older than I am, but we get along well. I think she wants a relationship."

Ron threw his arm around his brother's shoulder. Then get out there and see where God leads. Is your job still to your liking?"

"Yeah, and I'm up for a promotion. I may be getting my own hotel to manage."

"Wow, you have things happening. Whatever I can do to help you, let me know. First thing is this house. Let's get it ready to put on the market."

Jake grasped Ron's hand and pulled him into a rough hug. "Thanks, Ron. Thanks for being here for me."

Chapter 11

Lane Jennings scanned the documents he drew up for the purchase of the Wimberley Cottage. He was surprised when Betty agreed to sell it to Sheila. He shamefully recalled the way he acted at the estate sale banquet, trying to build up his real estate business when guests were sharing their story of the legacy Mary Ludwig left to them. Thankfully his later apology was accepted and both Betty and Sheila forgave his rudeness.

"Lane," Sheila called from the hallway, "Betty and Brian just drove up."

"Great, I have the papers all ready," he said, rising to join his wife to welcome their guests.

After seating her friends in the study, Sheila brought in a tray of tea, setting it on the side table. She made sure to offer the accompanying cookies and then took a chair next to Betty. "I'm so excited and can't wait to get started," Sheila said.

"I'm happy for you," Brian started, "and can't wait to hear about your plans for the cottage."

Betty jumped into the conversation, almost as excited as Sheila. "When I heard what Sheila wanted to do, I decided to be part of it by selling the cottage. I haven't shared your plans with Brian; I knew you'd want to do that."

"Thanks for keeping it secret and agreeing to sell the property. I plan to create a special quilt shop. As you know, Mary Ludwig left me an inventory of antique quilts. I already told Seth that I'm donating some for use at their B & B because it will honor Mary. I sold one of the most valuable quilts and will put that towards the purchase of the cottage."

"What kind of quilt shop will it be?" Brian asked.

"You know we lost our son, David, years back and we have a quilt the hospital staff made for him. It's called "Pockets of Love". It brought us such comfort after David passed, because the back of it has pockets in which staff members each slipped a love note to David." Sheila's eyes pooled, but she continued.

"I want to create a quilt shop where bereaved mothers, grandmothers, or other family members can gather and work on a quilt in honor of their child. I've been in touch with a few quilting instructors who have pledged to volunteer their time to teach on a rotating basis. As the women work on their quilts it will help them through their grieving."

Betty grabbed her husband's hand excitedly. "Isn't that a wonderful idea for our cottage? I mean Sheila's cottage?"

"It's great. I'm just wondering how it will operate. Will you charge for the classes and materials?"

"No, I have suppliers willing to donate fabric and loan sewing machines. I just need to make room in the cottage for various classrooms."

"You'll be applying for a non-profit status then?" Brian asked, munching on his ginger cookie.

"Yes. Seth, being an attorney, said he would help us with all the legal stuff."

Lane smiled at his wife. "I'm so proud of her. She's even going to have an area for Mary Dee to play in while they are spending time there."

"Where is Mary Dee?" Betty asked, looking toward the doorway.

"Naptime," Lane whispered and laughed.

Betty sipped her tea. "I hope we get to see her before we leave. She's such a cutie."

"I'm sure you will, she's due to wake up in about half an hour," Sheila said softly.

Betty patted her hands together happily. "Okay, let's look at the paperwork and complete this transaction." She looked at Sheila. "I want to be part of this beautiful ministry."

Sheila glanced from Brian to Betty. "Thank you both! I know at first you were hesitant to sell the cottage."

Brian smiled. "Now that I've heard how it will be used you have my vote."

Betty laughed. "When I first told him I was planning to sell it, he thought I was crazy. Brian's been using it as sort of a writer's retreat as he works on his book about Clarence."

"Well, it was a quiet place – the perfect atmosphere for reflection --, which is why it will be great for how you'll be using it, Sheila."

"I appreciate your willingness, Brian, to give up your space."

Lane handed the paperwork to the Hills and then drank his tea. "Honey, tell them the name you decided on for the shop."

Sheila wore a broad grin. "I'm keeping that a secret, and you better too," she warned Lane with a shake of her finger.

Both Betty and Brian smiled. "Can't wait to find out," Betty said.

***

Emily watched her husband as he installed the last room nameplate on the door. It was the one she liked the best, The Legacy Room, named appropriately for Mary Ludwig, whose home this was. Mary left a powerful legacy behind and if not for her, Emily's life would not be so rich with love and truth. Mary's generous heart and love for others was proved by the way she lived. Mary loved the Lord and used what He gave her in life to benefit others after her death.

"How does that look?" Seth asked, stepping back to admire his handiwork.

"It's perfect, and I love the classy Legacy font. The curves on the double T's soften the handwritten look even more."

Seth looked closer at the writing. The brass scroll gleamed with black cursive lettering, spelling out the room name. The double T's on each end stand for the name of their Bed and Breakfast, Texas Tribute. He liked it enough to adapt as their logo on the sign, stationary, brochures, and menu. "Brian not only did an outstanding job in naming the rooms, but also in selecting the font design. What's great is that each plaque is unique to the room but they all have the double T's. I think my favorite room name is Summer Bride, the English manor Mary gave to you. I love the fact that Mary's parents gave the manor that name because they were married there, so it was the ideal place for us to have our own wedding. The name will always remind me of our beautiful wedding there and the beautiful bride I have," he said, planting a kiss on the tip of her nose.

Emily looped her arm around Seth's as they stood side-by-side, admiring the door plaque. "I enjoyed picking out the furnishings, and with the Double Wedding Ring quilt that Sheila donated to the room, it's perfect."

"I think naming the library for Brian was a great idea. Choosing The Scribe for it matched him exactly. He's a writer and avid reader, plus Mary left him her first edition collection.

"Okay, I'm hungry," she said, tugging on his arm a bit. "Too bad we aren't open yet. Then we'd have some great food prepared by Blanca and Rosie."

Seth laughed. "It won't be long, just one more month. Are you excited?"

"I am. Did you see the website your friend designed for us? It's fantastic."

"I looked at it the other day but I think Lonnie's done a lot since then."

"He added the photos I sent, including several of Mary."

"Great, I'll check it out after we get back."

"Back? Where are we going?"

Seth laughed. "I don't know, you're the one who's hungry. Which restaurant do you want to choose?"

Emily pursed her lips and tapped her temple. "Hmm, I'm craving shrimp."

Seth steered his wife toward the door. "Ahh, I know the perfect place for a pregnant woman's cravings. Hello 'Joe's', here we come."

***

Annie Donovan maneuvered her Nissan through the construction detour and its backed-up traffic at 20 mph. At this rate she'd never get home. It was at a time like this Annie wished she knew the back roads instead of depending on only the freeways.

Her mind wandered to the conversation she had at lunch with Jake. She still couldn't believe her ears when he told her he was putting his childhood home up for sale. It didn't make sense. After his mother, Lillian, died last year, he had moved from his apartment back to her house. Then just a couple weeks ago Annie helped him with a huge yard sale to clear out his mother's furniture and décor so he could purchase new furnishings which suited his taste.

Traffic came to a dead stop. She leaned to the left hoping to spot an opportunity to get in the other lane, but it too was at a standstill. "Thank You, Lord, for reminding me to fill my tank this morning," she said. I should call Jake and let him know so he won't be sitting out front waiting.

"Jake, you won't believe the back-up on the Interstate with the construction going on," she explained when he answered. "It's a parking lot."

"I'm sorry; do you have plenty of gas?"

Annie laughed. "I just looked at my gas gauge and thanked God for reminding me to stop for gas on my way to work. Maybe we should wait until tomorrow when I'm off to get together."

"Sure! I'm glad you called. I was just getting in my car to head your way. Call me when you get home so I know you're okay."

"I will. I'm sorry, but I do want to hear about your progress with the house and plans to move."

"It's not your fault! Don't worry. Just be careful and don't forget to call me."

"Hey, traffic is moving again, I'm doing 25 now. Okay, I'll call you when I get home."

***

Jake hung up his phone and went back in the house. He felt badly for Annie being stuck in traffic and for his not seeing her tonight. He always enjoyed time with her. She had a knack for helping him make sense of things. He was thinking of moving closer to her apartment and planned to mention that tonight. Jake wasn't sure if it was a good idea or not. Ron suggested he buy a house instead of renting an apartment and that made sense financially. He wasn't sure though about having to deal with home ownership. When he had his former apartment things were less complicated. For one thing, it was furnished. Also, he paid only the rent, and didn't have to worry about repairs.

Jake kicked off his shoes and padded into the kitchen for a glass of tea. *I might as well pop a frozen dinner in the microwave since I'm eating in tonight.* He chose a meatloaf meal from the freezer and after setting the timer, he turned on the small kitchen TV to watch *Jeopardy*. *This is exactly the kind of life I don't want. Ron was right on target when he told me to sell and start over.* The timer buzzed and he retrieved his meal, resettling at the table, guessing the right answer to the current question on *Jeopardy*. *At least I got the answer correct on something.* Tomorrow he'd see Annie and go to a nice restaurant. Jake had that to look forward to and hoped she was happy about seeing him too.

***

Annie punched in Jake's number on her phone. She hated calling him again, this time with even more bad news.

"Hi, Annie, you made it home okay I see."

"No, Jake, there's been an accident…I'm almost sure my ankle is broken."

Jake nearly dropped his phone in his meatloaf. "What?"

"I was finally moving along and a car zipped up on my right and nearly ran me off the road trying to get in front of me. I overcorrected to avoid a truck and … well…"

"Where are you? I'll come get you."

Annie laughed. "I'm in an ambulance at the moment. They're taking me to Dallas Regional Med Center. I'm sure I'll be there a while."

"I'm on my way," he said, scooping up his keys and hunting his shoes in the living room. "I'll be there in twenty minutes."

"Please drive carefully; I don't want you in the bed next to me."

Jake laughed. "Thanks a lot. I'll see you soon."

He locked the front door, jumped in the car, and headed to the highway.

***

Annie was greeted at the hospital by some of the doctors and nurses she'd worked with at Scott & White several years back. The injection they gave her helped relieve the pain and now she waited for X-Ray results. She knew Jake was on his way and prayed that God would protect him as he drove. Annie felt foolish allowing herself to get into this predicament. She had seen enough broken ankles at the hospital to know what one looked like. It was conceivable there could even be worse damage. She suddenly thought about her car. *How badly was that damaged?* She sighed deeply, wishing Jake were here.

"Nurse Heartie," boomed a voice pulling back the curtain around her bed," I haven't seen you in at least three years."

Annie smiled at the nickname given to her years ago by her coworkers and at the familiar face of her friend. "Doctor Rawlings, it's great to see you, although not in these circumstances."

He shook her hand. "I agree. What happened to you?"

"Someone was in a hurry to get a car's length ahead of me in a traffic backup and he didn't mind shoving my car over."

"Road rage gets bad during rush hour. I'm sorry you're paying for his. Now, I've looked at your X-Rays and I'm afraid you have significant damage to your right foot."

"How bad is it?"

Doctor Rawlings turned his computer screen so Annie could see as he explained. "Being a nurse you will understand so I won't sugarcoat it.

"Annie..." Jake started as he swung the curtain open. "Oh, I'm sorry," he apologized, seeing the doctor. "I'll come back in when you're finished."

"No, stay," Annie said quickly, looking at Doctor Rawlings, "He's a good friend and I asked him to come."

"If Nurse Heartie doesn't mind, it's fine by me," Doctor Rawlings said, turning to Annie and his computer. "As I was saying, you have a fractured ankle. Fortunately, it's not displaced so we can get you into a cast. I've called in an orthopedic specialist to take care of you."

"Will she need to stay in the hospital?" Jake asked.

"No, we'll patch her up and send her home." Doctor Rawlings laughed. "Nurses don't make very good patients."

"I'll need crutches, I'm sure."

"We'll get you fitted and you'll mend well, as long as you behave and don't overdo things."

Annie pouted. "I hate having to take time off work."

The doctor shook his finger at her and grinned. "They will manage without you for a few weeks. You can follow up with the ortho doctor and you'll be good as new. You're lucky to have escaped with just a broken ankle."

"Not lucky, I'm blessed. God was watching out for me," she said as he rolled his computer out of the room. She heard him respond with an Amen.

"Okay, sweet friend," Jake said, bending down to kiss her forehead, "when they get your foot dressed and release you, I'm taking you back to my place for a few days. The guest room is untouched and I'll be able to keep an eye on you."

"Jake, that's not necessary, I do have medical training," she joked. "I'll be able to manage."

"Oh yes, I can see you going up those outside stairs on crutches to your apartment." He mimicked the action, limping up pretend stairs.

Annie laughed. "Well, maybe for just a couple days until I get used to using them."

Jake smiled as a nurse came to transfer her to a procedure room. "I'll be in the waiting room...waiting," he said, chuckling.

***

Rita stepped back and lifted her welder's mask. She examined the neck of the peacock, fashioned from a pair of needle nose pliers, minus one side of the handle. It looked smooth, and with polishing, the weld would be undetectable.

Finding the antique typewriter was a gift from God, she was sure. Rita wanted to give Ron a unique wedding present and this would be a one-of-a-kind gift. The tip of the pliers worked perfectly for the beak, and the top handle piece to the curved typewriter key section and then begin standing the keys upward to become the feathered display. She laughed out loud at this curious creature in the making. Ron, being an art lover of strange oddities, will fall in love with it.

Rita glanced at the calendar above her workspace. She would be moving into their new home next week. She had boxed up most of her things and had taken them to the new residence. Her small studio apartment felt empty. *It's a good thing it came furnished or I'd be sleeping on the floor.* Her lease would be up Monday so she'd officially move into her new home then.

She smiled as she covered her half-done art piece. *I can't believe I'll be Mrs. Ron Davis next month.* "Mrs. Ron Davis," she said out loud. Hearing her voice, Pekoe came around the corner and padded toward Rita. She laughed. "Did I disturb you, my friend?" Pekoe brushed against her until she picked him up. He ran his rough tongue across her hand, then buried his head in the crook of her elbow. "I guess you know," Rita said softly, "you can't honeymoon with us. You're going to stay with Kat and her dog, Crackers." Pekoe didn't move. "You may not care now but we'll see when you have your first play date with him later this week. It's time to go home, Puddy Tat. Your mom has to finalize some wedding details," she said, hugging her feline and placing him in his crate.

***

Annie sat quietly in the guest room, listening to the sounds of lunch being prepared in Jake's kitchen. The whirr of the can opener, a pan's being removed from the cupboard, bowls being placed on the table, and Jake's humming. He sounded content in what he was doing— fixing soup and grilled cheese sandwiches for each of them.

She looked at her disabled foot all tidy in its walking cast. Annie knew Jake was enjoying waiting on her, but she felt she was a helpless burden. He kept reminding her she was instructed to stay off of it for the weekend and Jake followed rules. She laughed a soft chuckle remembering his carrying her from the car to the guest room. She was a handful for sure but he managed well until he set her down on the chair. It was more of a plop than a setting down. They had both laughed to the point of tears. She promised not to go against doctor's orders but not without some reservations. She reminded him more than once that she was a nurse and knew what to do.

Annie held off on pain medication until late in the night and was glad Jake left a glass of water next to her pill bottle and the small bell he supplied for emergencies. Thankfully, he found a wheelchair for her to use temporarily.

"Your chariot awaits," Jake sang out as he came down the hall and tapped on the door before opening it and rolling the mobile chair through the door frame. "Lunch is ready and I hope you're as hungry as I am."

Annie smiled. "You are such an awesome caregiver, thank you." She sat upright, carefully lowering her foot to the floor. She allowed him to help her turn and maneuver onto the seat. "I think my appetite is improving now that I smell the tomato soup."

Jake laughed. "Your soup and grilled cheese turned out perfect, but my sandwich came out a bit charred."

"Oh no, what happened?"

He rolled her chair toward the kitchen. "I was dressing yours up to look nice on the plate and neglected to keep time on mine. It's good I don't do any cooking at the hotel," he said, helping her out of the chair onto the bar height stool.

"I'm sure it's tasty – like toasted marshmallows."

Jake wrinkled his nose into a scowl. "I hate toasted marshmallows."

Annie reached for his hand as he settled across from her. "May I ask the blessing on the food?"

Jake nodded and bowed his head.

Chapter 12

"We're going to have to delay the grand opening of our B&B," Seth blurted out to Emily.

Emily set the knife down and turned from her dinner preparations. "What? Why?"

Seth scowled, shaking his head as he took a seat at the table. "The new appliances have been delayed."

"No, we ordered them in January," Emily snapped back.

"Apparently there was a backlog of orders because they ran out and they're still waiting for delivery, which won't be until the end of May. We can't open until we have the commercial kitchen equipment."

Emily sat down opposite her husband. She looked at the discouraged frown he wore and knew he needed some cheerful news.

"Let's look at this in a different way," she began. "The delay of three months will give us time to fine tune everything. Blanca and Rosie still have to complete their food handling certification and the stationary will be in soon. We can take our time finishing the website and we will find out if we're having a boy or a girl this fall." She sat still, waiting for him to catch her last line.

Seth jerked his head up. "When is your sonogram?"

She loved the excitement on his face. "Next month on the 20th."

He rose to come around, pull her to him, and lay gentle kisses on her cheek. "I love you," he whispered.

She wrapped her arms around him as far as she could reach. "The feeling is mutual dear husband. Let's focus on what we're able to get done and trust God for the rest. Things will happen in God's timing."

"You're right, as always." He released her from his hug, patted her baby bump, and smiled. "Thank you."

"For what?"

"For being my wife. For being the mother of our child. For being the optimist always knowing how to change my mood in just the right way."

It was Emily's turn to smile. "I think the time I spent being Mary's caregiver and nurse enabled me to see the bright side of things. She taught me the truth about living: loving the best out of people."

"Mary was an exceptional woman. I miss her."

"She knew what was important in life."

"Speaking of what's important, weren't you starting something for dinner?" he teased, looking at the vegetables on the counter.

They laughed together. "You can help by getting out of my way," she said as she playfully pushed him toward the door.

***

Greta kept a slow pace as she ambled down the hall toward the director's office. She meant to talk to him sooner but the days got away from her. She liked Mr. Cavanaugh and his sweet wife, Jewel. They treated her and Clarence well and now that Clarence was gone, Greta knew she needed to make a few changes. Hopefully the director would agree without an argument.

She smoothed down the side of her hair; the side with the unruly strands refusing to stay behind her ear. Greta needed to find a hairdresser familiar with thin hair. Maybe she would call Betty later for a recommendation.

Greta heard Jewel's voice coming from the director's office as she gave a soft knock on the door frame.

"Come in, Greta, have a seat." Kenneth Cavanaugh greeted her at the door and escorted her thin body to a cushioned chair. "You relax and I'll get your special coffee."

"Thank you, and, Jewel, it's wonderful seeing you again," she said, shifting her eyes from the director to his wife.

"We always enjoy your company, Greta, and we are here for you."

Kenneth set a coffee mug on the side table and pulled up a chair so the three of them were in a circle. "How can we help you, Greta?"

Greta took a sip of coffee and set the cup carefully on the table. She leaned back in the chair, looking first at the director and then at Jewel.

"I'm not getting any younger," she blurted out.

Kenneth grinned. "Nor am I."

Greta wasn't grinning. "Of course, none of us are, but I'm 91 and now that Clarence is gone, I'm alone.

"You have us, Greta," Jewel said.

Greta smiled. "I know, and I have made other friends over the past year. Truthfully, I wasn't a very friendly person when I first came here. My life turned around after Mrs. Hills and her group entered my life. It's because of them I came to realize how much I needed the Lord."

Kenneth took a long drink of his coffee and then cradled the mug in his hands as he sat back in his chair. He contemplated a bit before speaking.

"Greta, you do know that God loved you even when you were less friendly, right?"

She looked straight at the director. "Yes, but unfortunately I didn't love me very much then. Mrs. Hills helped me forgive myself and others from my past. Once I did, I had room in my heart for love. God brought Clarence into my life and for the first time I was able to love someone enough to trust him."

Jewel was on the verge of tears. "We know losing Clarence was hard on you, but you will see him again one day."

Greta nodded. "Yes, and that brings me to why I wanted to meet with you."

Kenneth's eyebrows rose. "Oh? How exactly can we help you?"

***

Sarah entered Tim's diner quietly, hoping to surprise her former boss. She hadn't been by in a while and was curious how Leila, the new hire, was working out. As soon as the door closed behind her Tim poked his head out from the kitchen.

"Hey, Sarah," Tim shouted, making his way toward his former server, "How's the new job going? Have you created some show stopping yards yet?"

Sarah laughed. "Hi, Tim," she said affectionately as he hugged her shoulders. "I'm still working inside the nursery trying to learn as much as I can. I did create a cornerscape for the nursery yard though."

Tim escorted her to a table near the kitchen and they each took a seat. "I'll bet it was a show-stopper," he said, smiling.

"My supervisor took pictures and said it was beautiful, so I guess I did okay."

"I'm thinking you did better than okay. So what brings you here?"

"I'm off today and thought I'd stop by and see how Leila was working out and how you're doing."

"We're both doing fantastic. Thank you for bringing her in to interview. She is more than a waitress. In fact, I made her a manager."

Sarah's eyes widened. "What? Already?"

Tim chuckled. "She is a woman who can handle more than some men when it comes to putting in the effort. Leila's great with customers and our business has doubled since she came."

"Wow, I had no idea. That's great, Tim."

"I'm thinking of hiring another Sarah, if I can find one as dependable as you."

Sarah laughed out loud. "Well, where is Leila?"

"She'll be in at four. She needed time to take care of some business regarding her brother's house, so I told her to come in late today and she can close for me."

"Wish I could hang around to visit with her but I have things to do at home. I had better be going," Sarah said, glancing at the clock on the wall. "Mom's making meatloaf for supper and I need to stop at the store on my way home."

Tim stood and took Sarah's hand, helping her from the chair. "It was great seeing you again, don't wait so long the next time."

They walked to the door and she gave Tim a hug before heading out to her car. "Tell Leila I said hi, and I'll try to come back when she's here," she called out as the door closed.

Tim nodded and went back to the kitchen and resumed preparations for the soup and chili for supper. *As soon as Leila shows up I'm heading out to the bowling alley.*

Sarah slid into the driver's seat, started the engine, and backed out onto the street. *Things are sure changing this year: my job, college looming in the fall, my relationship with Jared, and Leila's working with Tim.*

Jared crossed her mind and she wondered how he was doing, working with his brother, Gus, fulltime. She wished he would give her a call but, then again, neither of them had time for a relationship. Sarah felt he wanted a deeper relationship with her and that scared her a bit. She wasn't sure about how she felt towards him. Maybe their being separated for several months would be good, giving them each time to focus on their futures. But, she did miss him and his sweet smile.

***

Kicking off her shoes, Betty padded across the tile floor to make a cup of Earl Gray. Fatigue suddenly struck her. *I tried to get too much done too quickly. All I wanted was to get home.* When the kettle sang she poured water over the teabag in her favorite mug and waited as it steeped several minutes. Even removing the teabag seemed to tire her.

What's going on with me today? I haven't done anything that required heavy labor. She didn't sleep well last night but still! She sipped her tea, feeling its warmth travel through her body. *Maybe I'll make a doctor's appointment and see if there's anything brewing.*

Her phone rang, rousing her from her thoughts. "Hello," she answered, without even looking at the caller ID.

"Hi, Betty, this is Kenneth Cavanaugh, from Mt. Laurel. How are you doing today?"

"Hello, Kenneth. I'm okay except for feeling a bit tired. I probably need more sleep. How can I help you? Is Greta okay?"

"Well, she is the reason I'm calling."

"She's not sick I hope."

"No, it's nothing like that. Greta came to see my wife and me the other day. We had a nice chat and I wanted to know if you'd have time today or tomorrow to stop by and visit with us."

"No hints on what it's about?"

Kenneth laughed. "It would be easier to explain in person, if you have the time."

"Okay, let's make it tomorrow morning though. I'll rest up this afternoon and try to get some decent sleep so I'll be fresh. Will ten o'clock work for you?"

"Ten is perfect, we'll see you then. Hope you feel better fast."

"Thanks, I'm sure I will. Bye."

Betty hung up the phone and wrapped both hands around her mug, taking a slow sip. *I wonder what Greta is up to now?* Betty had grown to admire her stamina and creative spirit. Since Greta lost Clarence she managed to find her way alone and be an inspiration to others. Her paintings were poignant and perceptive, expressing feelings better than words. *If she needed to talk with the Cavanaugh's, she must have something going on. But what?*

Crackers stirred from his basket in the corner, stretching his front legs and arching his back like a cat. His face had a sleepy look and he gave a big yawn.

"Did you have a good nap?" she said softly, allowing him time to get fully awake.

He slowly approached Betty's leg and rubbed the top of his head against her.

She scratched his ears and the back of his neck before scooping him up. "I bet you'd like a snack before Kat gets home." She carried him to the counter and retrieved a small biscuit from the doggy snack jar. He sniffed it and politely took it from Betty's hand.

"Okay, little guy, let's go get comfy on the couch and wait for Kat. Maybe I can catch a little nap."

Together they curled up against a big throw pillow. Crackers nuzzled next to her and licked her arm before she dozed off.

***

Rosie hung up her phone and excitedly rushed from her bedroom toward the kitchen where Blanca was stirring something in the stockpot on the stove.

"Blanca, guess what?" she asked and then answered before Blanca could guess. "Ro agreed to come as my guest to Rita and Ron's wedding in April."

Looking into her friend's eyes, she could see the delight and love Rosie had for her son. "I'm so happy for you," she said pulling her into a big hug. "Did you invite his girlfriend as well?"

Rosie hugged back and smiled. "I asked Rita if it would be okay and she said yes. Ro told me he would see if Monica wanted to come along."

"Either way, you'll get him for a couple days at least. I'm glad you're both on good terms."

Rosie took a seat at the table while Blanca added a few seasonings to the pot. "It's just that ..."

"That what?" Blanca quizzed.

"Well, if she doesn't come then he might back out."

"Let's give that to God and let Him work it all out. I have a feeling they will both show up and who knows, maybe Rita's wedding will promote another?"

Rosie shuddered. "I'm not praying for that to happen."

"I'm just kidding," Blanca said, laughing.

"What are you cooking?"

Blanca put the lid on the pot and set the spoon on the counter. "This, dear friend is my chicken tortilla soup."

"It smells terrific. Is it our meal tonight? Please say yes."

"It is indeed. By the way, I talked to Bree earlier. She called me from Mexico City."

"How is she? There's nothing wrong is there?"

"No, a few of the teachers left the village and traveled to Mexico City for a few days off. They've been working so hard. I asked if she would be able to come back for Rita's wedding and she said it might be possible."

"Oh, I hope so. I know it would please you so much."

"It all depends on whether or not another group of missionary teachers comes through, so she asked us to be praying about it."

Rosie nodded. "I will certainly keep that in prayer. It would be wonderful for both of you to have some time together."

Blanca thought for a moment. "You know, Rosie, I'm not sure why, but I think this wedding may do more than unite Rita and Ron in marriage."

***

Greta couldn't sleep. She went to bed early after putting in three hours of painting. Her mind didn't want to shut down. She prayed during her wakefulness but still she lay there wide-eyed. Thoughts of Clarence raced through her mind and she missed him dearly. Knowing he was with Jesus didn't lessen the ache in her heart for him. One day they would be reunited though and that was comforting.

She slid her legs over the side of the bed and flipped on the light switch. Digital numbers on the clock displayed two o'clock. Tomorrow she would meet with the director and his wife, Jewel, along with Betty Hills. It was exciting to see their reaction when she shared her idea with the director and his wife yesterday. Hopefully Betty would react the same and help her put things into motion. She wished it had been possible to make this happen when Clarence was alive, before he took sick, but she knew he would be ecstatic about it. Their marriage was a whirlwind, filled with love, humor, and adventure. It was also short. *Thank You, Lord, for bringing Clarence into my life. I treasure the time we had because it was filled with love I never knew before. Amen.*

Greta rose and went to the easel. She loved how this painting turned out. The lighthouse had exactly the right tones and reflections; the rocks jagged out perfectly, and the stormy sea revealed a ship approaching. There, in the ray of light was Jesus, hands raised, calming the waves. She had chills just gazing at it in the dimly lit room. Her eyes pooled and her thoughts of Clarence gave her peace. Perhaps now she could sleep.

She left the easel and returned to her bed, turning off the light. *Goodnight Clarence, I love you forever.*

Chapter 13

"Good morning, Betty," Kenneth said as he greeted her at his office door. "How are you feeling today?"

"I'm better, just a bit tired, but I did sleep a little more last night."

"That's good news. Jewel will be here shortly and then we'll meet with Greta in the sunroom. Would you like some coffee or tea?"

"Tea would be wonderful, thank you."

Jewel came through the doorway carrying two cups of tea, setting one down for Betty and keeping the other for herself.

"You're a mind reader, my love," Kenneth said, giving his wife a kiss on the cheek. "I was just going to get Betty a cup."

Betty laughed. "Your timing was right on cue," she said before taking a sip. "This is perfect, thank you, Jewel."

Jewel took a seat. "I figured we would have time before we meet with Greta."

Betty set her cup down on the side table. "Okay, I'm dying of curiosity about what's going on. Can you fill me in a little?"

Kenneth started. "We really want her to share what she wants to do, but I can tell you a few things. You know better than we do about Greta's younger life, her mother's death, and the relationship with her father. The documentary you and your crew put together about Greta and Clarence was terrific."

"Yes, Greta didn't have a happy childhood—or young adulthood for that matter," Betty said.

Jewel spoke up. "I think she wants to end happier than she began."

"In what way?"

"At her age, she's almost ninety-two, Greta realizes that she never really had any opportunity to do things or go places when she was growing up."

Betty's eyes widened. "She wants to travel?"

Kenneth gave a hearty laugh. "That's all we're going to tell you," he said, glancing at his watch. "Let's walk down to the sunroom. She should be there by now."

Betty finished her cup of tea and placed the Styrofoam container in the trash can as they made their way out of Kenneth's office. *She wants to travel? Where would she want to go?*

***

Ron parked the car near the entrance to the River Walk so they wouldn't have so far to walk. Visiting *Marriage Island* was on their to-do list today. Getting married on the heart-shaped island on the San Antonio River Walk was Rita's idea of the perfect wedding. He had to agree it would be romantic saying their vows outdoors underneath the towering cypress.

"Here we are," he said, giving her a hug as they locked the car and started down the steps to the River Walk. "It's still chilly and it's almost lunchtime," Ron commented.

Rita felt the breeze and shivered a bit. "Let's pray it'll be warm on April 15th." She gripped Ron's hand tightly as they descended the stairs. "I love the way everything is lit up."

They passed restaurants as they followed the stone steps winding along the river. Mariachis were playing at one table of guests, possibly a birthday celebration. Dining outdoors was fun, but now the aroma of a mixture of flavors wafted through the air, making Rita hungry as they forged ahead to Marriage Island.

"There it is, right in front of the Hotel Contessa," Ron said.

"Oh how lovely," she gushed. "The man said the cypress tree root ball is actually the island. Can you believe we'll be married on a root ball?"

Ron almost doubled over laughing. "That's hysterical. It must be one huge root ball."

They walked carefully onto the island, following the stone steps imbedded and sat on one of the small benches installed.

"It's perfect, Ron," she said, leaning her head against his arm. "I wish we were having the ceremony today. Next month seems so far away."

"Hmmm, I do too," he whispered, caressing her arm. "It can't get here soon enough."

"Let's have lunch down here and then go pay for the wedding package."

Ron reluctantly released his bride-to-be, rose, and pulled her to him for a quick kiss. He heard her stomach growl. "I guess you really are hungry. Where do you want to eat? We certainly have our pick."

"How about Café Ole? It's right over there," she said, pointing straight ahead.

"Sounds good to me," he said slipping his arm around her as they picked up their pace.

***

A light rain made Sheila and Lane's drive to Wimberley slightly dangerous. The highway was slick in places, slowing them to less than the speed limit. They received the keys to the cottage after getting paperwork signed and Betty wished them well in their new adventure. Transforming the cottage into a nonprofit quilt shop would take time.

Mary Dee, fastened snugly into her car seat, played happily with her puzzle box as Lane guided the car safely down the road. Her occasional "wha dat?" and squeals of joy when she picked the right square on the puzzle box proved she was travel friendly.

Sheila turned in her seat to watch Mary Dee's gleeful smile as she cuddled her stuffed bear under one arm. It was difficult to think about her parents' being killed in a horrific car wreck, leaving her an orphan. Sheila couldn't stop thanking God that they had left Mary Dee with a babysitter that night. Whenever she and Lane took her with them in the car, they always prayed before leaving and asked God to protect them on the road.

Lane turned off the windshield wipers. "It won't be long. I think we take a right about half a mile up the road."

Sheila turned her attention back to the road sign. "I think the rain has stopped. I see the sun trying to break through the clouds."

"Do you want to grab a bite to eat before we head to the cottage?"

"No, why don't we check the cottage out first. Mary Dee probably needs changing by now, and we can stretch our legs a bit. That way she can burn off a little energy too."

"A little energy?" Lane asked.

"Well, okay, a lot of energy."

"Me go," the toddler blurted loudly in her highest pitch. "Me go," she repeated, grabbing her teddy bear by one paw.

"Okay," Sheila assured her in a soft tone. "We're going."

Lane laughed. "I think she's excited."

"More like tired of sitting in one place too long," Sheila said.

Lane took the exit and followed the signs toward Wimberley. "Should be a few blocks down."

"Down," Mary Dee repeated after Lane, "me want down."

"Hang in there a few more minutes, Sunshine, we're almost there," Lane assured her.

Sheila glanced at Mary Dee's huge smile. "God added more sunshine to our lives when she came to us."

Lane reached over and patted his wife's hand. "Even on rainy days."

"Look, there's the cottage," Sheila said, pointing to a board and batten structure on the right. "Betty said to look for the house with eight windows trimmed in white."

"This is definitely it," Lane said, pulling into the driveway. "It looks like the drive goes around to the back. That will be great for parking."

"My heart is beating so fast, Lane. It's more than I could have imagined. The photos they showed us did not do it justice."

"You're right. I'm really impressed." He shut the engine off, exited the car, and removed the baby tote bag from the back seat.

Sheila hurriedly got out, unbuckled Mary Dee, and lifted her from the car seat.

Together, they walked to the porch.

"Honey, this house is the beginning of a new chapter in our life," Sheila said. "God is going to use it to help a lot of grieving families."

Lane hugged her, even as Mary Dee pulled on his face to give him a wet kiss.

***

Betty and the Cavanaughs found Greta in the sunroom sipping her coffee. Her face was bright. She wore emerald green slacks, topped with a crisp white, long-sleeved blouse. Betty noticed that Greta had applied a bit of makeup, which accounted for her lively look. Her hair was in a bun with a few tendrils escaping on her neck.

"Hello, Greta," Betty greeted her friend, "You look radiant this morning."

"Thank you," Greta said, tapping the back of the chair next to her. "Come, sit down. Good morning," she added, looking at Kenneth and Jewel. "I'm glad we could all get together."

The Cavanaughs took seats at the round table. "We're glad to see you in such good spirits," Kenneth said.

"Thank you, I'm feeling spirited."

"So, Greta," Betty started, "tell me what it is you have in mind to do that you wanted us all together to discuss."

Greta looked at Kenneth and Jewel to see if they had told Betty anything, but Kenneth shook his head.

"I have a birthday coming up soon and I'll be ninety-two years old. I haven't done much in my life — at least nothing adventurous or exciting. Since I met you, Betty," she continued, placing her hand on Betty's arm, "things have changed. The film you did, introducing me to Jesus, and becoming a trusted friend has made me a different person."

Betty's eyes pooled and she patted Greta's hand. "You're an amazing woman."

Greta smiled and continued. "I took up painting and then lost my dear Clarence. I wanted to go with him." She paused and pulled a tissue from her pocket, wiping her eyes. "Then the day you and Mr. Hills took me to lunch I suddenly realized that God has allowed me to live this long for a reason and He's not ready for me yet."

"Amen," Jewel chimed in.

"The lighthouses I've been painting have a purpose, a message. I've done a large number of them and the other day I felt a spark to do something, but I will need assistance."

Betty stared at Greta and saw the sparkle in her eyes. "Tell me, what is it that we can help you do?"

"I want to plan a trip and visit some of the great lighthouses in person. Now, before you say anything about me traveling at my age, that's where you come in. I'd like you and your daughter to accompany me. Clarence's life insurance left me some money, plus he had some socked away that I didn't know about. I also have enough to do what I want to do."

Betty couldn't think of one word to say. She stared first at Greta, then at Kenneth, and lastly at Jewel, hoping for some suggestions. Finally, Betty grasped at a response. "Greta, wow, this is a shock. I'm speechless. How long of a trip and what area of the country are you planning?"

Greta laughed. "I'm not planning to be gone all year if that's what you're thinking. I think two weeks should be enough time to visit either the lighthouses on the east coast or the many lighthouses around the coast of Michigan. You see, I feel God speaking to me through the lighthouses and the craggy rocks, smashing waves, and beams of light. I need to see them with my own eyes."

Jewel spoke with a knowing voice. "Greta, I can see the passion in your eyes and I hear it in your voice. I've always said that if we feel God is leading us or calling us to do something, then we should do it." She looked pleadingly at Betty, hoping for a yes answer.

"Thank you for understanding," Greta said.

Betty cleared her throat. "Of course, I'll have to run this by Brian and Kat, but I think we can assist you. It will be kind of fun — three generations on a girls travel adventure." She smiled at Greta. "Like I said, you are an amazing woman. When did you plan to leave?"

"I know it will take a lot of planning and setting things up, but early next month perhaps? I asked Kenneth and Jewel to help by checking on the tours offered in each location and see what is available that would fit my purpose. They work wonders on the computer. I've never touched one."

"Okay, I'll get my family together tonight for a discussion and let you know. I think Brian will be a bit jealous."

They all chuckled.

Greta hugged Betty, whispering, "Thank you," in her ear.

***

Gus plopped the hot pizza box onto the table and set a roll of paper towels within easy reach of both himself and Jared. "Pizza's here," he called out, "come eat while its hot!" He and Jared had a long hard day and were both too tired to drive anywhere for food. Ordering in was the only option because neither of them planned on cooking.

"Be right there, I'm on the phone," Jared answered.

"I'm starting without you," he said, then bowed his head to thank God for provisions.

He managed one bite before Jake emerged from his room and grabbed a slice of the pepperoni pizza as he sat down.

"Who were you on the phone with?" Gus asked.

"I called Sarah," he said between bites.

"You two seeing each other again?"

"I don't know. We're trying to figure out how we feel and how to work out schedules. I called to see if we could get together this weekend."

Gus took a long drink of his Coke. "Are you?" he asked casually.

Jared swallowed the last bite and sighed. "She has to work Saturday until six so I told her I'd be there and we could get something to eat or just hang out together."

"What did she say to that?"

"She needs time to clean up after work but she said if I come at seven that would be okay."

"Sounds like a date to me." Gus noticed the frown on his brother's face. "Isn't it?"

"We have to start somewhere I guess. She didn't seem overly enthusiastic about it though. I really like Sarah, maybe too much, but ..."

"But what?"

"In the beginning we had fun together. We talked, went places, laughed, and seemed close. Now, I'm confused because it's such an effort to even see each other. She has plans for her future and I have mine all laid out. Factor in her living in Blanco and me here in San Antonio, and you have the driving element problem."

Gus took another slice of pizza and set it on his plate. "I'm no expert on relationships because I'm not in one. But I do know that they take an investment of time and energy. The truth is, you both have to invest equally. If one is pouring ninety percent into developing something and the other is half-heartedly contributing only ten, it won't succeed."

Jared chewed his food and nodded. He finished off his Coke and tore off a paper towel from the roll.

"You're right, Gus, and I feel I'm doing the ninety."

"May I make an observation?" Gus asked.

"I'm all ears."

"I don't think you're putting much into a relationship at all. I'm not trying to sink your boat or upset you. I don't believe either of you are putting much into it. Maybe the timing isn't right or she's not the one."

Jared stared at Gus. "So you think I should stop calling her and just give up?"

"I'm not telling you what to do. How you handle it is something for you to decide. I'm just saying what I think is reality. Have you prayed about all this?"

"Truthfully? No." Jared took his plate and stood up. "Thanks, Gus. I appreciate your offering your thoughts. I will pray about it and see what happens." He threw the paper plate and napkin in the trash and headed back to his room.

"Any time, Jared," Gus called after him. "I'll be praying too."

***

Brian shut down his computer and rose from his desk. He had made progress on the book he was writing, delving into Clarence's life. It had been a challenge getting information from him last year. He wasn't a man who talked about himself much, and he didn't want the limelight. When Betty and her film crew made the film, he finally opened up a little. Brian spent time with him in private after that, just man-to-man talk. Some of what Clarence told him touched Brian deeply and that's why this book needed to be written.

He glanced at his watch and realized that Betty was probably downstairs with Kat waiting for him. All she said was *a family meeting at seven o'clock'.* He had three minutes to spare as he headed to the dining room.

"Here he comes now, Kat," Betty said, "right on time."

"He's always on time, Mum."

"I'm here," Brian announced, flying around the corner of the doorway. "What's the big mystery meeting about?"

"You need to sit down for this one," Betty warned.

They both sat, wide-eyed, staring at Betty, waiting.

She took a deep breath and began. "I was asked to meet with the Cavanaughs and Greta yesterday, at Greta's request."

"Is she okay?" Brian asked.

"More than okay, I'd say." Betty laughed. "Greta feels she needs to travel and she wants Kat and me to accompany her."

Jaws dropped.

"You're kidding, right?" Kat asked with a smile on her face.

Betty shook her head. "No, I'm very serious. She has a purpose and there's really no reason she can't travel."

"But she's over ninety ..." Brian said.

"She is proud of the fact that she will soon be ninety-two. She's in good health and has a sound mind. She does admit it wouldn't be wise to travel alone at that age, so that's why she wants us to go."

"Where to?" Kat asked.

"Her plan is to visit some lighthouses either on the east coast or around the coast of Michigan. Kenneth is going to research both and see which would be the most enjoyable and still easy to cover in two weeks."

Brian's eyebrows arched. "Two weeks? Did she invite me to go along?"

Betty couldn't contain her laughter. "No, this will be a girls adventure."

Kat clapped her hands together. "YES!" she shouted. "When do we leave?"

"Early next month if Kenneth gets the travel plans lined up quickly. The only thing, Brian, Greta was adamant about footing the bill for our travel. There's no way I'll allow her to do that."

"Of course not," Brian agreed. "We should cover her airfare as well."

Betty nodded. "I think we can sneak that by her. So, are we all in agreement that Kat and I will trot across Texas and head either north or east with Greta next month? All in favor, say 'aye.'"

Three "ayes" sounded in unison.

"Good, I'll call her this evening and give her the good news. Kat, you and I have some shopping to do."

Kat beamed from ear to ear. "Yay, I'm ready when you are."

Betty rose and started upstairs to call Greta. She paused and asked, "When I'm through talking with Greta, who wants to go for a walk?"

Brian volunteered.

"Count me out," Kat said, "I'm expecting Ryan to call about eight. Oh no," she muttered, "I won't see him for two weeks next month."

"You both will survive," Brian assured her. "Think about me, I'll be a bachelor and have to settle for Cracker's company while you're gone."

Kat chuckled and gave her dad a quick hug. "Speaking of Crackers," she added, "I'm going to my room and spend some time with that little rascal before Ryan calls." She found him in the living room, snoozing on the couch. "Come on, Crackers," she cooed, picking him up and cradling him in her arm, "let's go find a ball and play." His eyes flashed at the sound of the name of his favorite toy and she saw his tail wagging fiercely.

***

Jake pulled his car into the apartment complex parking lot. He managed to find a spot close to the stairs to Annie's place.

"Here we are, do you think you're ready to be on your own?"

Annie looked down at her foot, encased in a walking boot. "I think I can manage now, thanks to your excellent care. I might need a little assistance getting up the stairs though."

Jake shut the motor off and exited the car. He approached the passenger door and opened it as far as possible. Holding out his arm for her grasp, he waited for Annie to turn and lower her feet to the ground. He took hold of her hand and helped her stand.

"I'm a bit shaky," she said, laughing at her wobbly stance.

123

"No worry, I've got you. Just take one step at a time and lean on me if necessary. When we get to the stairs, I'll help you."

Together they walked slowly, inching their way up the curb and to the stairs.

"It's now or never," she quipped, as she put her good foot on the first step and took hold of the railing. Hesitantly, she lifted the cumbersome foot and carefully placed it on the step. She took a deep breath and pulled herself up. She held tightly to the railing and exhaled. "I did it!" she announced proudly.

"Excellent job, only fifteen more to go."

"Thanks for reminding me, Coach."

Jake stayed one step lower each time as she made her way up the stairs.

"Okay," Annie said, "that was tiring."

"Want me to carry you to the door?"

"No, I need to get used to walking on it. We're close anyway."

One turn down the hall and they arrived at her apartment. She put her key in the lock and let them both in. Annie sat down on the chair nearest the door. "They should install chair lifts on the outside of apartments."

Jake laughed. "Good luck making that happen, but it's a great idea. Would you like me to fix some tea?"

"Oh, Jake, that would be lovely. I think you know where I keep everything."

"I do, this isn't my first cup of tea you know."

Annie rested and smiled to herself. Jake was humming.

"Tea is coming up in two minutes," he called out.

When Annie heard Jake pouring the tea, she asked, "You're having a cup too, right?"

"Of course," Jake said, carrying two cups into the dining room and setting them carefully on the table. "Do you want to stay there or sit here at the table?"

"I'd really prefer to sit in the living room on the sofa so I can prop my leg up."

Jake grinned as he walked over, swooped Annie into his arms and carried her to the sofa. "How's that?" he asked, helping her lift the booted foot onto the cushion.

"You're something else, Jake Davis, thank you."

"My pleasure," he said, and went to retrieve the teacups.

Jake took a seat across from Annie as they settled in, sipping the hot beverages.

"Have you had any prospects to look at your house yet?" she asked.

Jake groaned a bit. "Only one and I doubt it was what they were looking for."

"Selling a house is difficult right now. Have you found an apartment yet?"

"I've looked at a few. Actually, one is about two miles from here and I liked the place."

"Good, that's progress."

"You're making progress with your foot too, but you need to go slow. Are you sure you'll be okay here by yourself?"

"I'll be fine, Worry Wart. I have my phone so I can call for help if needed."

"You could have stayed in my guest room a few more days, you know. I enjoyed having you there."

"I know and you took such good care spoiling me. I could have gotten used to it and then coming here would have been harder. I have things I can do here until I see the doctor."

"Let me know ahead of time and I'll drive you to your appointment."

"You're sweet, thanks, but you have to get back to work also. I can take a cab or call Uber."

"Annie," Jake said, looking serious, "I care about you and I want to drive you and it's no trouble."

"Okay, and thank you." Annie yawned. "I'm sorry. I guess things are catching up with me."

"You're tired and should sleep. Do you want to lie down on the bed? I can carry you."

Annie chuckled. "No, this is fine." She reached for the afghan on the back of the sofa and pulled it over her.

Jake rose, took the now empty teacups into the kitchen and rinsed them out. As he returned to where Annie was, he found her asleep. He bent down and kissed her lightly on the forehead and quietly left, closing the door behind him.

As he made his way downstairs and into his car, his heart was beating quickly. He really cared about Annie and suddenly realized that he was falling in love with her. Now the big question, *what was he going to do about it?*

Chapter 14

Emily decided she was not getting up yet. She snuggled deeper into the Bear's Paw quilt and refused to open her eyes. She knew Seth had gone to the office to meet a client and wouldn't be home until late morning, so there was no rush to leave the comfort of her bed.

She wasn't sleepy, just tired. Patting her baby bump, she smiled. "You're probably the reason your mommy is tired." *What will our life be like when the baby comes?* Emily was excited but also a little scared. Would she be a good mommy? She thought about her own mother and the way she raised Emily. Emily was taught good manners, respect for authority, cleanliness, and so much more. Emily knew she learned so much about what love is from her mother. Love for Jesus came at an early age, and then loving others seemed easy. The compassion Emily had for people came from the Lord. It was a gift and led her to become a nurse.

She opened her eyes gradually and saw a stream of sunlight peeking through the window. *Thank You, Lord, for another day. Help me use it for Your glory. Thank You for my hardworking husband and this precious little one in my womb. Please watch over us all and help me to be a good mother to our child. Amen.*

Emily threw off the quilt and sat on the side of the bed, stretching a bit before heading to the kitchen for that wonderful first cup of the day — tea. She thought about breakfast but realized she wasn't even hungry. The one thing on her mind was to call Ruth and Teddy, the caretakers at her place in Essex, England. They contacted her last week about some things that needed to be done in the Manor house and Emily promised to get back to them after discussing it with Seth. *Where did the week go?* Seth and Emily had been so busy at the bed and breakfast, making sure each of the guest rooms looked perfect and working with their web designer. Emily took photos of all the rooms and the outside so they could be uploaded for viewing, plus ordering the brochures. To find out they couldn't open as planned because the commercial appliances were delayed, was frustrating. Seth was still upset but she did not give up her attempts to calm him down. Emily still thought God slowed their plans down for a reason.

She would love to fly back to England and check on the Manor, but Seth wanted to wait until her next doctor appointment to make sure she would be safe flying. Since the grand opening of the bed and breakfast was postponed, she thought it would be a great time to go. Also, Rita and Ron's wedding was coming up and Emily didn't want to miss that. Everything seemed to be hitting at the same time.

She sighed and slipped her feet into the fuzzy slippers by the bed. "Lord, please work things out and show us Your perfect timing," she prayed out loud.

***

Emily splashed a few drops of Half & Half into her cup of English Breakfast Tea and set the cream back in the fridge. She sat at the table and thought about the Manor house Mary had left to Emily in her will. The time she spent in England was so precious. The house was magnificent and the garden was the most beautiful she'd ever seen. After meeting Ruth and Teddy, and their having taught her so much about the house and its history, Emily felt she belonged there. It was a hard decision to come back. Even the neighbors there welcomed her warmly. Some of them were close friends with Mary's parents, even watching Mary and her twin sister, Bertha, grow up.

Emily and Seth made the decision to get married at Summer Bride and invited Betty and Brian to come make it a double wedding. She sipped her tea and smiled, remembering that day as if it were yesterday. When they came back to San Antonio, they discussed what to do with Summer Bride — move there and live or transform Summer Bride into a wedding venue, so other couples could be married in such a beautiful setting. There were changes that had to be made of course, but the end result was awesome. They scheduled weddings only during the summer so when they wanted to stay in the Manor, it would be just Seth and she. Of course, it wouldn't be long until baby would accompany them.

Mary wanted her legacy of love to be carried on and Emily often wondered if she was doing that in using the Manor house for weddings. Emily knew that at some point Ruth and Teddy would be unable to continue doing the work they've been performing. Teddy especially because he tended the garden and did the landscaping by himself. Emily promised Ruth that she and Seth would discuss what to do. Ruth didn't want Teddy to feel he wasn't able to do the work, but she also didn't like seeing him so exhausted every night. "A wife has to look out for her husband when he thinks he can physically do more than he really should," she told Emily on the phone. Emily agreed with her. Seth said it would be no problem finding someone to help Teddy, but it needed to be done in a way that wouldn't hurt Teddy's feelings. Emily suggested they encourage Teddy to train a young man as his protégé so the traditional landscaping of an English Manor wouldn't be lost to future generations. Seth liked the sound of that.

Emily finished her tea and decided to have a slice of quiche that was left over from yesterday's lunch. She looked at the clock, deciding the time difference would be perfect. Teddy would be in from the garden so she could speak to both of them. *I'll have breakfast and then give Ruth and Teddy a call.*

***

Rita loved small restaurants with a quiet atmosphere. She sat across from Ron, who was perusing the menu, while she had made her dinner choice quickly, as the salmon was her favorite. She knew the server would return any minute.

"Have you decided what you want yet?"

"Hmmm, I've narrowed it down to either the chicken and dumplings or the chicken Alfredo."

"They both sound good," she said, looking toward the counter where the server went. "You love the Alfredo, I know. I'm having the blackened salmon."

"You're right," he agreed, closing the menu and smiling at Rita. "Chicken Alfredo it is."

Rita looked again at where the server was and smiled. He took the cue and headed toward them.

"Are you ready to order?" he asked.

"Yes, it'll be blackened salmon for the lady and chicken Alfredo for me. We could use tea refills when you have time, iced for me and hot for her."

Ron handed his and Rita's menus to the young server, whose name tag said, Donnie. "Thank you, Donnie."

"You're welcome," the young man answered, "I'll have your refills shortly."

Rita smiled as he left. "I wonder if he is related to the owners. Maybe he's a grandson."

"He could be. I liked his personality — very polite and friendly."

Rita reached out her hand and took hold of Ron's. "When we're done I'd like to stop by the studio before you take me home."

"Sure, did you leave something there?"

"No, I want to give you something. I created something special as my wedding gift to you, and I finished it yesterday."

Ron's eyes widened. "I can't wait to see it. I am an ardent fan of your sculptures and I know it must be really special."

Rita squeezed his hand and felt him return it before releasing her hand.

"Speaking of art," Ron said, "I have been thinking about something and want to run it by you."

"Oh?"

The server, Donnie, appeared with their refills, along with a crusty hot loaf of bread and dipping oil.

"Here are your refills," he said, removing them from the tray. "And I brought bread for you to munch on till your meal is ready."

"Yum!" Ron said, taking a piece of the pre sliced loaf and spooning the oil into the small dish provided.

"I never am able to resist hot fresh bread," Rita commented as she indulged. "Now, what did you want to talk to me about?"

Ron finished chewing his bread, swallowed, and dabbed his mouth with the napkin. "I was contemplating opening my own art studio."

Rita swallowed her bread quickly. "Your own art studio?"

Ron laughed. "Yes, but nothing huge, just a small studio where I can feature local artists."

Rita was quiet for a moment.

Donnie returned to their table. "Dinner is served," he said in a friendly tone. He placed the salmon in front of Rita and passed the chicken Alfredo over to Ron. "Will there be anything else?"

"This is fine, thank you," Ron said.

The server left and Rita took a first bite of her salmon. "This is heavenly," she swooned.

Ron nodded. "Same here," he said.

"Okay, back to the art studio subject," Rita started. "How and when would you proceed with it?"

"First I'll have to see what's available. Real estate in the area I want is limited but there are a couple of sites I'd like to look at."

"Before or after our wedding and honeymoon?"

Ron smiled. "Nothing comes before our wedding and honeymoon, my dear. I thought I'd just inquire about them. I don't want to rush into anything."

Rita felt relieved. "I don't think it's a bad idea, in fact, I know you would be successful. We have a lot going on with the wedding and then we'll be gone for two weeks. Taking on a project like that means full focus."

"I agree. I just wanted to see how you felt about it. I enjoy my work at Blue Star but would really like to have my own studio. I can continue with Blue Star while I'm building my place."

Rita put her fork down and sipped her tea. "I do like the idea and you have my full support. Maybe you'll feature some of my sculptures in your studio," she said, while wearing a wide grin.

"Not just my studio," he quipped, "our studio."

***

Rita unlocked the door to Rita's Artsy Kids; at least it would be named that when they opened in the summer. Since Ron bought her this new building as a wedding present, she wanted to take time to make it perfect for the inner city kids.

"Okay, now close your eyes," she ordered Ron, "until I tell you to look."

Ron laughed. "It's dark in here — I can't see anything with them open!"

"Nevertheless, keep them closed and stay right here," she said, releasing his hand and making her way to the display table where she had placed her peacock typewriter sculpture.

"Okay, get ready, one — two — Threeee!"

She switched on the light and carefully removed the white cloth that shielded her creation, and then stood in front of it. "Okay, open your eyes," she sang.

Ron blinked to adjust his eyes to the light. He glanced around and seeing nothing unusual, he joked. "You're my wedding gift? I like that idea," he said, moving teasingly toward her.

When he was an arm's length from Rita, she moved to the right, exposing his gift. "Ta da!" she exclaimed with a wave of her hand.

Ron looked at the strange looking peacock, and then turned it to view the back, running his finger along the curve of the peacock's neck. He noticed the vintage keys standing upright — a sort of plumage he supposed. The standing keys that caught his eye were Y-O-U + I. Even though they were upside down and backwards, they stood out and were legible. His heart melted at the off-the-wall sculpture. Rita knew him so well.

"Honey, this is the most touching gift you could have given to me." He reached out with one arm and slipped it around Rita's waist, pulling her close. "Thank you," he whispered, kissing her on the cheek. "I'll make this the star of the new studio when we open it!" he boasted.

"I'm glad you like it. We are a team, *you and I.*"

"We are and will always be," Ron said, taking her in his arms and kissing her warmly.

***

"Hi, Kat," Ryan said over the phone, "I hope you had a good day today — better than mine anyway."

"Ryan, you are always so punctual. You said you'd call at eight and you nailed it," Kat said, glancing at the clock. "I've had some excitement today, but before I tell you about my day, what's going on with yours?"

"It started out like any other day. Checking the fire truck to make sure it was ready to roll when needed, breakfast with the guys, and just normal everyday firehouse stuff. But then, a call came in."

"Was it a bad fire?"

"Bad doesn't come close, Kat — it was a nightmare. There were burglar bars on all the windows and the fire was in full bloom when we arrived. We heard screams coming from somewhere inside but the noise from the fire was so loud we couldn't tell which part of the house they came from."

"Oh, Ryan, that must have been devastating. I'm so sorry. Did you find anyone inside?"

"Piper did! You remember I told you about him – he saved Crackers."

"Yes, I remember him."

Crackers pawed at Kat's leg and she picked him up with one hand and settled him on her lap.

"Well, Piper broke through a door in the back and found a woman huddled with a young girl. Both were burned already, but Piper managed to get the woman out and yelled for me to grab the daughter before that room exploded. Piper suffered a messed-up arm trying to carry the woman to safety. I only suffered smoke inhalation, but I'm fine now."

"I'm so sorry, Ryan. Will the three of them be okay? Were they the only ones inside?"

"Piper will be out of commission for a month or so. The girl was shielded by her mother so she had only a few burns and smoke inhalation, but the mother is in critical condition."

Kat had tears flowing. "I'll be praying for all of them. I'm glad you are okay. You are, right?"

"Physically I'm fine. I was in the back of the structure, trying to locate where the screams were at. But I can't unsee what took place."

Kat's heart was hurting for the family, and also for Ryan. *He has such a sensitive spirit and to witness such a tragic event will certainly stay with him a long time.*

"I know, and I wish I could help you in some way."

"You have, just by being on the other end of this conversation. It helps talking to you. I always feel comforted."

"I'm glad. May I pray with you right now?"

"I'd like that."

"Lord, thank you for keeping Ryan safe today. He means so much to me and I know he means much more to You. Help the mother and daughter who were injured in the fire, heal their bodies completely. Help Ryan emotionally as he must still be there for future fires. Place Your healing hand on Piper and help him get well. Amen."

"Thank you, Kat. I feel less stressed already."

"Call me anytime, but when you have your off days, I'd love to see you and give you a big hug."

"I'll be off day after tomorrow, and I expect to collect that hug."

Kat smiled into the phone as they both disconnected. She headed downstairs with Crackers at her heels. She wanted to ask her dad and Betty to keep the fire victims in prayer. As she reached the last step, Brian and Betty came in the front door.

Brian looked at his daughter and knew immediately something was wrong. He walked to Kat and put his arms around her. "What's going on?"

Kat broke down and her dad waited patiently until she composed herself enough to share what she learned from Ryan about the fire.

"Honey, I'm sorry. Ryan must be saddened by it all. We will pray for all of them."

"Thanks, Daddy, I know you will." She looked at Betty who was drying tears with her arm. "I know you both will. I'm really tired so I think I'll go up to bed."

Crackers let out a little yip and tried to jump up on Kat. She picked him up and cradled him, burying her face in his fur. "You, too, Crackers. It's bedtime."

***

"Seth, I talked to Ruth and Teddy earlier," Emily said, as she opened her planner and took a seat at the table on the patio.

Seth relaxed on the rollback porch swing, looking through the newspaper. "I'm glad you caught them both at the same time. Was Teddy open to the idea of bringing on someone to help with landscaping?"

Emily smiled excitedly. "He was and even suggested that we give him some time to find someone before we start looking."

"Wow, I'm surprised. I thought he would balk at the idea since he takes so much pride in doing the work himself."

"Ruth is probably the reason," Emily suggested. "I think she has been dropping not-so-subtle hints to him."

"Sometimes wives do that," Seth said, winking at Emily. "I'm just glad he's agreeable and I hope he can find someone soon. Let's keep up with his progress so we can step in if necessary."

"I'd really like to fly there soon. How about if I call Dr. Sanders tomorrow and ask her about my flying? That way we'd be back for the grand opening of our B&B and also for Rita and Ron's wedding."

Seth thought for a moment. "Okay, give her a call and see what she says. If she has even the slightest doubt about your and the baby's safety, we're not going to risk it. Agreed?"

"Of course. You know I wouldn't jeopardize either of us."

Seth smiled. "It'll be fun going back there. Summer Bride is such a beautiful place and brings back wonderful memories of our wedding there."

Emily rose from her chair and joined Seth on the swing. "It is and it does. I have often wondered what it would be like if we lived there."

Seth put the paper down on his lap. "Is that something you would want to do one day?"

She leaned her head on Seth's shoulder and was quiet for a moment. "Maybe."

"We have a lot going on with the B & B opening in the very near future, not to mention our new addition to the family coming this fall."

"I know, and it will all be exciting. I'm just daydreaming a little, playing the 'what if' game."

"I'll play along," Seth offered, swinging his arm around his wife, "What if we get our B & B off the ground and hire others to manage it?"

Emily sat upright and stared at her husband. She smiled. "Can we even do that?"

"It's ours; we can do whatever we want to do with it. We could even sell it."

Emily shook her head. "I wouldn't ask you to sell it. You, we have poured a lot into that place. It's very special. But, if later we decide to make a change and hire someone to manage/run it, that would give us options."

Seth put on his most serious face as he turned to look into her eyes. "Honey, I want you to be happy. I want us to be happy. We can pray about what to do once we open and get established. The Manor House isn't going anywhere, so we have plenty of time to mull it over and see what God wants us to do."

Emily kissed him and smiled. "Thank you," she whispered.

***

Blanca hung up the phone and all but ran into the living room to give Rosie the good news.

"Rosie," she said rather loudly, causing her friend to almost drop her recipe box onto the floor, "Guess what?"

Rosie bent to put the box on the coffee table. "What? I'm no good at guessing games. You look super excited so it must be good news."

Blanca took hold of Rosie's hands and squeezed them tightly. "Bree is coming home for a visit and she'll be here to attend Rita and Ron's wedding. Isn't that the most wonderful news?"

Rosie noticed her friend's eyes pooled. "I'm so happy for you. I know you've missed her and she must have missed you even more. When will she arrive?"

"She gets in the first of April. I can't believe my little girl will soon be home and I can give her some real hugging."

Rosie laughed. "Our kiddos need lots of love and plenty of hugs, that's for sure. We should prepare a special meal for her first night home."

"That's a great idea!" Blanca said. "It will be wonderful to hear about all her work in Mexico."

"I haven't seen her in a long time, so I'm sure she's grown up a lot."

Blanca finally calmed down. "Would you like some hot chocolate, Rosie?"

"I'd love a cup. You always make it so that it's perfect."

"I have my own recipe and I've never divulged it to anyone — not even to Bree!"

Rosie laughed. "Really? Not even to your own daughter?"

"Nope. I told her I would leave the recipe in a sealed envelope for her to open after I die."

Rosie laughed even harder. When she finally stopped and dried her eyes, Rosie looked at Blanca, expecting her to say she was just kidding. "You're serious aren't you?" she said.

"I am. I want to leave her something she can hand down. Not material somethings, but a special secret she can share with her future children."

"Awww, that is so sweet."

Blanca suddenly remembered — "Bree will be here for the grand opening of the Texas Tribute B&B. She will love that."

"Wonderful. You'll have your daughter here and I'll have my son."

Blanca reached out and hugged Rosie tight. "God is good to bless us this way." Releasing her friend, Blanca moved toward the kitchen.

"Since my hot chocolate recipe is secret, why don't you finish what you were doing with your recipe box while I put my concoction together?"

"Sounds like a plan to me," Rosie said, picking up her box and seating herself on the sofa. "I'll know when it's ready by the rich aroma that travels through the house."

***

Jared headed out Highway 281 to Blanco, Texas, intent on being at the Blooms-A-Lot nursery when Sarah finished work. She told him on the phone last night she would get off a couple hours early and invited him to drive up. Hearing her say she'd enjoy seeing him and agreeing on their dinner plans, Jared was one happy guy.

He had asked Gus if he could leave a little early and Gus said it wasn't a problem, so Jared didn't waste any time. He jumped in the shower, changed out of his work clothes, and filled his gas tank.

He glanced at the speedometer and quickly let his foot off the gas a little. Doing eight-five in a seventy wouldn't get him anything but a speeding ticket. He looked forward to seeing Sarah and hoped she was equally excited to see him.

***

Sarah clocked out and headed to her car. She loved her job and often got so involved with creating new arrangements in the outdoor area that she worked past quitting time. Today her supervisor told her to take off early because of the extra time she had accumulated. They laughed about her eagerness and creative abilities piling up overtime, but Sarah agreed that she would leave early.

She unlocked her car and slid into the driver's seat. Jared should arrive in about an hour so she'd have time to run home and get ready. He wanted to take her to dinner. *It'll be good to see him.* She sighed. Sarah enjoyed spending time with Jared and she had feelings for him, but she was afraid to get too involved. They both needed to focus on their careers and living in two different towns made dating difficult.

Sarah pulled out of the parking lot and headed toward home. Her parents would be there and she knew her mom had supper in progress. Sarah told her she would be going out to eat with Jared. Both her parents liked Jared and probably wished she would see him more often. She sighed again. Turning into the driveway, she put the car in park, shut the motor off, and sat for a moment. *Being an adult sure can be complicated.* Sometimes she wished she was still in high school and didn't have to make adult decisions about her life. But then she smiled. Sarah was pleased with her most recent decision to attend college and work on her future in landscaping. She loved her job and knew in her heart it was what God wanted for her.

"Sarah," her mother called from the front door, "are you coming in?"

Sarah was startled from her thoughts by her mother's voice. "In a minute, Mom," she called back. Sarah picked up her phone and dialed Jared's number. She would have him pick her up here instead of from the nursery.

***

"How's your steak?" Jared asked.

Sarah smiled. "It's so tender I can cut it with my fork. I love the seasoning they used."

"I knew you would like it. They have a special butter they brush on it and the flavor is fantastic."

"Thanks for bringing me here," Sarah said, putting her fork down and taking a drink of her iced tea. She relaxed in her chair and gazed at Jared, who was finishing his steak and mashed potatoes.

"I know a lot of places I'd like us to see together. Maybe we can plan on them in the near future. One reason I brought you to Roadhouse Café is so we could enjoy a quiet evening together."

"You're so thoughtful, Jared. I really enjoy being with you."

Jared dabbed his napkin across his mouth, took a drink of his coffee, and sat back. "I don't get it," he said. He shook his head as though he wanted the answer to his thoughts to come falling out.

"You don't get what?"

He looked her in the eyes. "I love being with you and you enjoy being with me, but yet it seems so hard for us to connect. I know we have jobs and plans for our future but I don't want to work and plan without its having some meaning."

Sarah lowered her head trying to find the right words. She finally looked up at Jared. "I understand what you're saying, and I agree with you. It's just that I feel I need to be independent and able to provide for myself. I worked at Tim's diner right out of high school and that's not the kind of job I want or could possibly live on."

"I'm not saying you should quit working or not continue your education. I know those things are important to you. They're important to me too. I'm only concerned that we are allowing our relationship to be put on hold while we're pursuing those things. I've heard it said that we make time for what's important to us. My half-brother, Gus, told me to pray about us and I really did. That's why I called you."

Sarah nodded. "Yes, you're right, and you are important to me."

Jared noticed her eyes were watery. "Why don't we leave and go for a ride," he suggested, hoping to continue their conversation.

Sarah smiled and picked up her purse as Jared rose, offering his hand to assist her.

He left the money for the tip on the table along with the dinner bill, and together, he and Sarah left. Jared slipped his arm around her waist and when they reached the car, he helped her in. Settling into the driver's side, he buckled up and they headed out of the parking lot.

"Jared," Sarah started, "I don't want to mislead you."

"What does that mean?"

"You are important to me. Since I first met you, I felt something special toward you. I'm not sure what it is. I care deeply for you."

"I think I'm falling in love with you, Sarah."

Sarah turned her attention to him. "Jared ..."

"No, let me finish. I was praying after Gus and I talked and I told the Lord everything I felt about our relationship, you, and our future. It wasn't until the next morning when I woke up that I realized I want our relationship to grow because I love you."

Sarah was silent.

Jared saw Tim's diner ahead. It was closed. He turned left into the vacant parking lot, shut off the engine, and turned to face Sarah. "This is where it started. This is where I first began falling in love with you."

Sarah smiled. "I remember that day when you first came in and ordered George's special. I loved your smile."

"That day I had reason to smile. George helped to turn my life around. When I asked Jesus to forgive me and be Lord of my life, I finally understood what real love was. I know that God put a special love in my heart for you that day. I might not have known it then, but I do now."

Sarah reached over to grasp his hand. "When I said I didn't want to mislead you, I meant that I didn't want you to think I didn't care about you or didn't want a relationship. I'm not sure about love just yet, Jared, but I want our relationship to grow."

"That's all I ask. Let's build on what we have and see where God takes us." Jared leaned toward her, gently cupping her chin in his hand. He felt his hand tremble a bit as he kissed her softly.

Sarah responded to Jared's sweet kiss and then pulled away slowly.

"I'm staying in town tonight. I spoke to George on my way here and he invited me to spend the night. May I see you tomorrow?"

Sarah grinned widely. "I was going to ask if you'd like to attend church with me tomorrow."

"I'd love that. George mentioned it, too, so I'm going for sure."

They laughed as he restarted the car. "I guess I better get you home so I can get to George's place before it's too late. I wouldn't want to keep him up."

Jared left the parking lot. "I'm glad I followed George's advice in his suggestion I go to Tim's. I may not have met you otherwise."

"If God in His plans has us together, we would have met regardless," Sarah assured him.

Chapter 15

Greta stared out the window of the aircraft. Her amazement at seeing the ground disappear couldn't be contained. "I can't believe I'm actually on an airplane."

Kat laughed. "Is this your first time to fly?"

"Yes." She turned from the window and looked at her seat companions. Kat and her mum had agreed to accompany her on a tour of lighthouses. "Here I am almost ninety-two years old and flying for the first time. This is so exciting!"

Betty watched Greta's face bloom with happiness. Her cheeks were rosy and her eyes sparkled. "I wouldn't have missed seeing you this excited for anything. I'm happy that Kat and I were able to come with you. We'll have fun and celebrate your birthday early."

"Mum, we could look for a nice restaurant in Portland and celebrate her birthday there."

"That's an idea. What do you think, Greta?"

"Let's be flexible and see what the week brings. We can always end our trip with a celebration in Michigan before heading home."

Betty chuckled. "This is your excursion so we'll follow your cue."

"I'm so anxious to see the Portland Headlight. I read that it's the oldest lighthouse in Maine," Greta said.

"Didn't you use it as a model for one of your paintings?" Kat asked.

"Roughly, yes. My interpretation was similar but only in the after painting. Remember, I was creating before and after pictures that illustrated transformation from a broken-down state to a new life."

"You did a great job," Betty said. "Wasn't that the pair of paintings purchased by Kenneth and Jewel?"

Greta shifted in her seat, adjusting her lap belt a little. "Yes, they wanted those two so much but I wouldn't sell them."

"But I thought – "

"I told the director and his wife I wouldn't sell the paintings to them, but I wanted to give them as a gift."

Betty smiled broadly. "That was sweet of you."

"My paintings have never been about the money. It's always been about the message."

Kat leaned her head on Greta's shoulder. "You're a very special lady," she whispered.

Greta reached over and patted Kat's cheek. "Thank you and you are too, my dear. Don't ever forget that."

***

Brian hung up the phone, satisfied knowing his wife, daughter, and Greta were safely on the ground in Portland, Maine. *Well, maybe not on the ground considering they're on the fourth floor of the Hilton. Betty sounded excited and from all the background chattering from Kat and Greta, it sounded like it was a shared emotion.*

Crackers had even let out a little woof when he heard their voices on the phone. Kat talked to him and told him nighty-night. Brian looked at the little guy's face and sad expression. His heart melted. "Come on, Crackers, let's go find some little fishy crackers." Brian doubted the dog knew the difference between his name and the cheese crackers from which he got his name. It didn't matter as long as there were some in the box.

Crackers barked as Brian pulled the box of treats from the pantry shelf. When he held one up, the furry guy sat obediently, waiting for his cue to stand and turn in a circle, for which he would be rewarded with a cheesy fish-shaped cracker. Brian gave him a few more than he should have but since Kat wasn't here, he felt it would ease the dog's loneliness. *Two whole weeks of trying to figure out how to keep the fellow happy and not miss Kat too much. I wonder how I'll figure out how to do the same for me, missing Betty that long.* He popped a fish cracker into his mouth, crunched it, and poured a few more into his hand. "You may be on to something, boy," he said, looking down

143

at Cracker's open mouth and wagging tail, "these are pretty yummy." He gave the dog one more before closing the box and putting it back on the shelf.

"Okay, let's go watch a movie," Brian said in an enticing voice. "I'll find one with a pretty girl dog in it."

As if he understood, Crackers dutifully followed Brian into the living room, jumped onto the sofa, and snuggled against the cushion while Brian turned on the television and joined him. He propped his feet on the foot stool and Crackers stretched his neck and laid his head on Brian's lap.

"We're good, little buddy — at least for tonight. We have only have thirteen more days and nights to get through." He stroked Cracker's fur and turned his attention to the channels as he flipped through them absentmindedly. His mind was absent here but present in Portland, Maine.

***

Ryan Ladderman sat quietly in the counselor's office, not really sure he should have kept this appointment. With Kat gone to Maine, he needed to talk to someone. He had told her about the fire but hadn't gone into a lot of detail. Ryan had seen a sign at the firehouse about grief counseling and had heard that first responders were often in need of someone to share their pain with, but he associated it with police and EMS servants. Thinking about getting counseling for himself had never been on Ryan's radar. Sure, he'd seen tragedy during his few years since becoming a firefighter – a few fatal fires – children injured ... that was the worst. He had been shaken at the sight of burned pets and, of course, seeing other firefighters injured always haunted him. In each of those events it never occurred to Ryan to ask for help in dealing with his emotional responses because he considered himself strong and always asked God to help him work through each situation.

Last month's fire was different. He felt helpless, even with all his training, to stop the screams for help calling through the raging fire that destroyed the house and dreams of one family. Ryan could only imagine Piper's state of mind, after his finding the badly burned woman, with her little girl shielded beneath her body, in a corner of a bedroom. Ryan shook his head at the memory of that day. *Piper should be here, too, getting counseling.*

Lucas Patone came through the doorway, closed the door softly, and extended his hand to Ryan. "Hello, Mr. Ladderman," the counselor said, "I'm Lucas Patone, and I've been given the privilege to talk with you about what's going on in your life."

Ryan rose and shook hands with the stout man, clad in starched jeans and a pullover shirt with a collar. He didn't look like a counselor — more like a guy going to a bowling alley. Ryan relaxed. "I'm glad to meet you, Mr. Patone," he said before sitting back down.

"Please, call me Lucas."

"Only if you call me Ryan."

"Ryan it is. Would you like coffee, a Coke, or anything?"

"No thanks, I'm good," he said, holding up his bottle of water. "I developed the habit of carrying a bottle of water with me wherever I go," Ryan said.

"Good habit. I should try it," Lucas responded as he leaned back in his leather chair. "I see from my notes when we talked on the phone that you're from Maryland and have been a firefighter for five years."

"Yes, Sir, I was in the Air Force a couple years – that's how I came to Texas – and then I saw an opening to become a firefighter, so I took the leap. I love what I do."

"That's admirable. I know your parents must be proud of you."

Ryan smiled and took a drink of his water, then replaced the cap. "I'm sure they are. They always wanted me to become a firefighter. When I was a kid I always received firetrucks and things associated with them as gifts. With a last name like Ladderman, I was teased a lot about what I would do in the future. I guess it was inevitable."

"Do you think if your last name had been Houndsman or something else, you would have made the same career choice?"

Ryan thought about the question. "Probably, because I believe God placed that desire in me. I didn't really choose to be a firefighter — God led me to serve Him in that capacity."

"You told me on the phone that you've had nightmares recently. Why don't we talk about that for a minute?"

"It's been more of a haunting dream than a nightmare. Since the horrible house fire last month, I can't seem to shake the echo of a woman screaming in pain and my inability to find her."

Lucas studied Ryan's face, noticing the tense furrow between his brows. The ease Ryan seemed to have at the beginning of their conversation was gone. "Is the woman you hear visible in your dream?"

"No, and the odd thing is that there's no fire. There's only darkness and a void. Her screams are muffled and distant like an echo returning them over and over. I wake up feeling I failed to help her."

"Was the woman in the house fire badly injured?"

Ryan lowered his head. "Yes, she's still in critical condition. Her daughter has been released from the hospital, though, and is doing well with relatives."

"I know this might be asking a lot of you right now, but would you consider paying the girl's mother a visit? Or maybe going to see the daughter?"

Ryan looked surprised at the suggestion.

"You would need to check with the hospital, of course, to see if they would allow it," Lucas said quickly.

"I wasn't the one who found her. It was my friend, Piper, who located and carried her out. He shouted out to me in the smoke-filled house to come and get the daughter. It was difficult finding where they were. I kept to the back of the place because others were putting out the flames on the other end. I finally found the room Piper and the injured were in. He had the woman and I picked up the girl. I thought she was dead but then I felt a pulse. We both hurried toward the back door but we had to go through two rooms of smoke to get there."

"That must have been a terrible thing to witness. Perhaps you and Piper could go together to see how she's doing and then take the daughter a small gift."

Ryan listened to the counselor's suggestion and wondered if he could muster up the courage to go. He would talk to Piper and see if he'd like to do it together. "Thanks, Lucas," Ryan said as he stood, "I'll talk to Piper later and we'll see what happens. I appreciate your time."

"That's what I'm here for, Ryan. Call me anytime. Please update me on what happens."

The two men shook hands and Ryan left the office, glad that he followed through and kept the appointment. He liked this guy.

***

Ryan and Piper arrived at the Methodist Hospital burn unit and donned protective garments. They were unrecognizable underneath the gown, mask, cap, and gloves. The doctor who gave permission for the two firefighters to visit Mrs. Thompson, had briefed the men about her condition and explained that the need to prevent infection necessitated the protective garments. He said she had suffered third degree burns over twenty-eight percent of her body and they were planning her first surgery the following week to do skin grafts on her left leg, arms, and hands. She had just come off the respirator two days before and was breathing on her own, but the doctor warned them not to stay more than ten minutes.

Ryan looked at Piper and they gave each other thumbs up to go in. Once inside, they quietly approached the bed. Angie Thompson lying face up with her eyes closed. Ryan whispered to Piper, "She's sleeping. Let's come back when she wakes up."

"I'm awake," said a soft voice coming from the bed. "I like keeping my eyes closed so I can picture my daughter better."

"We don't want to tire you, Mrs. Thompson," Piper said. "We are the two firefighters who brought you out of the burning house. We have been concerned about you and wanted to see how you were doing and if there is something you need that we can help with."

Angie opened her eyes and stared at the two masked strangers standing at the foot of her bed. "Bless you both, and thank you for saving my life. The medical team told me your names but I'm sorry, I don't remember."

"I'm Ryan and this is Piper," he said, pointing to his friend.

Angie gave a big smile. "Please call me Angie. Which of you helped my daughter, Sandie?"

"I found and carried her out after Piper lifted you off of her," Ryan explained. "You did an awesome job of shielding your daughter. She's doing great after being treated for smoke inhalation."

"Yes, the Fire Chief came in to see me and he mentioned that, too. She was all I could think of." Angie looked down at her bandaged left leg, arms, and hands. Tears rolled from her eyes. "I'm thankful Sandie doesn't have to endure this."

Piper swiped his eyes with a gloved hand. "Ma'am, is there anything you need or something we can do for you or your daughter?"

"You've already done it! You saved our lives and I can't ever repay you."

Ryan took the slip of paper on which he had written his phone number and placed it on the table next to her bed. "If you think of anything we can do, please call or have someone call me. Piper and I will gladly help anyway we can."

"Thank you both. I'm going to be here quite a while, they told me. I'm having my first surgery next week, and if possible I'd like to see you both afterward."

Ryan smiled under his mask. "That we can and will be happy to do. I'll let the medical team know to call us when you can have visitors."

A nurse entered the room. "Gentlemen, time is up. This young woman needs to rest," she said approaching the bed. She took a tissue from the box on the table and lightly pressed it to Angie's eyes, dabbing the remaining tears.

"Goodbye, Angie," the men both said at the same time. "We'll be praying for you as you go into surgery and we'll be back to visit."

"Thank you, both," she whispered, before closing her eyes again.

***

Kat took advantage of some alone time while Betty and Greta were napping. The morning had been full, with visiting the Portland Headlight, taking photos out front to capture the quartzite rock formations, hunting for souvenirs, and watching Greta soak up the history of the oldest lighthouse in Maine. Greta was in her element and relished every moment. When she told the tour guide, she did a painting of the Headlight and threw in the fact that she was almost ninety-two years old, he gave her every tidbit of information he had stored in his memory bank about that lighthouse. Kat laughed when the tour guide, Ronald, wanted his picture taken with Greta.

After the trio returned to their hotel room, Kat was the only one not wanting a nap, so she went downstairs to the lobby to place a call to Ryan, hoping to catch him off duty. She pressed the speed dial on her phone and waited.

"Hello, Kat," Ryan answered, "I was just thinking of you and wondering how the trip is going. Is everyone having a great time?"

"Yes," Kat said, "but Mum and Greta needed some down time so I thought I'd call. How are you doing? I am really missing you a lot."

"Not half as much as I miss you."

Kat detected something in his voice. Sadness? She couldn't tell if it was because she was away or if something deeper was going on.

"Ryan, what's wrong. You're not your usual high-note self."

"I'm good, really. We can talk when you get back."

"No, that's too long," Kat insisted. "I'll just worry all the time I'm here."

"Actually, I'm better today. A couple days ago I was feeling weird after having nightmares."

The word, nightmares, got Kat's attention. "Nightmares? About what?"

Ryan relayed the nightmares and told her about visiting Lucas, the grief counselor, and the visit he and Piper made to the hospital to see Mrs. Thompson, the lady they pulled from the house fire. "My mind and heart were so heavy, carrying the weight of the screams I heard. They were in my dreams and I felt so helpless."

"Oh, Ryan, I'm sorry I wasn't there for you."

"Please don't feel like that. This was something I had to work through with a professional and since seeing him, I feel a lot better."

"So how is the lady? What about her daughter?"

"Mrs. Thompson is still in critical condition. They are doing the first skin graft this week. She'll be in the hospital burn unit for some time. The little girl is staying with relatives and is doing well."

"I think it's wonderful that you and Piper visited. You have a compassionate heart."

"Well, Lucas suggested it. I'm a little ashamed that I didn't think of doing it on my own."

"Ryan, you've been dealing with so many emotions since that happened. Don't beat yourself up. I'm so proud of you for being a hero."

"I'm no hero, just serving God the way He called me to do. On another note, I stopped by your house today to see how Crackers and your dad are getting along."

"Oh? That was sweet of you. How are they doing, really? He told me they are becoming good friends."

Ryan laughed. "I'll say. Crackers has your dad eating those fish crackers. I noticed two big boxes of them on the table. He told me they were watching movies together, and Brian even taught him a couple new tricks."

It was Kat's turn to laugh. "Crackers may not have anything to do with me when I get home."

"That's okay, it'll mean more time for me to spend with you. I really miss you, Kat."

"I'm missing you more!"

"That's not possible," Ryan argued. "One good thing is that I'll be working seven straight days before I'm off. I'll stay pretty busy and the time will zoom by and then you'll be back."

"That makes two of us who'll be running crazy. We have so much packed into this trip. Tomorrow we're traveling to Quoddy Head State Park in Lubec, Maine, to visit the West Quoddy Head Lighthouse."

"The what?"

"I know, a crazy name, isn't it? So far all I know is that it's candy-striped."

"I hope you and the others have fun, but please be careful. I don't want anything to happen to you."

"We will and don't worry. I'll be praying for you and you can pray for me."

"Done! Hurry back."

Kat ended the call and sat back in the lobby chair. *I should get back upstairs and see if Mum and Greta are awake and ready for the next part of our adventure. Kat's stomach growled. I know what part of the adventure I'm ready for.*

Ryan placed his phone on the table and went in to change into his running clothes. The next day would start his seven-day stretch at work so he wanted to get in some running before he would be hefting hoses and climbing ladders. When he was done he'd grab a meal in Southtown and then head back home. Home for him was a small apartment, meagerly furnished and convenient to everything he needed to access. One day he would invest in a home, that is, when he had someone to share it with. *Maybe that would be Kat Hills,* he thought, as he pulled his running shoes from the closet.

Chapter 16

"Hey, Ron," Jake said, spilling his news into the phone as soon as his brother answered, "I have a buyer for the house!"

"Wow! That didn't take long. Did you get your asking price?"

"Close, I made a few concessions, but I'm happy with their offer."

"Good for you. Have you found a new place to live yet?"

"Not really. I plan to look at a couple more this weekend. I asked Annie to go with me now that she's finally out of the walking boot and can maneuver stairs."

"I'm happy for you. If you need any help with the house let me know. By the way, will you be able to come down for our rehearsal dinner in a couple weeks?"

"I'm planning on it and have it on my calendar. The best man has to be there, you know."

Ron laughed. "You are the best in my book."

"I have some other news, although it's not as good as selling the house."

"What's up?"

"Remember me telling you I might be getting my own hotel to manage?"

"Yes."

"Well, it's not happening. Seems there was a relative of the big shot who needed employment and he got the job. Of course, they didn't actually say that, but his name showed up on the promotion list."

"That's a bummer, Jake. I know you were excited about moving up."

"Yeah, well, that's life I suppose."

"There may be a bright side to it though. Now that the house is sold, or soon will be, you're not tied down there."

"I wasn't planning on moving away."

"No, but you're free to look at other options now. God may have something better planned for you."

Jake was quiet. "Hmmm, could be. But Annie lives here."

"Like I said, God may have other plans, so don't rule anything out. I'll be praying about the situation and you pray too."

"I will, thanks."

"That's what brothers are for. We'll see you in a couple weeks."

***

Seth and Emily were excited as they sat in the exam room waiting for Emily's obstetrician, Dr. Havel, to share the results of the ultrasound. Emily had been nervous about it.

Dr. Sanders smiled. "The baby is developing fine," "I'm sending a copy of the ultrasound to both your oncologist and primary doctors." She clicked send on the computer screen, and then turned to Emily. "Your baby is right on track. I know we couldn't tell the gender this time, but hopefully when you come in next time the baby will be more cooperative."

"Thank you doctor," Emily said. "I do have a question."

"Certainly, what is it?"

"We are thinking about flying to England soon and we wondered if it would be safe for me to do that."

"Well, you're right at sixteen weeks, so I would give you permission to fly. How long do you think you'd be gone?"

Seth spoke up. "We're not sure but possibly a couple two or three weeks."

"You should be okay. If you will give me your location there, I'll find an obstetrician in the area, just in case you need someone."

Emily clapped her hands. "That's wonderful, thank you so much."

Dr. Sanders stood. "You're welcome, and I'll have my physician assistant provide you with a packet we have for pregnant patients who must fly."

Seth rose from his chair, thanking her. "You've made this lady," he said, motioning to Emily, "very happy."

"You're welcome. I like happy patients. We'll set up your next appointment and you're good to go."

Emily stood and wrapped her arms around Seth. "Now, we need to look at the calendar and get some plane tickets."

Seth couldn't help but see the joy in his wife ... she wore a broad smile, the happiest one he'd ever seen on her.

***

Leila Farmington finished working on the new spring menu, adding several of her own recipes. She planned to introduce them next weekend so Tim could be her first taster. *He'll either love them or fire me,* she chuckled to herself. Growing up in New Mexico, Leila was taught how to cook reginal dishes early in her life. She learned to prepare her aunt's So-So-Salsa Salmon when she was barely twelve. The pear and pineapple salsa was the secret weapon for the award her aunt won at the festival. She could already taste the fruity flavor spiked with red chiles.

The other recipe she hoped Tim would allow her to add to the menu is the Chile Willy's Chili, named for her dad, who loved the dish. It was a cross between a gumbo sans okra and a kitchen sink veggie soup with chicken thrown in. Leila's mom would save all the vegetable leftovers during the week and toss them in with Hatch chiles and diced chicken. This was their traditional Saturday meal.

Tomorrow she would go to work early and get the Chili started early so Tim would be able to sample it. Maybe he would agree to give free samples to customers. The following day she would make the So-So-Salsa Salmon and repeat the tastings in the evening.

Leila closed her recipe book, stood, and stretched. It was almost ten o'clock and she wanted to catch the news before going to bed. She placed the book on the shelf above the counter and began preparing a cup of decaf to take to her bedroom. She would shower and slip into her pj's, make a cup of coffee, watch the news, and read for fifteen minutes. She'd love to read longer but her eyes shut down any chance of that happening. She took her coffee to the bedroom and placed it on the nightstand on top of her latest read, a mystery by an unknown author. Leila found it at the library used book sale, buried under a deluge of famous authors. She felt obligated to buy it for fifty cents and who knows; maybe she would discover a great writer.

Leila once considered writing a book – a recipe collection of dishes made by her grandmother and handed down. Granny never measured anything; she added a handful of this and a scoop of that. When Leila was growing up, her mom taught her the same way. No cookbook would sell using that system of measuring ingredients. Now, Leila felt she had perfected the recipes enough that she could put actual measurements down. *I wonder if I could really create a cookbook and get it published.*

She reached for her cup of decaf, took a slow sip, and retrieved her mystery novel. Staring at the man on the cover, half hidden in the shadows to depict something sinister was on his mind; she blinked a couple times and looked closer. His features, what she could see of them, reminded her of her brother and dad rolled into one. Darrell favored his father greatly in the brooding eyes, shallow cheeks, and his height. They definitely made good mystery cover subjects. She wondered how Darrell was doing in Arizona. She hadn't heard from him in a month or so, but he preferred his seclusion since retiring. Leila wanted to discuss buying this house from him but he always avoided the conversation. *I'll try calling him tomorrow after work.* She wanted to at least make sure he was okay.

Leila opened her book, removed the yellow tab that marked her place and settled back against the pillow. She took another sip of coffee and chided herself humorously. *Maybe I can finish this chapter before nodding off.*

***

Annie walked confidently into the hospital, ready to get back to work after being on short term leave to heal from the accident. She knew her coworkers were waiting for their chance to spring their surprise welcome back on her the moment she walked in. She took her time as she made her way down the hallway and as she pushed the double doors there was ... nothing ... no yay, you're back. No welcome banner or smiling faces to greet her. Annie stopped in her tracks and looked around. Nurses were tending patients in the surgical holding rooms, several techs pushed carts down the wing toward the supply room, and one nurse's aide was on the phone. *This is eerie! What's going on?*

Annie headed around the corner to the nurse's lounge to put her purse away and check in. She arrived early as was her usual habit, to give herself a few minutes to get familiar with any new happenings. Since she had been out so long she figured she needed extra time. Annie used her name tag to unlock the door and enter.

Suddenly the room was filled with light as paper streamers exploded in the air and shouts of welcome echoed from every corner. Doctors, nurses, techs, and even volunteers rushed to greet her with hugs and hellos. Tears spilled as she took in the sight.

"Nurse Heartie! Welcome back!" voices called in unison.

Annie cried a bit more hearing the nickname by which she had become famous for after word went out that she loved watching the Hallmark Christmas shows. Everyone said she had a soft heart. She did have a soft heart and it showed in how she cared for her patients.

"Thank you, all, so much. It's great to be back – without the boot –" she added, lifting her right foot. "I'm anxious to get to work and find out what all happened while I was out."

"You'll find out soon enough," Cindy, one of the RN's on the night shift, joked. "You may want to extend your sick leave when you do. But before you begin your day, you might want to have a slice of this." Cindy stepped aside to reveal a large cake. A fondant foot in a boot with icing signatures of her coworkers all over the boot adorned the top.

They all laughed as Cindy snapped a photo of the cake and several girls began cutting and handing out slices.

"Thank you again, for going to all this trouble. I've really missed each of you and I'm sorry I wasn't here to help carry the load."

Annie was inundated with hugs as they ate their cake quickly before getting back to work. *I love working here and being part of helping people.*

Some coworkers finished eating and headed back to work. Doctor Rawlings, her former associate from earlier years, and the doctor who treated her in the ER, motioned he wanted to talk with her. Annie set her paper plate down and joined him.

"Annie, I'm happy to see you followed my instructions and have healed nicely."

Annie smiled. "Thanks to your expert diagnosis and treatment, too."

"I would like to talk to you privately when you are not on the clock."

"Oh, is something wrong?"

Doctor Rawlings grinned. "No, nothing negative, but it could turn out to be life-changing for you."

Annie's eyebrows rose. "You have my full attention, Doctor Rawlings. What's going on?"

"I can't talk about it now. Call me if you're off work and perhaps you can come to my hospital for a cup of coffee. I really need to get back to the emergency room." He placed his plate with a small bite of cake still remaining, in the receptacle by the door. "I must go, but I'll look for your call, soon."

Annie glanced at her watch. "Yes, I need to wrap up my celebration here and clock in. I will let you know when I can come by."

"Great," he said, giving her a quick hug before scurrying out the door.

By now, the room was empty and Annie stood quietly wondering what just happened. *What could possibly be so important to discuss that Doctor Rawlings wanted to talk privately?* Myriad of things whirled through her mind as she mechanically clocked in and prepared for the change of shifts and reports. She had an unsettled feeling about her, not to mention a growing knot in her stomach. *He said it wasn't negative.* Annie exhaled as she rounded the corner and approached the nurse's station. *But, he also said it could change my life!*

Hearing her name called, Annie looked up quickly. Cindy was holding a clipboard and staring at her.

"Are you alright?" Cindy asked.

"Yes, I'm sorry, I was lost in thought for a moment."

"I wanted to go over stats on a patient with you before I leave."

"Certainly, where do you want to sit?" Annie said, looking at the now crowded nurses' station.

"Let's go to the conference room."

Annie followed her coworker down the hall and they took a seat at the small table in the corner.

"I have a patient named, Mrs. Brooks. She has not responded well and I'd like you to care for her. I trust you," she added in a whisper.

Annie was baffled. First, Doctor Rawlings requests a private meeting to discuss something that might change her life. Now, Cindy, who is a fantastic and compassionate RN, wants to turn over her patient to Annie. *God, please guide me through whatever you have planned for me.*

"Why me?" Annie asked.

"Truthfully, you're the one nurse who I believe can help Mrs. Brooks. The doctors are doing all they know to do but she seems to have just given up. I don't want to see her die. She only has one son and he travels a lot, so it's rare when he visits. Her doctor wants to transfer her to a nursing home, but I'm afraid she won't make it. Here's her chart," Cindy said, passing the clipboard to Annie. "I'm hoping that you can reach her somehow and help her want to respond to treatment. I've tried but nothing has worked."

Annie glanced over the chart, assessing what had been done and how the patient had responded. It broke Annie's heart to know this woman, only fifty-eight years old, has such a dire prognosis. The treatment she's had should be working."

"Okay, I'll look in on her and study her chart. Hopefully, I can help her. There's no guarantee of course. It says here that she is Doctor Sherman's patient. Is he new? I don't remember him."

"Yes, I forgot to tell you. He came here from the east coast. I think he started a few days after you went on short term leave for your foot. I like him, and he is really good–looking."

Annie smiled. "Well, that's fine, but how is he with the patients?"

Cindy stood and laughed. "He's a great doctor, very caring. I was just putting in a plug for him in case you were interested."

"Cindy!" Annie said with a loud gush. "I would never. You know I have never dated anyone I've worked with."

"I know, I'm trying to lighten the mood here. I need to go," she said, looking at her watch.

Annie watched Cindy as she headed out, leaving Annie to ponder about Mrs. Brooks, on top of everything else. She sighed. *Okay, Mrs. Brooks, we are going to see what's going on with you and I'm going to find a way into keeping you out of a nursing home.*

Annie tucked the clipboard under her left arm and walked slowly down the hall to room 203. When she arrived, the door was closed but she heard a muffled sound coming from inside. She pushed the door open slowly and approached the curtained bed. Annie was able to see her new patient in the light of the early morning dawn. She was crying into her pillow. Annie's heart broke.

***

"I'll talk to Ron tomorrow," Seth promised, satisfied that Emily was in agreement about their decision. "Of course, ultimately, the outcome will depend on whether Ron's brother would even consider such a move."

"I know," Emily said, folding her robe over the chair by the bed and slipping between the fresh, linen-scented sheets, "but we can at least offer him the opportunity. He has hotel experience and we already have the cooking solved by adding Blanca and Rosie to the staff."

Seth plumped his pillow and turned on his side facing his wife. "He may not want to move down here from Mesquite." Seth wanted to prepare Emily just in case their idea didn't work out. Hiring Ron's brother to manage the Texas Tribute Bed & Breakfast so he and Emily could make a trip to England and decide what to do about the Manor house seemed like the perfect solution. The chance of Jake accepting the position was good since the salary offer was above the average rate.

"Maybe Ron won't want his brother to move here."

Emily pulled the sheet to her shoulders and nestled snuggly on her side to face her husband. "Nonsense, Ron will probably welcome the move. They seem to be close."

"You're so optimistic, my dear," Seth whispered as he kissed the tip of her nose."

"It's better than being negative, don't you think?"

Seth laughed, pulling Emily close. "You've got me there. That's yet another reason I love you so much."

***

Standing in front of the Brant Point Light Station, Greta was in awe of the history behind the structure. "You know," she commented to her two traveling companions, "I see myself in the struggle to stand strong and be a light, in this light station."

"What do you mean?" Betty asked.

"This lighthouse is the ninth one built here."

"Wow," Kat said, "what happened to the others?"

"It's tragic. The original wooden one was destroyed by fire in1757. Actually, two others were also taken by fire. A couple later ones were wrecked in storms, and others were taken over and rebuilt."

"How do you fit that into a picture of your life?" Betty asked.

"I've experienced loss and tragedy in my past, but I was somehow able to come back from it. Then finally, thanks to you, Betty, I experienced a rebirth through Christ. I hope my life, through my paintings of these beautiful lighthouses, might help navigate someone else into God's safe harbor."

Betty put her arm around Greta and hugged her close. "You are such an inspiration to me, Greta, and I think for Kat too."

"You are," Kat added. "I hope to be like you when I grow up."

"It's starting to rain a bit," Betty commented. "Why don't we find a place to grab some lunch."

In agreement, they made their way back to the rental car, covering their heads with the brochures they carried.

"I think next time we need to bring the umbrellas instead of leaving them in the car," Kat suggested.

They laughed as they reached the parking area and scrambled into the car just as the rain became heavier.

***

Brian finished washing the few dishes he used for his supper, rinsed out Cracker's water bowl before refilling it, and then poured himself a cup of coffee. He was anxious to settle in and work on his book about Clarence. He finally was near completing it and then get the editing started. If all went well, he'd have it out by summer. He felt good about the progression and the direction the ending was headed.

He could see Clarence shaking his head in disbelief if he held a book about him in his hands. Clarence was such a humble man. Brian hoped readers would see this man's heart and soul on the pages, not just because of his service to his country, but as a man who lived simply and treated others compassionately.

He looked at his notes for marketing the book. He had already talked with several VFW locations about having a book signing, and he was excited about that. Brian also spoke with the person at the public television station and planned to offer book copies as gifts when they play the documentary that Betty and her film crew did last year about Clarence and Greta. When viewers sent in their donation in support of public television, they would get a free copy of the documentary plus a book. *I think Clarence would approve.*

He pulled up the file titled, *The Heart and Soul of a Man*. He already had the cover design, a side view of Clarence saluting the American flag. Now he needed to buckle down and get the last few chapters written. Betty and Kat wouldn't be back for another week, so this was the ideal time to get the book done.

"Woof, woof," came a determined sound from Crackers, nudging Brian's foot.

"Crackers, now what? I fed you, gave you fresh water, and even some fish crackers. What else is there that you could possibly want or need?"

He looked down to discover the little guy brought a tennis ball and dropped it between Brian's feet." Brian sighed. He picked up the ball. "Okay, five minutes of fetch and then I have to get back to work," he said, rising from the chair. Together, they walked down the stairs and out to the back yard. "Five minutes!" he reminded Crackers, "five!"

***

Kat dialed her dad's cell phone number; she wanted to check on Crackers.

"Hey, Kat," Brian answered, what's up?"

"Hi Dad, I thought I'd see how you're doing with Crackers. Is he behaving?"

"We're good. He's training me to pitch a tennis ball."

Kat laughed. "I miss him, and you, of course."

Chapter 17

"Greta, are you sure?" Betty asked in astonishment. "We're set to go to the Lighthouse in Michigan tomorrow."

"And we're planning to celebrate your birthday there, too," Kat added.

"I'm sure. You've both been wonderful travel companions and I love all we've done, but truthfully, I'm tired, and having seen the Brant Point Light Station, I feel I've seen what God brought me here to see."

Betty looked at Greta, propped up by three pillows in her bed. She did look tired. Traveling always tired Betty, so it must be taxing to Greta even more. Although, she also had a look of satisfaction on her face.

"We could have a birthday breakfast here in the hotel first thing in the morning," Kat said. "It'll be fun."

Betty smiled. "Leave it to Kat to find the fun in every circumstance."

They all laughed.

"Then it's settled," Greta said in her determined voice. "Betty, would you check with the airline and see if we can change our return flight time?"

"Certainly, I'll see if I can get us home tomorrow. We won't tell anyone though, let's surprise them."

"Ooooh, Dad and Crackers will sure be blown away when we walk in unexpected." Kat was quiet for a minute. "Ryan will really be happy," she added with exuberance.

Greta lay still thinking about the obvious. She had no one who would be surprised or excited about her early return. Clarence would have been. She refused to dwell on his passing. She was moving forward, which was one reason for this trip. She'd get home and begin working on the next lighthouse painting, now that she knew which one it would be. Greta was excited about going home early. That was what mattered.

"I think I'll turn in now, if that's okay with you ladies. My tiredness has overtaken my excitedness."

Betty and Kat laughed together.

"Goodnight, Greta, we'll see you for breakfast," Betty said quietly, as she and Kat rose to go to their own room.

"Goodnight to you both."

***

Jake sat across from Seth in his office at the Texas Tribute Bed & Breakfast. Seth's wife, Emily, had left the room briefly.

"You have a beautiful place here," Jake commented.

"Thank you, it took a lot of work and patience, but we think the original owner, Mary, would approve. Since we talked last, have you had time to consider everything or do you have additional questions about the job?"

"Your offer really has me intrigued," Jake said. "I've been a hotel manager since I finished college and I like what I do. I have to say though, running a B & B – this B & B – is something I could grow to love. The quality is top notch and San Antonio is a great place."

"Thank you, Jake. When we spoke earlier, I indicated that the position is more than just being a manager. You would essentially take over operations, a turnkey position. My wife is pregnant and we want to travel back to England where she has a home. Timing is important because of her condition and being able to fly. We have to go very soon and with the grand opening coming up, we need to make sure we have someone we can trust."

"Have you considered selling this place?" Jake asked. "I mean if you don't plan to return to San Antonio."

Seth shook his head. "No, not now anyway. We poured our hearts into making it happen, and we'd like to know it will be a success. We're not sure exactly what our future looks like at this point. I know you need to give notice where you're currently employed, and I hate to rush you, but...."

"Well, I have vacation coming, so I could use that. I also have a very efficient assistant manager who could certainly take over. There is the matter of finding a place to live though."

"You are welcome to utilize the suite off the back. We call it the Homeroom. We put that in just in case we would need to accommodate speakers or even use it for ourselves." Seth rose and walked around his desk. "We can go take a look at it and see if it works for you."

"That would be great," Jake said, and followed Seth out.

Emily greeted the two men in the hallway. "Well, I see smiles, so that must be good news."

Seth took Emily's hand and they escorted Jake to the Homeroom. "I think we have found our resident manager," Seth told his wife.

Emily looked at Jake, who nodded his head and smiled. "I'm so happy, Jake. Thank you."

"I'm the one who should be thanking you both. This position is one of a kind and I will make sure the Texas Tribute B & B is a success!"

They reached the Homeroom and Seth unlocked the door, swinging it wide. "Welcome to your new home, Jake."

Jake stepped into the room and couldn't believe his eyes. He turned to his employers. "May I move in this weekend?"

They all laughed.

"We were hoping you would say that," Emily said.

***

Annie couldn't wait to see Jake tonight. He sounded so excited when he called, saying he had some unbelievable news. She had never heard him bubble over with happiness in his voice like he had today. She turned and looked at herself in the full-length mirror in her bedroom. *This dress is too drab,* she thought, unzipping it and tossing the gray shirt dress on the bed. *I need something that doesn't scream matron, something flowery.* She pushed hangers aside in her closet, examining each dress or outfit before moving to the next. *I need to go shopping!* She plopped herself on the bed and stared into the closet. Annie didn't have a vast wardrobe, mostly functional clothes for work, and casual. She wasn't a material girl who bought into fad clothes or brand labels. She laughed out loud. "You're not a girl anymore," she said to the image in the mirror. She pulled her hair down out of the knot she usually wore. Her shoulder length, cocoa shaded strands fell below her neck. She seldom wore her hair down, but it felt nice for a change. Annie got up, grabbed her handbag and headed for the door, glancing at her watch. I have three hours before Jake gets here. *I can find something nice to wear before then, I'm sure.*

***

Jake stared at Annie from across from the table at El Tipico. She looked different, brighter, and livelier than he could recall ever seeing her. He smiled and lifted his iced tea glass.

"A Toast!" he proclaimed.

Annie met his glass in the air with hers. "To what are we toasting?" she inquired. Annie felt excitement build in her. She couldn't wait to tell him about her job offer. When Jake said he had something he wanted to discuss with her, she thought it might involve their future, possibly together. He'd been acting a little different lately. Would he propose? If so, how would he react to her good news?

"This is a toast to change!" he said, before clinking his glass to hers.

Annie responded. "To change!" She took a sip and set the glass down. "So, when do you plan to share your news with me?"

"I'm hoping to as soon as our food arrives and the server disappears," he said, looking in the direction of the kitchen. "They usually don't take this long."

Annie's heart grew anxious. *If he proposes, how can I tell him what I've decided?*

***

Ryan was thankful he had days off over the weekend. Since Kat surprised him with her early return, he hurriedly spruced up his apartment and made a quick run to the laundry room. He wasn't much of a housekeeper; after all, he spent more time at the fire station than at home. Ryan wished for the first time that he had a fireplace. Being a firefighter, Ryan disliked fireplaces because he saw too many homes burn to the ground because the owners didn't

165

clean their chimney. But it would be nice to have a cozy fire going while he and Kat talk and get caught up on what's been going on. He wanted to share with her about his visit to the grief counselor and how much it helped him. Ryan also couldn't wait to hear about Greta's reaction to the lighthouses and find out why the ended their trip so suddenly with another week to go. Ryan figured they could talk more easily here than in a restaurant. He was glad he thought to stop at the flower shop on his way back from doing laundry. *Hope she likes daffodils.* Ryan found the brightest yellow blooms the florist had.

He glanced at the clock and knew he better leave. Ryan couldn't wait to hug Kat. Two weeks had gone by slowly. Grabbing his keys from the bowl on the counter, he whistled as he closed the door behind him

Ryan planned a full weekend with Kat and hoped she would enjoy going to the antique mall tomorrow. He remembered her saying she loved estate sales, so Ryan figured the antique mall was a good choice. He knew the guy who owned it and they always had a huge inventory from estate sales. He got in the car and backed out ... smiling.

***

Greta was happy to be back from her adventure trip, even though she had no one waiting for her. She loved being with Betty and Kat. They doted on Greta and treated her like part of their family instead of an old woman. Of course, she was old, but being with Betty and her stepdaughter infused Greta with life.

She looked around her suite, once shared with her husband, Clarence. It looked different now that she brought her painting tools in and set up her own little studio, but she still missed his presence. When he died, Greta lost some of her own life, or so she thought. Finding love this late in life made it more valuable. Clarence brightened her days with his humor and gave her all his support. *I still miss you, Clarence.*

The director had picked up Greta and her travel companions from the airport and saw to it that they all arrived home safely. Greta was indebted to him for all his help in arranging the trip. But now that she was back, Greta knew the course her painting would take and she needed to get started tomorrow. *First things first, a good night's sleep in my own bed, and then I'll be able to think more clearly.*

Greta slipped into bed. The moment her head was on the pillow she closed her eyes and saw the Brant Point Light Station in her mind. She made a mental note to ask the director if he would pull up information on that computer of his about the history of Brant Point. Maybe he could find photos of the other eight structures and how they were destroyed before the current one was built. She needed more background than what she read in the brochure they handed out.

Now that her mind was whirling, she doubted sleep would come anytime soon. *Why do I think of these things at night?* She tried clearing her mind by thinking about Clarence. He would laugh at her now, laying here trying to fall asleep. He would tell her to count from one hundred down to one and she would begin but couldn't recall ever reaching fifty. *At my age I'm doing good to count to ten forward. One hundred, ninety-nine, ninety-eight, ninety-seven ....*

***

Annie stared at Jake, dumbfounded. Certainly, she did not hear him correctly. It sounded like he said he was moving to San Antonio to take a position as hotelier for a Bed and Breakfast. She shook her head as if to reset her hearing.

"Did I just hear you tell me that you're moving to San Antonio for a new job?"

Jake was taken back a bit by the look on Annie's face. He couldn't tell if she was happy, sad, or angry.

"That's right, but there's more to it than just taking on a new job. I would be in full charge of the place and if the owners decide to stay in England, who knows, I might have an opportunity to buy the place. My brother lives in San Antonio and I think since I have a buyer for my mom's house, this is all in God's timing."

Annie's jaw dropped. She still couldn't believe what she heard. "Okay, let's back this up for a minute. Remember I said I had some news to share with you?"

"I do."

"Well, you won't believe what I'm about to tell you. I agree that things happening right now are in God's timing." Annie drew in a deep breath and then relayed the conversation she had with Doctor Rawlings and her subsequent visit with him.

"I've been offered a position at the Metropolitan Methodist Hospital in San Antonio. There is a shortage of nurses there and he is on some board connected with the hospital. They had a meeting and he brought up my name. I've had a virtual interview and they all but wrote me out a sign-on bonus if I start right away."

Jake's eyebrows nearly reached his hairline.

"You're not joking with me, are you?"

"Not in the least. "I've been so on edge about telling you because I'd be moving away."

Jake reached across the table, knocking over the saltshaker, and took Annie's hand in his. He smiled. "Then I steal the moment by telling you I'm moving instead. I'm sorry. I should have let you tell your news first."

"It doesn't matter now. We're both moving. We're both taking new positions. We'll both be close by. That's what matters."

***

Emily pointed to the calendar she'd been writing on. "I've been looking. If we leave right away, we could have two weeks in Essex at Summer Bride, and then come back for Rita and Ron's wedding. We wouldn't want to miss that."

"They would be disappointed if we weren't there," Seth agreed. "But ... "

"But what?"

"I'm more concerned about the effect of our jaunting across the pond twice in two weeks would have on you and the baby."

"Doctor Sanders said it was okay to fly to England right now."

Seth scooted closer to Emily on the sofa. "I know, but the purpose of the trip is to decide whether we want to make Summer Bride our home or stay here. I know where your heart is and I'm afraid that once the wedding is over, you'll want to go back to England. That's another trip."

Emily sighed. "You're right, as usual. I know I sprung this on you without warning, but something in me just says we need to go. The baby isn't due until fall, so if worst case scenario happens and

I'm not able to fly back, you could come home and tend to what needs to be done."

"No way would I leave you in another country like that. Two will both go and stay or two will both go and come back – together. I think the best solution is for us to let Rita and Ron know there's a possibility we won't be able to attend. They will understand."

"Okay. If you'll make the flight arrangements, I'll talk to Rita."

"That's my girl," Seth said, brushing a stray lock of hair from the edge of her eye.

"Now that we have that settled, how about some hot chocolate with marshmallows?"

"Sounds good to me," Seth answered.

"The cocoa and marshmallows are in the pantry,"

"Oh, you want me to make it?" Seth said, pointing his index finger to his chest.

They both laughed as he rose and headed toward the kitchen.

***

"Did I tell you that my brother will be the new manager of the Texas Tribute Bed & Breakfast?" Ron asked as he helped Rita address the wedding invitations.

Rita straightened her back, stiff from hunching over the envelopes. "You said he was interviewing for the position. So, he accepted the job? That's great. Is he looking for a house or apartment here?"

Ron rubbed his fiancé's back. "He did accept and no, he won't need to find a place. Apparently, he'll be living on the premises – at least for now."

"I wonder what his moving here will do to his relationship with Annie."

"I don't know, but I'm sure they'll figure something out. I'm glad he took the job though. He wasn't happy where he was and since he sold mom's house he can make a clean break by moving away."

Rita's phone rang. She mouthed the words, I'm sorry, to Ron as she stood and walked to the window as she answered. "Hi Emily, how are you?"

Rita listened as Emily relayed their plans to fly to England and hoped, but couldn't guarantee, they would be back in time for the wedding. Rita assured her friend it was okay and not to worry. "Have a good trip and if you make it back, we'll see you at the wedding." She hung up and looked at Ron.

"What was that all about?" he asked.

"Emily and Seth are flying out to her Manor House, Summer Bride, for a couple weeks to see if they want to make it their permanent home."

"What? Really?"

"Yes, and depending on how well she does with flying, they might not get back in time for our wedding."

"I'd miss having them but I'm sure Emily loves that home Mary gifted to her."

"I wonder what it would be like, living in another country," Rita said wistfully, staring out the window.

"Hey, don't get any ideas. We just invested a lot of money in a new home for us and a new studio for you, Ron said, winking at his future bride.

Rita laughed. "Just kidding." she said, walking over to Ron. She sat in his lap.

He wrapped his arms around her and squeezed gently. "Those envelopes aren't going to address themselves, you know."

Rita slid from his lap to the other cushion and picked up her pen. "It's a good thing the venue limits the number of people or we'd never get done. I only have five more."

"Hmmm, let's see. I still have ten. How about we finish these and after we drop them at the post office, we go grab something to eat?"

"Works for me."

***

Ryan seated Kat at his table, pausing to kiss her cheek after moving her chair up a bit. He had plated their meal from the caterer and placed the daffodils on the table. He took his seat across from her and smiled.

"I hope you like comfort food."

Kat looked at the chicken and dumplings and nodded. "This is one of my favorites."

He reached for her hands and they locked fingers.

"Heavenly Father," Ryan began his prayer, *"thank You for bringing Kat back safely and early, You know how much I missed her. Bless this food as we seek to serve You with the body you gave each of us. May we do it for Your glory. Amen"*

"Amen." Kat agreed.

"Tell me about your excursion on the east coast, and don't leave out anything."

Kat laughed as she glanced at the daffodils. "I will, but first I need to thank you for providing the flowers. There's a story about them I'd like to tell you."

"I'm all ears."

"When I was in high school and head over heels about a guy, he broke my heart. I thought my world was coming to an end." Kat noticed the caring look in Ryan's eyes. "I told my mom what happened and that evening she brought me some daffodils. She told me there would be other boys who would probably break my heart before I found the right one and it was better to laugh than cry. So she renamed the flowers *laughadills.*"

Ryan laughed, but he wanted to get up and hug Kat. "I won't break your heart," he promised as he looked deep into her eyes.

Kat put her spoon down and wiped the dampness from her eyes with the napkin by her dish. She didn't know how to respond to his promise.

"Okay, what have you been doing while I was gone?" she asked quickly to change the subject.

"Not yet. First tell me about your trip." Ryan insisted, setting his now empty dish to the side.

"I'll condense it because there was so much. I'll show you photos of some of it, but the best part was when Greta had a lightbulb moment concerning the last lighthouse we visited. It gave her the purpose she was looking for regarding her paintings. I'll take you to visit her one day and show you some of her work. She is awesome. Oh, the other great part was her birthday breakfast the morning we left. We actually had it at the airport restaurant and the whole staff came out and sang to her. She was the star of the morning."

"I'll bet she was," Ryan chuckled. "I can see it now."

"It's your turn," Kat said.

Ryan started slowly, explaining about the haunting dreams he had after he and Piper rescued the woman and her daughter from the fire. "I needed to talk to someone and sure didn't want to burden you while you were on your trip. I remembered seeing a phone number on the bulletin board at the firehouse for a grief counselor. I called and was able to get in right away."

"Oh Ryan, I'm so glad you did. How was the counseling session?"

He explained how at first, he didn't think the guy could help him, but as they talked, Ryan relaxed and began feeling much better. He told her about visiting the woman and the prognosis for her. "Me and Piper plan to keep in touch with her so we can help that family recover. She has a long road ahead with many surgeries."

"I'm so proud of you and Piper for what you're doing. You're so compassionate. That's one of the things I love about you."

Ryan beamed.

"Have you had that dream anymore?"

"No, and I'm so glad. It was terrible." He stood and offered his hand to Kat. "Let's go for a walk."

Kat took his hand and when she stood, he pulled her close, kissing her with such passion, he pulled back suddenly. "I'm sorry, I didn't mean...."

Kat took a step back and composed herself. "I need to freshen up a bit before we leave," she said, looking around for the restroom.

Ryan recovered enough to point toward the hall. "First door on the right," he said.

After Kat left the room, Ryan did a high five on his forehead. *What were you thinking? Get a hold of yourself!* He ran his fingers through his hair and as she appeared, he saw nothing but love in her eyes. At least he convinced himself it was love. He smiled back at her. "Ready?"

"Let's go, the night air is perfect for a walk," she said.

Chapter 18

"I know you've taken the position at the Texas Tribute B & B, and next week is the open house," Ron said, "but I'm hoping you'll be able to come to our wedding rehearsal dinner."

Jake smiled. "I wouldn't miss it. The dinner is at night and most of the activity at the B & B is morning and lunch time. Besides, Seth hired an assistant before he and Mrs. Gardley left for England, and I've been training her."

Ron slapped his brother on the back as they headed for the cashier. "I'm glad, and I really enjoyed having lunch with you today. We need to do it more often after Rita and I get back from our honeymoon."

Jake pulled out his wallet and fished a credit card from the slot, handing it to the cashier with their ticket. "I'm happy for you both. You're made for each other. I hope one day I'll find my soul mate, too." He closed his wallet and they headed for the parking lot.

"How is Annie? Has she moved here yet and started her new job?"

"Yeah, actually, Monday is her first day. I wish I could help her get settled this weekend, but with the open house and all, there's no way. She understood and told me not to worry about it."

"It's tough starting over. You both have a lot on your plates right now. There's plenty of time to work on a relationship."

Jake was quiet.

Ron looked at his brother. "There is still a relationship isn't there?"

Jake answered quickly. "Sure, we knew we would have to slow down when we each discovered the other was moving here." Jake stood by his car and leaned against the door. "It just seems like I can't seem to pull things together like you do."

"Like me?" Ron was shocked at Jake's remark. "What things are you talking about?"

"I don't know, everything. You've always managed to land on your feet. Me, I bounce all over the place when I make changes. Remember the decorating I tried at Mom's house?"

Ron burst into a hearty laugh. "That was a huge bounce, but it helped you make a decision to change things. Now you have a great position, a new place to live, and your possible soul mate moved here too. I think that's a pretty good bounce."

Jake hugged Ron's shoulder. "You always seem to know how to make me feel better."

"Like I said many times, that's what brothers do."

Ron looked at his watch. "I gotta run. I'll see you next week at the dinner!"

Jake watched his brother head back to his car before he got into his own. On impulse, he hit speed dial on his phone to call Annie. *I just need to hear her voice.* It rang four times before going to voice mail. He listened to her short, recorded greeting but decided to not leave a message. Jake tossed the phone onto the passenger seat, started the car, and headed out of the parking lot. He needed to get back to the B & B to go over the details of the open house with his assistant, Becky Frost. He hoped she was a fast learner.

***

The taxi slowed as it approached the drive that would take Seth and Emily up to the manor house, Summer Bride. The driver turned and ambled up the wet pavement.

"It's been raining for three days," he told Seth.

"I suspect it'll continue for a few more, if the weathermen are correct," Seth said, laughing.

Emily pulled closer to her husband, enjoying the slow drizzle running down the window of the taxi. "I love the rain," she said softly. "I can't believe we're really here."

Seth patted Emily's hand. "How are you holding up? Do you feel okay?"

Emily smiled. "I've never felt better."

The taxi came to a stop in front of the manor and was greeted by Teddy and Ruth, the caretakers, along with a younger man. Teddy held an umbrella to block the drizzle.

The taxi driver exited the car to remove the luggage, while Seth assisted Emily. Teddy hugged the pair and handed the umbrella to Seth as they exchanged greetings before introducing them to the caretaker in training, Rusty Dolby.

"We're so happy to meet you," Seth said, shaking the young man's hand. "We hope you like working here. You have a great guy to learn from," he stated, pointing to Teddy.

"Yes, Sir, Mr. Gardley. I really enjoy it here and Mr. Ted has taught me a lot."

"That's great. Rusty, this is my wife, Emily."

Rusty removed his cap quickly. "It's nice to meet you, Ma'am."

"I'm pleased to know you, Rusty. I look forward to learning more about you in the coming weeks."

"Come," Ruth encouraged Emily, "let's get out of this bloody rain and have some tea while the men bring in the luggage."

Emily stepped under Ruth's umbrella as they made their way into the manor, leaving the men to gather suitcases in what had turned into a steady rain. Once inside, she immediately felt the warmth from the fire and smelled the aroma of Ruth's delicious stew wafting through the rooms.

"Ruth, it smells delicious in here. Thank you for having something cooking. I'm starving."

"No trouble at all. In this weather you have to get warm on your inside before you feel it on the outside."

Emily laughed. "I won't argue with that, but first we have tea!"

"I have the kettle on. We can talk while we sip. I'm anxious to hear about your trip, but most of all, I want to know about the baby."

Emily instinctively placed her hands on her abdomen. "We are so excited, Ruth. The baby is the main reason we decided to make this trip."

Ruth poured hot water into the waiting teapot and removed china cups and saucers from the cabinet. Emily sat at the breakfast table and memories of her first visit here came rushing back.

"I remember when you prepared a full English breakfast for us and I was amazed at how much food was on my plate."

Ruth gave a hearty laugh. "Your eyes were so big when I set that plate down, I thought you might pass out. But you ate almost half of it."

"I sampled some of everything because you worked so hard on it."

"Posh, I'm used to cooking large." Ruth poured the steeped tea into the cups and set one in front of Emily. "This Earl Gray is very smooth. It has Silver Tips in it. It will warm your bones." Emily swirled in some honey and a dollop of milk, stirring until it blended. She took one sip and rolled her eyes. "You're so right, Ruth, I feel warmer already."

"Good," Ruth said firmly, "now, I want to know how you're doing and all about that baby."

Just as Emily began, Seth and Teddy shuffled into the kitchen.

"It's really pouring down out there," Seth said, running his hands through his hair.

"Would you like a cuppa or do you prefer coffee?" Ruth asked.

"Coffee if it's made."

Teddy was already pouring their mocha-colored brew into mugs. "We can go in the study, Seth, and let the women have some time together."

Seth took the mug Teddy offered and kissed Emily's cheek before disappearing through the doorway.

Emily chuckled and took another drink of her tea. "Ruth, I think I want to move back here permanently."

Ruth's eyes grew large, and then her face blossomed into a huge smile.

"That would be lovely, my dear. I cannot think of anything I would like more than to be part of raising your wee one." She stopped talking abruptly. "That's if you want me to of course."

Emily reached across the table and pressed her hand on top of Ruth's. "I would be highly disappointed if you didn't want to."

The two women were quiet for a moment.

"How soon would you move back?" Ruth asked.

"We have some thinking and planning to do. We have a lot going on in San Antonio with the bed and breakfast just opening, and there's also Seth's law practice. But, we've been praying about it, trusting that God will show us what to do and when to do it."

"You're very wise, my dear. It's really all about His timing."

"Thank you, Ruth. Now, tell me about Rusty. How is he working out?"

"Teddy has taken to him like he's his son. They get along great. He's an orphan and he struggled so much. Now that he's here, we think he's happy for the first time."

"Wonderful. He seems very polite. I noticed when we shook hands, that he had calluses. He must be a hard worker."

"You won't find many young men nowadays, who work as hard as Rusty."

"I know Teddy appreciates that quality."

"He does, and so do I. Teddy isn't getting any younger, so it's good he has someone to follow behind him."

Emily yawned. "I'm so sorry. I think jet lag is catching up with me. I'm going to take a nap. Would you let Seth know when they come back in?"

"Certainly, your room is all prepared. When you wake up I'll have a hot bowl of stew ready for you."

"Thanks, Ruth," Emily said, stifling another yawn, "You're such a blessing to me."

"I care about you and, of course, Seth, too. You go on now and take your nap."

Emily rose and headed for the stairway but met Seth just as she was going up. "Hi, Honey, did you and Teddy have some guy time?"

Seth reached his arm around his wife's waist and hugged her. "Sure did. Where are you going?"

"I nearly yawned Ruth to death so I'm gonna take a little nap."

"Good, I was going to suggest it. You looked tired." He promptly kissed the end of her nose and urged her to go.

She smiled and nodded. "I'm on my way," she said as she ascended the stairs.

Seth watched his wife until she reached the top and turned the corner, before returning to the kitchen to refill his coffee mug. *Thank You, God, for such a beautiful wife.*

***

Seth took his coffee and entered the drawing room, taking a seat on the bench in the Inglenook fireplace. He set his mug down and leaned back. Closing his eyes he listened to the crackle of the fire, thankful Teddy had started it up early. Somehow, a rainy day and a crackling fireplace go together.

He loved this house as much as Emily did and could see them living here. Soon it would no longer be just the two of them. The baby would come in the fall, and their lives would be changed dramatically. Seth knew he could work his law practice from here thanks to technology. Sure, he'd have to travel back once in a while, but his partners were equipped to handle things in Texas. He wanted the move to happen, but he couldn't shake the feeling that he was needed at the bed and breakfast. Hiring Ron's brother, Jake, to oversee the place seemed to work out. After talking with him earlier, Seth felt confident that Jake could run things — at least for the present. Somehow, Seth felt like he abandoned the project that they had worked so hard and long on. *I wonder how Mary would feel.*

Mary, having been the benefactor in leaving this manor house to Emily, was his client but more so his friend, even before they selected Emily to be her caregiver. Once the estate sale was over and the will was read, Seth felt that Mary would have been happy at how it all turned out. She bequeathed him her San Antonio home to do with as he pleased. That was the problem – he wanted to please Mary in how he handled the house. He tried selling it, but that didn't work out well, so he took it off the market and made the decision to transform it into Texas Tribute Bed & Breakfast. He wanted it to be a tribute to Mary and her legacy of generosity and love for others.

Seth took a drink of his now lukewarm coffee and stood to stretch. The house was quiet. He hoped Emily was sleeping well. He was concerned about making the long trip to Essex, but she did great. After a couple days, the jet lag should wear off and they would be able to talk about what they wanted to do. For now, Seth planned to enjoy this time away from all that was happening in Texas and help Emily do the same.

Ruth entered the room, calling Seth's name. It startled him out of his thoughts.

"Hi, Ruth, can I help with something?"

"It's Teddy, can you please come quickly? He slipped on the wet stones out back."

Seth put his mug down on the table and rushed ahead of Ruth. "Certainly, is he hurt?"

"I think so, but I'm not sure where," she said in a raspy tone. "It might be his back."

***

Annie surveyed her new apartment. Boxes stacked everywhere and piles of clothes draped over furniture. It would take weeks to get unpacked and organized. She had rented a U-Haul and asked a couple friends to help load everything. They followed her to San Antonio and helped lug everything upstairs. She couldn't have done it without them.

Annie decided what she needed was food and there was no way she was equipped to cook. Actually, there was no food in the fridge and the few canned things she brought wouldn't qualify as a meal. She opened the app on her phone and ordered sweet and sour chicken plus a couple eggrolls. Now she had thirty minutes to wait for delivery. Annie would start work in two days, so a lot would have to get done to be able to live here. Finding bed linens, clothes for work, makeup, and toiletries was priority. The rest could wait until she had a day off.

Annie wondered how Jake was doing in his new job at the bed & breakfast. He lucked out by being able to move into the place without having to search for an apartment, at least for now. She wanted to call him but he would be super busy right now. I'll call him tomorrow. She leaned back on the sofa and closed her eyes. She was so tired. Annie hoped she made the right decision in taking this new job and moving to San Antonio. It would be a new chapter in her life. She wondered if it included Jake. Did he want to be included? Annie tried to picture her future with Jake and for some reason, she just couldn't see what that would look like. Maybe it was because she was older than him? It could just be that she was used to living by herself.

The doorbell jolted Annie awake. She must have dozed off. She jumped up and looked through the peephole, then opened the door to receive her Chinese food. "Ooooh, this smells delicious," she told the young Asian man, "Thank you." She slipped him an additional tip above what was charged on her app. "Have a blessed day," she said. He thanked her and headed downstairs. Annie inhaled the aroma from the sweet and sour chicken as she set everything on the table. She quickly removed a bottle of water from her fridge and sat down, bowing her head.

"Lord, thank You, for all You've provided, including this apartment and new job. Help me adjust to the changes. Bless this food and the young man who delivered it. Amen."

She bit into one egg roll and the crispy crunch was delicious. *"Mmmmm, good! Thank You again, Lord,"* she added, *"today I am truly blessed."*

***

Sheila held Mary Dee on her lap and watched her husband put finishing touches on the last wall to be painted. She couldn't believe that very soon this cottage would become David's Legacy, a place for grieving mothers to transform fabric into a beautiful legacy of the child they lost. The quilt Sheila and Lane received from the hospital staff after their son, David, passed away would hang in the main quilting room. She wanted others to see the beauty and comfort it provided for her.

"Me down, me pway," Mary Dee insisted, squirming off her mother's lap.

"Okay, Sweetie," Sheila agreed, "Daddy's almost done so let's get ready and we'll have lunch."

"Me pway pwuzzle," Mary Dee hollered as she ran to the play area.

"You can play for a few minutes and then we're going to get some lunch," Sheila said, knowing her daughter's love of puzzles and how difficult it would be to pull her away from the large cardboard pieces.

Lane came out of the quilt room, paint on his forehead and light blue streaks in his hair.

"What's the commotion out here?" he asked.

Sheila laughed. "Only the usual persistence of your daughter's will when it comes to puzzles."

Lane glanced over to the play area filled with books, toys, and puzzles. "I should have known. Oh, well, let her play. Come look at the walls and give me your approval, please."

Sheila followed Lane into the quilting room and admired his painting skills. "I'm glad we went with the more delicate blue you suggested. It feels calm in here. You did a great job, Lane." She slipped her arm around his elbow, snuggling close. "Have you heard from the sign company yet on when they'll be delivering our sign for the cottage?"

"The other day they said it should be ready Monday."

"Good. Are you planning to come back here then, or do you have clients to meet?"

"I think I'm clear, but if I have any meetings set, maybe you could be here and then I'll join you when I'm done."

Suddenly Sheila felt a tug on her leg. Looking down, she spied Mary Dee.

"Me hungwy."

Lane scooped her up. "I'm hungry too, Princess, we're all ready to go eat."

Sheila smiled. "I'm hungry for barbeque. Let's go to Bill Millers."

"That sounds good to me, how about you, Mary Dee?"

"Me good too!" she responded with an affirmative nod for emphasis.

Lane handed his daughter off to Sheila. "Let me put the brush and roller away, wash my hands, and we'll be on our way."

"Come on, Mary Dee, Mommy will check your diaper before we go eat."

Mary Dee clapped her small hands. "Go eat!"

***

Leila loved seeing the diner crowded. Today customers came in and out most all day except for a slight lull about three o'clock. Last week, Leila couldn't believe that Tim became so excited about the new recipes for the menu. He was astounded that she had prepared both so he could sample them. He especially enjoyed her Chili Willy's Chili, of which he ate two bowls. She had made enough to provide samples that evening for the customers. They all gave it a ten. The So-So Salsa Salmon was a hit too. Leila had worked hard at her computer to create a new menu and had then printed out a master so she could have professional ones made. She had added some artwork to the menu just for fun. They were all set for the new lineup as soon as they menus arrived.

Leila noticed the couple at a booth near the door was finished with their meal. They had been very cordial to her. The man looked much older than his dining companion. She scurried over so they wouldn't have to wait to check out.

"If y'all are finished, I can clear these dishes so they'll be out of your way."

"Thanks," the gentleman said. "Would you bring us a cup of coffee when you return with the ticket?"

"Certainly, I just made a fresh pot."

"I can smell the wonderful aroma from here," the young woman said.

Leila laughed. "I'll be right back."

When she returned with their coffees and sales ticket, the two seemed to be in an intimate conversation. Leila hesitated a moment before approaching the booth, until the man looked up and they stopped talking.

"I'm sorry," Leila said, "I didn't mean to interrupt."

"You're fine," he replied, "thank you for the fresh coffee."

Leila placed the ticket on the table and started to leave.

"Ma'am," the gentleman said, "may I say something?"

Leila turned back to the couple. "Certainly, is there anything wrong?"

"No, not at all. We just wanted you to know how much we appreciated the service you gave us today. You're an outstanding server and we wanted to tell you face to face."

If Leila didn't know better she thought she was blushing; something she never did. No one had ever complimented her spontaneously like that. "Thank you," she told them both, "you have made my day. I hope you'll be regular diners here. I've enjoyed serving you."

She held her head a bit higher as she made her way back to the kitchen. *What a sweet gesture that was. There are some nice people around.*

Later, after the couple left, Leila went to remove the coffee cups from the booth and under the ticket she was startled to find a note on top of a hundred-dollar bill along with the exact amount for their meal. The note said simply, *be blessed.*

Leila felt tears on her cheeks. *Lord, thank you for this blessing, and please shower that couple with their own personal blessings.* She tucked the bill into her pocket and finished clearing the table. She didn't understand what just happened, but then, she didn't understand a lot of things God did. Truthfully, all she needed was to accept it.

Chapter 19

Greta put the finishing touches on her painting, then stood back and critiqued it. She normally created two paintings of the same lighthouse, one showing it in great need of repair, allowing the observer to see the structure at its worst. The companion painting captured the restoration and showed the lighthouse in shining glory. Greta wanted people to see how God restores His creations, giving them new life after their suffering great devastation.

This lighthouse painting of the Brant Point Light Station depicted on her canvas was almost 3D when the light cast from the side. She had decided to do graduated lines; each piece of the lighthouse rose above the first until she had eight small lighthouses in various stages of repair. The ninth was a completed final rendition. What made this painting stand out, at least in her opinion, was how she managed to sketch in bits and pieces of her life among the brokenness of the first eight drawings and her renewed life in Christ around the last structure.

Losing her parents, being alone, searching for something, self-pity, and so much more swirled around the canvas from the bottom to the middle of the lighthouse. Then, the angels appear, almost iridescent. Happiness glimmered as a beam of light shown out onto the sea. A ship on the water headed in, guided by the light. Clarence was in the ship, coming into her life. The brief time she had with him crashed as a wave against the rock at the water's edge.

Greta sat down, quite tired. She picked up her brush and quickly signed her painting. She titled the piece simply, *My Life*. She picked up her supplies, putting them neatly away, and then turned her easel toward the wall. Greta changed into her nightgown and slipped between the sheets. Smiling, she thought of Clarence. *Goodnight my love. I'll see you soon.*

***

Betty hung up her phone and buried her face in her hands. Her sobs brought Brian swiftly to her side.

"What's wrong?" he asked in a worried voice as he wrapped his arms around his wife.

"It's Greta," she managed to choke out, "she's gone."

"Gone where? Y'all just got back."

Betty turned and put her face against Brian's chest. "Kenneth just called and said that Greta passed away." More sobs erupted and Brian choked back tears.

"I'm so sorry, Honey. I know you were close to her. We all grew to love her as our own. How and when did it happen, did Ken say?"

"They checked on her when she didn't come for breakfast this morning and found her in her bed." Betty moved to sit at the table and reached for a tissue. Drying her eyes, she continued. "He said she died peacefully with a smile on her face."

Brian went to the sink and started a kettle to make Betty some tea. "I think she wanted to be with Clarence. She really missed him, but it was like she had to complete the task God wanted her to do."

"Kenneth asked us to come by. There is something he wants to show us."

"Did he say what?"

"No, only that it was something he found in Greta's room, along with an envelope with my name on it."

"Do you want to go now?"

"Let's have tea first so I can collect myself."

"Good idea. We should call Kat and let her know, she may want to go along."

Betty rose and walked toward the phone. "You're right. I'll see if I can get ahold of her."

The kettle whistled and Brian busied himself preparing their tea while Betty called Kat. He hated Kat's having to hear it over the phone.

As he poured the boiling water over the tea, he thought about Betty's words, "Ken wanted to show them something he found." *What could he have discovered that would concern him and Betty?*

***

April fool's Day didn't fool around with the weather. It rained three days in a row, and Rita was getting concerned that it would reappear on her wedding day. Ron assured her he made alternate plans just in case, but Rita had her heart set on being married outdoors on Marrying Island down on the San Antonio Riverwalk. Two weeks from now she would become Mrs. Ron Davis. She felt so blessed to have a man like Ron. They were certainly made for each other. Rita's past was filled with loneliness and abandonment, something Ron assured her she would not experience with him. She believed him too.

Rita sat in the breakfast nook in the house the two of them would share in a couple weeks and watched the rain drops bounce on the small patio. The concrete slab suddenly reminded her of the day she walked home from school when she was seventeen only to discover the trailer she and her family lived in was gone, leaving a bare slab. Her parents had abandoned her, taking Rita's older sister and moving. A note had been attached to her bag of belongings and said they didn't want her. A tear slid down her cheek, and she quickly brushed it away. Rita sipped her cup of tea and remembered that God had watched over her through the years and now she would soon marry the man God chose for her — a man who would never abandon her.

The doorbell rang, and Rita left her thoughts in the breakfast nook as she went to answer the door. When she peeked through the peephole she smiled, seeing Ron making a silly face. She flung open the door and all but threw herself into his arms.

"I'm so glad to see you," she said.

"I saw you just last night," he teased, "but I'm happy you're so excited I'm here."

She clung a little tighter to him.

"What's up, is something wrong?" he asked, holding her away a bit so he could look into her eyes. "Have you been crying?"

She patted her eyes and shook her head. "No, I'm just happy that soon we'll be married."

"You and I both," he said as they entered the house and closed the door.

Rita took his hand and led him to the kitchen. "Coffee?" she asked.

"That sounds perfect. I hope the rain stops soon. I need to go back to Blue Star and check on the preparations for the art show this weekend. Do you want to ride with me?"

"Yes!"

Ron was a little puzzled at her responses. She seemed melancholy or something. He hoped she wasn't having wedding day jitters or anything.

Rita handed him a mug of coffee, and they went to the breakfast nook. As they sat at the oak table she looked out again at the patio.

"I'd like to do something different with the patio," she said.

"Like what?

"I'm not sure, but it looks bare. We could put a glider and plants, or fire pit. I'd like some wind chimes, too."

"Wow, you want to fill it up."

"I don't want it to look empty or barren."

"When we get back from our honeymoon you can fill it however you want," he said, leaning over to kiss his soon-to-be bride.

Rita's heart was full and she knew she was right where God intended her to be. She looked at Ron's face and saw love. She decided right then and there that the legacy her parents left would never be carried on in her life. If and when she and Ron had children, they would know they were loved, and they would always feel wanted.

"What are these tears for?" Ron asked, smearing them away with his thumbs.

"A legacy of truth and happiness," she whispered.

***

"Ro! Hijo mio, te he echado de menos," Rosie blurted out when her son broke through the crowd at the airport.

"Hi, Mom, I've missed you too," Roland said more quietly, looking around before being enveloped into his mother's arms.

"Ro, this is my friend, Blanca Moreno," Rosie said, releasing her son from the hug she held him in. "She has been such a blessing to me."

"How do you do, Mrs. Moreno, It's a pleasure meeting you," he said, reaching out his hand.

Rather than shake, Blanca grasped it and pulled him in for a quick hug. "This is Texas, Roland, and I'm a hugger." She noticed that he stiffened a little at first, but she saw a bit of a smile when she stood away from him.

"Let's go get your baggage, Ro," Rosie suggested.

"I have it right here," he indicated, nodding down at the one suitcase and then he patted the backpack slung over his shoulder.

"Wow, you travel light!" Blanca said, laughing.

They began trekking down the corridor toward the exit when Rosie spoke softly. "I'm sorry Monica didn't want to come."

"It's okay, she said she would probably feel out of place. I think she was right. We needed a little break from each other anyway."

Outside, they crossed the traffic dropping off people and made their way to the short-term parking. Blanca clicked her key fob when they approached her car. "Are you sure you won't stay with us, Roland?

"I made a reservation at a hotel not too far from your address, so I'll be fine. Thanks for offering though."

"You're most welcome but if you change your mind, the rollaway is still available. My daughter, Bree will be driving in from Mexico day after tomorrow. She'll bunk with me so we have room."

"I'll keep that in mind," Ro said, placing his suitcase into the trunk. "I look forward to meeting her."

They all settled into the car and Blanca started the engine. "I know you must be tired from your flight. Your mother and I prepared a good meal, so we thought we'd all go to our place, eat, relax and then, if you still want to go to the hotel, we'll drop you off. You could stay overnight with us and check in tomorrow."

"I'm really bushed. I appreciate the invitation but I'd like to go to the hotel tonight if you don't mind. I'm going to get a rental car tomorrow so I can get around."

Rosie gave Blanca a side glance and noticed a look of concern on her face. Maybe he just needs some alone time.

"Marriott Hotel," Blanca teased to lighten the moment, "coming right up!"

***

"Welcome to the Texas Tribute Bed & Breakfast, Ms. Witte," Jake greeted the young woman at the desk. He handed her driver's license back to her along with her credit card.

"Thank you," Sarah said, smiling as she gazed around the lobby. "I'm looking forward to a fun weekend in San Antonio. I'll be attending San Antonio College in the fall and wanted to get to know the city a bit before then."

"We're happy to have you here during our grand opening. If you need anything, please don't hesitate to let me or my assistant, Becky, know. We want your stay to be a great experience." He turned to Becky, who was checking in another guest. "Becky, I'll be showing Ms. Witte to her room, and I'll be right back."

Becky nodded and smiled, then continued getting the couple checked in.

"When I registered online I had difficulty deciding which room to reserve. I loved all the photos, and the names were so interesting."

"I think you'll enjoy the Rustic Romantic, and the story of the name. The person it's named for is actually getting married next weekend."

"Really? That's so exciting."

"Yes," Jake answered. "There's a story card in the room for you to read."

They approached the room and Jake opened the door, then handed Sarah the key. "Here we are," he said, "The Rustic Romantic. Please make yourself at home, and if you need anything, just call the desk. Breakfast is served in the dining room at nine, but coffee, juice, and sweet rolls are available at the coffee bar at six, in case you are an early bird."

"Thank you," Sarah said, looking around the room. "This is lovely." She spotted a photograph on the dresser. "Is that the lady the room is named for?"

Jake nodded. "Yes, her name is Rita."

Sarah handed a folded bill to Jake as she thanked him once again.

Jake looked surprised at receiving a tip. In all his years in the hotel management business, he had never received one. "Ma'am, this isn't necessary," he stuttered slightly.

"Please accept it," she insisted.

Jake tucked the bill into his pocket and eased himself toward the door. "Thank you, and I hope your time with us is all you hope it to be."

Sarah smiled. "I know it will be."

***

Jared scrubbed the grease off his hands and dried them on the shop towel next to the sink. He enjoyed working in his half-brother's auto repair shop, but he hated getting greasy. He always tried to keep the muck from getting under his nails. He glanced at his now dry hands and spotted the tarry gunk at the edge of his thumbnails. Mumbling under his breath as he headed to the house, he looked forward to the fall, when he would start back to college.

He opened the door and heard his phone. He used a still-smudged thumb to press the talk button. "Hi, Sweetie," he answered in a better tone than his previous mumbling, "What's going on?"

"I just wanted to hear your voice," Sarah said.

He could see her smiling in his mind. Her voice even smiled. "Well, you've heard it. I hope it's all you imagined," he teased.

She laughed. "Are you done working for the day?"

"Matter of fact, I am. I just came in from the shop, and I was trying to decide if I would have my thumbnails removed or find a different job."

"More grease?" she asked.

"You know me well. How are you doing at the nursery?"

"Very good. I'm actually off for the weekend and I am currently checked into the new Texas Tribute Bed & Breakfast here in San Antonio."

"What? Really? You're in town? All weekend?"

Sarah started laughing as she assured him she was. "I figured since I'll be starting college here in the fall, I'd play tourist. I reserved a room here, and I'm hoping that you and I could find something to do this weekend."

Jared's spirits exploded. "Wow, what a surprise. I can find plenty for us to do. Give me time to clean up and change clothes, then I'll pick you up. How about dinner?"

"Dinner sounds great. The bed & breakfast serves only breakfast and lunch, so that works perfectly. Make sure those thumbs are clean," she teased.

Jared smiled. "As a whistle! I'll pick you up about five?"

"I'll be ready. Do you know where this place is?"

"Sure do, it's in the King William District. See you soon"

***

Blanca couldn't believe how her daughter had changed since she last saw her. Bree had been in Mexico heading up a missionary team, providing a school in one of the villages. Bree left as a young college graduate and returned a young woman. She had confidence, compassion, and a hunger for the Lord that wasn't there when she left. Blanca was so proud of the woman Bree had turned into. Watching her now as she stirred the soup on the stove, Blanca thanked God for her.

"I'm happy that you made it home for Rita and Ron's wedding. She will be thrilled to see you."

"I'm thrilled too, Mama, but I didn't come just for the wedding. I've missed you a lot and couldn't wait to see you. After the wedding, I want us to talk about some things."

Blanca's eyes widened a bit. "Is something wrong Mija?"

Bree set the spoon on the counter and came to sit opposite her mom at the table. "No, nothing's wrong. I just want us to talk about the future. Mine and yours."

"Are you thinking of not going back to Mexico?"

"Let's not discuss it now. I have several options, or maybe I should say I want to look at other options. I enjoy what I'm doing but it may not be what God wants me to be doing forever. I miss my home. I miss you."

Blanca looked into her daughter's eyes and they weren't as bright as she remembered. She reached out and clasped Bree's hand. "I've missed you, too. After the wedding we will sit down together and talk about our future." She noticed a tear slide down Bree's cheek.

***

Seth loved sitting across from his wife next to the Inglenook fireplace. The crackling fire set the mood for the evening, and enjoying tea and biscuits together made it perfect. Well, Emily had her Earl Gray tea, while Seth preferred coffee. She sat quietly, watching the flames lick the grate and seemed lost in thought.

"What is going around in that pretty head of yours," Seth whispered, almost afraid to disturb the unspoken thoughts she had whirling about.

Emily smiled. "Imagining our life after the baby comes, and hoping we never stop having moments like this," she said softly.

Whatever Seth thought she might be thinking about, that was not part of it. "We'll always make time for us, my dear," he said quickly. "Don't think our baby will change that part of our life. Our little one will bring us even closer, because we will both be present in his or her life."

Emily relaxed and leaned back against the bench. "I know, but are we prepared for what raising a child requires?"

Laughing, Seth rose from his side of the table and came to sit next to Emily, placing his arm around her shoulder. "Honey, I doubt whether any parent is fully prepared for raising their first child. I think its called OJT, On-the-Job Training. If we choose to stay here at Summer Bride, we'll have Ruth to help out and give us some good English training. If we choose to return to Texas, we have friends to help us learn. But more than anything, we have the Lord to guide us." He pointed to his Bible sitting on the table by his leather chair. "That's our parent's guidebook, and with that, we have the best manual around."

"You're right," Emily agreed, resting her head against his chest. "I think I want to stay here," she added. "Would you mind terribly?"

"Not at all, I love this place. I can still handle my practice long distance with a couple trips back annually. If that's what you want, then that's what we'll do. I'll take care of what needs to be done with the bed and breakfast and set up a meeting with my associates at the office."

Emily hugged her husband. "I think we should return for Rita and Ron's wedding though."

"I think so too, as long as you're up to traveling."

"I'm fine. That way we can break the news to our friends together."

"I'll make arrangements and let them know we'll be there," he said, kissing the tip of her nose. "I love you."

***

Rosie and Roland sat opposite Blanca and her daughter, Bree, in the booth at IHOP. Blanca suggested they have supper there instead of cooking at home.

The server picked up the menus after taking their orders, promising coffee and juice would be brought to the table soon.

"Okay, that was quick," Blanca said in a low voice," with so many people here, I expected a longer wait time."

"You're right," Rosie agreed, "and after the meals we cooked at the bed and breakfast today, neither of us feel like cooking. Hope you kids don't mind eating out."

"Mom," Roland said a little too stern, "we're not kids, and I for one am used to eating out so this is fine."

A hush fell among the group before Bree spoke. "I ordered breakfast for supper. I'm used to eating in a small village where you don't have French toast with cream cheese and strawberries."

They all looked at Bree, and laughter broke out between the mothers, and even Roland had a grin on his face.

"I'm sorry," Roland offered, looking at his mom. "I've just been edgy since, well, you know." He didn't want to mention Monica's name, especially with Bree sitting there. She didn't need to know about his relationship problems.

"No Mijo," it's okay. Let's enjoy ourselves and laugh," Rosie said, hugging her son.

Roland smiled back at his mother, then at Bree. "Maybe I should have ordered breakfast too".

Both mothers looked at each other and silently exhaled just as the server brought their beverages and tableware.

"It won't be long," the young man explained, "we have an extra cook today. If you need anything else just let me know."

Blanca suggested they all see a movie after their meal, but no one seconded the motion.

Bree bounced her idea into the discussion. "We have some DVDs at home, so why not go back there and choose one? I'll make popcorn and we can relax."

The server approached their table, carefully making sure each received their correct meal.

"Is there anything else I can get for you?" he asked.

They all inspected their plates.

"Looks like we're good to go," Blanca said. "Thank you."

Roland started to cut his chicken fried steak when Rosie spoke. "Let's join hands and ask God's blessing on our food."

Roland set his knife and fork down, and tilted his head, more to hide his embarrassment for not waiting than anything. He accepted Bree's hand when she reached across the table to complete the circle.

"Lord," Rosie began, "thank You for all you have provided us. Thank you for family and good health. Bless this food as well as the ones who prepared and served it. May it nurture our body that we might serve You better. Amen."

A chorus of "Amens" echoed around the table as they began their meal.

Roland silently wondered what Monica was doing but then chastised himself for even thinking of her. She certainly didn't care that she hurt him when she talked against his mother when he invited Monica to come to Texas with him. He didn't understand why he never saw the selfishness in her earlier in their relationship. She accused Rosie of trying to come between them, but now he could see it was quite the opposite. Monica always tried isolating him from Rosie. He set his fork down and took a slow drink of iced tea. He noticed Bree looking at him. He lowered his eyes and set the glass down. When he looked up Bree was looking at her mom.

"This chicken fried steak is fantastic!" Roland blurted out.

"And huge," Blanca said. "You're in Texas, what else can I say?"

Rosie bumped shoulders with Roland. "You can handle it, Mijo," she teased.

Bree looked at her French toast and then at Roland's plate. "I should've ordered it too."

Roland laughed. "I'll share if you're up to it."

<h1 style="text-align:center">Chapter 20</h1>

Brian and Betty followed the director down the hall of Mt. Laurel Assisted Living to Greta's room. Since her passing, funeral, and burial, Kenneth and his wife, Jewel, had to go through her things and make decisions. With no family left, it seemed Greta had finalized everything and put the director in charge. Kenneth had Greta's handwritten, notarized will in his pocket, but what he wanted the Hill's to see had nothing to do with the will.

They reached the room once occupied by Greta and her husband, Clarence. Since Clarence died last year, Greta used the extra space as her painting studio, rather than having to haul all her supplies to the community room.

"Here we are," Kenneth said, turning the key in the lock and gently pushing the door open.

Brian and Betty hesitated entering the room until Kenneth went first.

"I want you both to see Greta's final painting as she left it," he said, walking over to the easel which was turned toward the wall, covered with a canvas.

Betty looked at Brian and then moved closer to the painting, watching as Kenneth carefully turned the easel to face them and slowly removed the covering. Slowly she brought both hands to her mouth, and her eyes widened in disbelief at what she saw.

Brian stood frozen as he gazed upon Greta's life story painted on canvas by the only artist capable of doing it — Greta herself.

"It almost has a 3-D effect," Betty exclaimed when she was finally able to speak. "Look at the progression of rebuilding the lighthouse and bits and pieces of Greta's life intermingled. You can see her as a child, and then her mom's passing. It's sad."

Brian inspected the painting closer, pointing to the darker area with a woman's outline faded in. "It looks like rain coming down but when you focus, it looks more like tears. This must have been her lonely years."

Kenneth had moved back so the couple could get a better view. He then opened the blinds a bit more, and the light hit the right side of the painting. "Look at what the sun reveals," he said.

There where the sunlight rested was Greta with Clarence in a ship coming into her life as she stood on the rocky shore with waves crashing around her. The lighthouse beam was focused down on Clarence, guiding him in.

Brian and Betty inhaled in unison. "Breathtaking," they both said.

Kenneth removed an envelope from the side table and handed it to Betty. "This is for you."

Betty recognized the handwriting as Greta's and she had penned Betty's name on the envelope with great precision. Each letter was the same height and aligned perfectly. Betty felt her eyes watering. She managed to choke out the words, "I need to be alone to read this," before her throat closed, shutting off her ability to speak further. She turned and left the room, heading for the small chapel on the other side of the building.

Kenneth replaced the covering on the painting and closed the blinds. "I have a copy of Greta's will. She made me the executor, so I'll be taking care of things soon," he said in a whisper. "Why don't we go have coffee and wait for Betty in my office, I'm sure she'll find us okay."

Brian brushed his eyes with the back of his hand. "That'll be the first place she'll look. We really appreciate your showing us the painting, Ken."

"Greta left me a note, too," Ken said, leading the way to the hall, "and that was one thing she emphasized, for you both to be the first, after me, to see it. She said that you two were responsible for her finding Jesus and Clarence, and she loved you both so much."

The men walked quietly down the hall toward the director's office. Words weren't necessary. Brian's heart was heavy, and yet he rejoiced that Greta found peace. He was, however, concerned about Betty and how she may be dealing with whatever was in the envelope given to her from Greta.

***

Betty sat quietly in the little chapel off the hall and stared at the envelope in her lap. She carefully opened the stationary bearing her name, written in Greta's beautiful handwriting. While it wasn't calligraphy, her cursive sway on each letter showed the importance she placed on detail. Every letter was even, and the Y had a distinct curlicue that carried it in a flourish. She sighed. Betty carefully opened the envelope and removed the single sheet. *Lord, give me courage,* she prayed silently before she unfolded the paper.

My Dear Friend, Betty,

I know you are sad as you read this but please know that I am at peace and in the presence of the Lord and my beloved Clarence. While I loved knowing you and am forever grateful for all you have done for me, I knew it was time to leave. I completed what I felt God gave me to do, painting His message, and I am content in having done so.

The final painting is my legacy. It is my story of how God transforms us when we allow Him to tear down and rebuild. You helped me understand that truth. I would like you to oversee the painting. Please be sure it never gets sold. Help others discover God's truth by making the painting available for viewing wherever possible. You are creative in your documentaries so I am sure you will find a place for it.

I love you and your precious family, along with the others from the estate sale group. Don't ever stop what you're doing because people are being blessed.

Love, Greta

A tear escaped Betty's eye and rolled onto the note. She quickly blotted the paper with her sleeve to prevent the ink from smearing. She waited until it was dry before refolding and tucking the paper back into the envelope.

Betty stood, steadying herself before looking up at the stained-glass window on the side of the room. *Thank You, Lord, for bringing Greta into my life. Give her a hug from me.* She turned, head high, and walked with purpose, to find Brian. She knew what her next steps would be.

***

Leila and Tim sat at one of the corner tables in the diner, enjoying a cup of coffee. The day had been busy, requiring both of them to put in a lot of energy.

"I think your new menu additions have increased our business," Tim said, sipping his hot coffee carefully.

Leila laughed as she stirred a teaspoon of sugar around in her coffee mug. "Maybe, but people like coming here and relaxing over home-cooked meals. They love listening to your stories, too."

"My tall tales you mean."

She placed her spoon on the table and enjoyed a quick drink of the rich dark coffee she loved so much. "Do you think we need to hire extra help?"

Tim nodded. "I was thinking the same thing this afternoon as I watched you serving and busing tables. I couldn't help much because of what I was cooking and then loading the dishwasher. How about getting some part-time help to bus tables and wash dishes during peak times?"

"I'll post an ad tomorrow and we'll see what we get. We might consider getting another part-time server, too," Leila suggested.

"Great idea, we might try hiring a student needing extra money. That's how I found Sarah. When she was graduated she wasn't sure what she wanted to do, so she took a year off before thinking about college. She stayed with me several years and just recently decided to go to college."

"She interviewed me for this job. I really liked her. That's a good idea, finding someone like that. And, speaking of money . . ."

"You want another raise?" Tim said jokingly.

Leila chuckled. "I would never turn one down, but, no, it's about the tip I received."

"The hundred dollar one I'm assuming?"

"Yes. It has been on my mind, and I'd like to do something special. I'd like to start something to 'pay it forward', as the saying goes."

"What did you have in mind?"

"I remember your telling me how George Banks finds people down on their luck, as he puts it. George sends them here and tells them to ask for George's Special, and then they get the meal free. He gives you the money in advance to cover the cost."

"Yes, George loves doing that. It's his ministry, as he calls it. But we don't have many people in need of a free meal around here."

"I know, but I thought, since we are looking at hiring students in between their graduation and career decision, they need extra money. Let's face it, Tim, a part-time dishwasher and server salary doesn't pay much."

"You're right about that. It can't be helped though. Normally they don't stick around long enough, and I can't afford to pay them a big salary."

"Of course, I understand. So, I was thinking about using my big tip to start an investment fund for students who work here. I'd also put aside a small percentage of my salary each month to keep it building. Would you consider adding a percent of profits to the fund?"

Time stroked his chin as though he had a beard, as he contemplated what Leila was presenting. "This could get complicated with our CPA. It's a noble idea and I'm all for helping kids get started in life, so we need to make sure we do it right. When

I talk to him next week, I'll discuss it and see how we can do this legally."

"Great!" Leila said, standing and picking up her coffee mug. "I need to rest my brain now, so I'm heading home. I think our busy day is catching up with me."

"Set that mug down," Tim said. "You go on home, and I'll close things up here. Have a good night. Don't forget, you don't come in tomorrow until three."

Leila smiled. "I didn't forget. Thanks, Tim, and have a good night," she called over her shoulder as she retrieved her handbag and headed out the door.

Tim sat for a while, thinking. *Leila has a big heart and wants to make a difference for other people.* He sipped the last of his now-cold coffee. He was blessed to have people like her and George in his life, reminding him of the good in mankind. Too often, people only hear about the bad. He'd make sure some folks knew about the good.

***

Kat and Rita sipped their tea, sitting on the patio at Starbucks. It was a beautiful day and Rita wanted to talk with her bridesmaid about the wedding.

"I hope the weather is just like this on the fifteenth. I can't believe by next weekend I'll be married and heading off on my honeymoon to somewhere," she said excitedly.

"I know, the time has gone by so fast, and so much has happened. With Mum and my taking off with Greta on her lighthouse tour and then her passing, the memorial, and everything . . ."

"Bless your heart," Rita said, patting Kat's hand, "it's been rough. I know you thought a lot of Greta."

"I did, but she wouldn't want me moping around, so I'm focusing on being your bridesmaid and taking care of Pekoe while you're off having an awesome honeymoon. You still don't know where he's taking you?"

"No, and it's making me crazy. I don't know what kind of clothes to pack."

"Did he give you hints?"

"Not yet but he promised he would before the wedding. Like he thinks I can pack overnight," she said in a high-pitched tone.

They laughed together as they munched on the muffins they bought with their Chai tea.

"Have you spent any time with Ryan since getting back?"

Kat smiled broadly. "Yes, and we have had good conversations, too. I really care deeply about him, Rita."

"I can tell. Do you love him?"

Kat hesitated before speaking. "I think I do. I've never been in love before, so I'm not sure. Remember when I told you about how my mom explained to me as a high school junior what a real kiss was?"

Rita thought for a minute. "Vaguely. Something like it made you feel very special?"

"She said it was a light touch of the lips that makes you think you're totally special and nothing else matters. That's how I am with Ryan. I think I'm very special and nothing else matters. My mom's description of a real kiss is just like being in love."

"That's so touching, Kat. You and your mom are right. I feel that way with Ron, too."

The two women hugged, and then decided they better get down to business and go over the wedding plans.

"I love getting married on Marriage Island because the space is small and we have our guest list limited to twenty people. When we actually move onto the island, there'll just be twelve of us, and that includes the pastor."

"That's more intimate anyway. Who are the others?" Kat said.

Rita was suddenly silent. She drank some of her tea before answering. "Remember the story of my childhood and how my parents and older sister moved and left me behind?"

Kat made a pained face. "Yes, that was so sad."

"I've known for some time where my sister lives so several weeks ago I wrote to Lacy and invited her to come to my wedding."

Kat pummeled back against the bistro chair she was sitting in. "What? Wow! I never saw that coming."

Rita gave a nervous laugh. "Yes, well, I didn't tell anyone because I really never thought she would answer me, let alone accept the invitation."

"So she did and she's coming?"

Rita nodded her head. "She lives in Alaska and will be here tomorrow. She lost her husband a year ago, and her daughter lives in Arizona. I'm very nervous."

"I'm dumbfounded." A thought struck Kat. "If you would like her to be your maid of honor, I totally understand."

Rita shook her head sharply. "No! She's coming but will sit with the other guests who aren't participating in the actual ceremony on the island. We have talked several times on the phone and gone over everything, so please forget that. You're my sidekick!"

Kat searched Rita's face for any sign of regret about her asking Kat to stand with her, but she looked sincere. "Okay, I'm even more honored. So, does Ron know?"

"Yes, I told him a few days ago when Lacy sent me her travel info. He's fine with her coming. He said as long as I'm happy about it, he is too."

Kat nodded. "That's great. By the way, I love the rust-color dress we chose for me, and I can't wait to see you in your gown this afternoon. Thanks for asking me to go along for your final fitting."

"Well, don't expect a lot of foo-foo. I wanted something to go with who I am, and so my dress is fitted, and the design features artistic swirls. I think it's beautiful."

"I'm getting excited just thinking about it," Kat said, finishing her cranberry muffin.

"I'm also looking forward to meeting your sister."

Rita picked up her napkin and blotted her lips after finishing her tea. "I am, too!"

"Since I'm an only child I can't imagine what it would be like having a sibling."

"After she and my parents left I was basically an only child. It wasn't fun. But what's past is done and can't be changed, so we agreed to focus on the future. Besides, none of what happened was her fault."

"That's true and I'm sure she felt horrible knowing what your parents did, but there was nothing she could do about it."

"Nope. I'm just sorry we waited so long before contacting one another."

"You'll have plenty of time to catch up now."

"Yes, we will." Rita looked at the clock. "Oh, my, we need to go so we'll get to my fitting on time."

They cleared their small table and dumped their cups and napkins in the trash can before leaving.

Outside, they hooked elbows and walked briskly to Kat's Volkswagen. She unlocked it, and they hurriedly jumped in, as Kat loudly hummed the wedding march.

Chapter 21

Rita paced nervously, checking to see if the living room was neat and cozy, so her sister would feel like she was in a warm, loving home. The tea kettle was ready to go, and she had prepared a tray using two special teacups Kat had surprised her with as a friendship gift. Rita glanced at the clock then took the tray of cookies she baked earlier and placed it next to the tea tray. All she needed now was for Lacy to show up. She had rented a car at the airport, and Rita prayed she didn't get lost. Whatever vehicle she was in must certainly have a GPS. Another glance at the clock reassured Rita that Lacy wasn't late, but the minutes were ticking away.

Five minutes later Rita heard a car drive up, and the motor stopped. She looked in the mirror in the foyer, checking her hair; she didn't do anything fancy, she only piled it on top of her head, allowing tendrils to cascade in front of her ears. She took a deep breath as the doorbell rang, composed herself, and calmly opened the door.

The woman standing in front of Rita looked nothing like the sister she remembered. The youthful shine to her face was gone, replaced with accordion lines on her forehead and long crevices along each side of her mouth. The look on Lacy's face reflected years of worry and hardscrabble. Neither of them spoke until Rita held out her arms, inviting her sister in. Lacy walked slowly into the house, and tears gushed out. Rita hugged her tightly and repeatedly said, "Shush, shush, it's okay." When the sobs ended, they looked at each other and hugged again before moving into the living room.

"You have a lovely home, Rita," Lacy said, looking around.

"Thank you," Rita said as she poured the hot water into the teapot, "I moved in a while back, so I didn't have to lease my small apartment again. Ron will move in after we're married. Well, most of his stuff is here, but he's still in his apartment." Rita poured the steeped tea into cups and carried the tray to the living room, going back to retrieve the cookies. "I hope you like Chai tea and coconut pecan cookies."

"It looks and smells delicious."

They settled in and after small talk Lacy set her cup down. "Rita, I'm so sorry about the lost years and what Mom and Dad did. I should have stood up and refused to go with them, but Dad . . . well, you know."

"I don't blame you at all, Lacy, and I've long since forgiven both of them. Jesus forgave me for all my sins, and so I need to forgive as well. The important thing is that we are together now, and we have the future to make memories . . . good memories, together. I'm the happiest I've ever been in my life, and I want you to experience happiness, too."

"Thank you. When Cain died I floundered for a while. I had my daughter, Tammie, for comfort. I really didn't have any work experience so I didn't make much money." Lacy picked up a cookie and then set it down without tasting it. "We struggled a great deal with having enough food and paying bills."

"I'm really sorry you had to go through that. How is Tammie doing?"

"She's working for an electric company and does well for herself. She says she doesn't want to get married. I'm afraid my marriage caused some fear in her. Cain and I weren't happy for a long time."

Rita looked long at the sister she really didn't know. Her heart broke inside, knowing that Lacy suffered unhappiness. "And how are you now?"

Lacy's expression brightened. "I'm doing much better. I work for an animal rescue organization and love what I do. Mistreated animals really appreciate love and affection from people willing to be patient with them. I spend a lot of time there and work hard to find good homes for them."

"That sounds rewarding. I agree with you about being patient with animals that have been mistreated or abandoned." As soon as Rita spoke the word abandoned, she regretted it. Lacy's face moved as if struck. Rita hurriedly changed the focus. "I have a kitten named Pekoe, who adopted me, but she's at my friend's house now. Kat is going to take care of her while Ron and I are on our honeymoon."

"Awww, I'm sorry I won't get to meet her."

"We could stop by there later if you like. I told you about Kat . . . she's my maid of honor. She actually adopted a small dog that was rehomed after his humans both perished in a fire at their home. His name is Crackers."

"I would love to meet him."

Lacy looked at her sister and touched her face lovingly with one hand. "Thank you for calling me and reconnecting. We need to work on rebuilding our relationship. I wish I didn't live so far away."

"Well, Ron and I can fly up to Alaska and visit you and you can come here anytime, after the honeymoon, of course." Rita laughed as she emphasized the last part of her invitation.

"That's a promise."

***

Sheila knotted off the last stitch in the Wedding Ring quilt she had been secretly making for Rita and Ron. With all the work she and Lane had been doing at the Wimberley shop, there were moments when Sheila doubted it would be finished in time. Now, just days before the wedding she could call it done and feel proud of her accomplishment in completing a not-so-easy pattern. Thankfully she found a couple experienced quilters to help her along the way. All that was left was to wrap it.

"Is it done?" Lane asked, removing his jacket and hanging it over the dining chair.

"Yes, finally," Sheila said, sighing a bit as she stared at the jacket.

"Oops, sorry," Lane apologized, remembering his promise to hang it in the hall closet. Since they replaced their old dining room furniture, Sheila had become obsessed with keeping the room dressed for company, and that meant no jackets tossed onto the chairs. After the woman from the foster program stopped by unexpectedly last month, Sheila was adamant about keeping things in order.

"I don't mean to harp about it, but . . ."

"I know, Honey, but you need to relax more. Mary Dee is our daughter now, and just because someone from the program visits, doesn't mean they want to take her away."

Sheila stood and placed the quilt in the box she prepared to wrap it in. "Of course I know that, I just want them to know we take good care of her."

Lane walked over to his wife and put his arms around her. "You're a good mother and wife. Mary Dee will never be neglected in this family." He kissed her on the cheek and massaged her shoulders. He knew the quilting tightened her shoulder muscles. "I'm glad the quilt is done. Now you can focus on other things."

"Do you think Rita will like the quilt?" she asked, smoothing the fabric with a soft touch of her hand.

"It's beautiful, I know she will. You know, you could have given her one of the quilts you received from Mary at the estate sale. They all have high value. It would have saved you a lot of time and work."

"I could have but then it would be Mary's legacy. I want us to pass on something of David. When we decided to open the quilt shop in Wimberley, we knew we would be leaving a legacy for our son. You and I must pass on to others the comfort God gave us. That's our legacy."

"You're right. And, this is also for Mary Dee. Speaking of our little angel, will she be waking from her nap soon? I'd like to take her to the park."

"Probably, let's go check. The park sounds good; we can walk the trail for exercise."

***

Emily and Seth arrived in San Antonio close to midnight due to a flight cancellation. Emily was exhausted from waiting in the airport for over three hours at Heathrow until another plane was available. Seth wasn't happy about it, fearing it might take a toll on his wife and their unborn baby.

Seth parked the car and softly awakened Emily. She had dozed off halfway home.

"Hmmm, what?" she answered as Seth stroked her arm gently.

"We're home. Let's get you inside, and I'll tuck you into bed."

Emily rubbed her eyes and looked around, suddenly realizing she wasn't in England, cocooned in their manor house, Summer Bride. "Oh, okay. Sorry I drifted off." She sat up straight, stretching her back a bit, before exiting the passenger side and joining Seth as they entered the house.

"I'll get our bags in the morning," Seth told her. "You, my sweet, are going straight to bed."

"I'm not arguing," she said sleepily. "You are, too, right?"

"I'm tucking you in and then I'll make sure everything is locked tight. It won't take me long."

Emily couldn't prevent the huge yawn that prevented her from responding.

They reached the bedroom, and Seth helped his wife get settled into bed. He pulled the comforter up over her arms and kissed her nose. "I'll be right in." He realized she was asleep and never heard a word. Seth quietly left the room and headed to the living room, taking a seat in his recliner. He wanted a few minutes to unwind from the long, international flight and drive from the airport. His mind was whirling with what still needed to be done. They came back to attend the wedding of Ron and Rita, but he knew he needed to check on how the bed and breakfast was doing. He'd call Jake first thing in the morning. After that Seth wanted to go to the office and see how everything there was running. There were still plans to be carried out to shift some of his caseloads coming to trial and spread them out to his partners.

He stretched out his legs on the footrest, and clicked on the lamp, and picked up a pen and paper from the side table. If he and Emily are really going to relocate to Essex, England, there was a lot to do, including finding someone to manage this house. He certainly didn't want to sell it, at least not right now. Nor did he want to sell the bed and breakfast yet. Seth knew the perils of making big decisions hastily.

Seth jotted down reminders of what he would do tomorrow and then next week. The wedding was two days away, and being on the weekend, he couldn't do business anyway. He wanted Emily to enjoy the wedding and just relax for a few days. Of course, when Betty knows Emily is back, they will have to get together. Seth would use that time to take care of his business. He yawned twice and decided it was time for bed. He put the notepad and pen on the table, rose from the recliner, and checked the lock on the door. The third yawn did him in. He walked to the lamp and turned it off, then headed for the bedroom. *Tomorrow is another day.*

***

"Hello, Mr. Gardley," Jake said, "it's good to hear from you. When did you get back?"

"Late last night," Seth related, "I just wanted to see how things are going there."

"We're booked and busy. All rooms have stayed full, and the meals are great. The two lady chefs outdid themselves."

Seth smiled into the phone. "They are quite a pair and very creative. Listen, I know you're best man at the wedding tomorrow afternoon and we, along with the two chefs, will be attending as well, so I thought you might be able to meet with Emily and me on Monday about three? We'd like to discuss some business with you."

"Certainly, Mr. Gardley, I'll let Becky know that I'll be unavailable during that time. She has really become a great help, and she knows what she's doing. I couldn't ask for a better assistant."

"I'm glad to hear that. Okay, we'll come by about two-forty-five and meet in the library."

"I'll see you then," Jake said, hanging up the phone. *I wonder what business they want to discuss.* Jake remembered suggesting that if they wanted to ever sell the bed and breakfast, he would be interested. Maybe that's what they decided. Of course, there was always the possibility they decided to stay here instead of moving to England, which might mean Jake could lose his job. He doubted that scenario would happen, though, what with Mrs. Gardley expecting a baby and their wanting to move to England. He wouldn't worry about it. *God is in control!*

Tomorrow Jake would stand with his brother, as Ron took Rita to be his wife. Jake was excited for them both. He was equally excited that Annie would be attending as his guest. She made it a point to get off work from the hospital. He couldn't wait to see her.

Maybe being at a wedding would help our relationship go up a notch. Jake didn't think Annie was ready for marriage, and, truthfully, he wasn't either. At least not now. They were both starting new jobs and moved to a new city. It would take time for them to adjust and build on what they had in Mesquite. Being a Registered Nurse, Annie was overloaded since starting this new position. Jake accepted his new job knowing there was a lot involved and much to learn. Neither of them had the time to put a lot of energy into being a couple.

"Hi," Sarah Witte, said, approaching the front desk, "Can you tell me how to get to the Riverwalk from here?"

Startled by her voice, Jake shook off his own thoughts and focused on the guest in front of him. "Certainly," he said, pulling a brochure from the stand on the counter. "Here's a map that shows you exactly how to find the area you want to be in. Will you be gone all day?"

"No, my boyfriend and I want to go tomorrow afternoon so I thought I'd check out the area first. Thanks, you've been a big help. By the way, the breakfast this morning was awesome. I loved the quiche."

"Great, I'll relay the complement to our chefs. Enjoy yourself on the Riverwalk tomorrow. Oh, I just remembered, I'll be down there, too. My brother is getting married tomorrow afternoon, and I'm the best man."

"That's right, you mentioned someone named Rita was getting married, but you didn't say it was to your brother. How exciting. Maybe I'll see you there."

"It's possible because they're getting married on Marriage Island. You can read about that romantic place in the brochure."

"I will, thanks for the heads up."

Jake watched the young guest head toward the community area and take a seat. She seemed very nice. He hoped her boyfriend was the same. *San Antonio seems to be a couples' place this weekend,* he mused to himself.

He made a note about being unavailable on Monday and posted it on Becky's computer monitor, before heading to his office to check the website for upcoming reservations.

Chapter 22

"Today is my wedding day!" Rita squealed to her sister. "At six o'clock this afternoon I will become Mrs. Ron Davis!"

Lacy sat at the breakfast table sipping a cup of English Breakfast Tea. Seeing the broad smile on Rita's face made her heart pulse rapidly. She was so happy for her sister and hoped the love she had for Ron would last forever.

"I'm thrilled for you, Rita, and I'm over-the-top happy that I get to witness it."

Rita removed a cup from the cabinet and sat down across from Lacy. She poured tea from the English Rose teapot, plopped in a splash of cream, and stirred it briskly. "I didn't sleep a lot because so much was going on in my head, but I feel like I'm flying this morning." She took a sip of tea and commended Lacy on brewing it just right.

"Well, you left good instructions and I wanted you to sleep in."

"That's good. Let me drink my tea, and I'll fix us an omelet, if that sounds good to you."

"It sounds great. I'll help with whatever you need me to do."

Rita paused a second. "You were always good in the kitchen when we were kids."

"That's my only talent. Look at you, a serious sculpture artist. I was looking through the album of all your artwork. You are really good."

"Awww, thanks, I've just learned to recycle things and transform them into new pieces."

"Well, you are very good at it. Ron is lucky to have you."

"He's talented, too, and we sort of meshed together at the Blue Star. I feel blessed to have him. God knew the kind of man I needed."

Lacy's eyes dimmed a bit. "What's on the agenda for this morning?"

"We, my dear sister, are going to get a Mani and Pedi, and then at one o'clock we are having our hair done. My maid of honor, Kat, is picking us up at nine so we need to get moving."

"Oh my, I haven't done anything like that in years. Come to think of it, I've never had a Mani or Pedi."

Rita rose and placed her cup in the sink. "Then you're in for a real treat. It's my gift to you and Kat."

Lacy rinsed out both cups, setting them upside down on a tea towel on the counter. "This will be so exciting. I really like Kat and her dog, Crackers. I was amazed how well he got along with Pekoe yesterday when we visited."

"I know, I was concerned at first, but seeing them together yesterday, I won't be worried on my honeymoon."

The two sisters joined arms and headed toward the bedrooms to get ready for their spa treatments.

"When will you leave for wherever you're going?"

"Ron said we take off Monday morning. We'll spend a couple nights at the hotel on the Riverwalk and take a cab to the airport early Monday. Now, let's get hoppin' because Kat will be here in forty-five minutes."

"I'll be done in thirty!" Lacy said excitedly.

***

Ron stood in the hotel room, in front of the full-length mirror, staring intently at his reflection. He and Rita had chosen to do modified Bohemian-style wedding attire. Now, gazing at his navy blue pants and blue checkered shirt, he wondered if he pulled it off. The blue and white striped suspenders helped. Once he donned the rustic newsboy cap, he might be more believable.

In just over an hour he would be married. His face softened at the thought of Rita becoming his wife, but he was also nervous, knowing it would bring significant change to his life. He loved her beyond eternity, and yet he suddenly felt inadequate in the role of husband. Ron knew Rita's childhood trauma regarding security, and he promised her that she would never have to worry about that with him; he would never abandon her. Ron knew of course that he was a mortal and his life and death were in God's hands. How could Ron promise to never abandon her when he had no control over the number of days God planned for him? *"Please, God, allow me to keep my promise to Rita. Give me the days on earth to fulfill that promise,"* he prayed quietly.

A knock on the bedroom door brought him out of his prayer.

"Ron," his brother called out, "how are you doing in there?"

"Come on in, I'm just having a last-minute prayer."

"Not getting cold feet, are you?" Jake teased as he checked Ron's tie. "You look sharp. This is a Ron I've never seen before."

"Ha, and one you may never see again. I'm not sure about this style. I wonder what Rita's gown will look like."

"She'll be a knockout, I'm sure. I think you look great. We better get going. I checked out Marriage Island and it's all set up. Guests have started arriving so we need to get down there."

"Do you have the ring?" Ron asked.

"Of course," Jake said, patting his vest pocket, "right here."

***

"You look beautiful," Kat told Rita as they did a last-minute check of the dress Rita chose to be married in. "You should make Bohemian-style your new look all the time. It becomes you. I love the textured-lace overlay. And, ooh," she swooned, "the thick embroidery that outlines the swirls and blooms on the lace! Rita, you picked the perfect dress for you."

"Does the neckline look okay?" Rita asked with a little self-doubt in her voice.

"V-neck on you works great. Now, we need to go. Your groom and guests wait."

"Give me a second, okay? Wait in the hall. I'll be right out."

Kat gave Rita a wary look. "Are you okay?"

"I'm fine, I just need a moment."

Left alone, Rita fingered the engagement ring on her left hand. "Lord, this is forever. Help me be the wife You want me to be for Ron." Rita felt the butterflies flitter in her stomach. She took one last look in the mirror, exited the hotel room, and was escorted by Kat and Lacy to Marriage Island.

In the lobby of the Contessa Hotel, Kat whispered to Rita, "Lacy will be your Matron of Honor. I'll stand with her as your Maid of Honor."

Rita looked quickly at the two women and realized they had matching dresses. Before she could respond, Lacy handed Rita a small bouquet of Texas wildflowers to carry and kissed her softly on the cheek. "Let's go, Sis," she said, urging her out the door.

Guests applauded as the bride emerged and all heads turned in her direction. Straight ahead on the heart-shaped island stood Ron, looking elegant, and his brother, Jake. The pastor of Ron's mother's church watched silently as Rita, Lacy, and Kat began walking slowly toward them. Mariachis nearby began playing their version of the *Wedding March*, and Rita felt her eyes watering. *I can't cry now, I can't cry now.* Seth stepped forward as Rita approached the island and folded Rita's arm around his elbow. Rita was overcome with emotion. She had no father to give her away.

Standing now, in front of Pastor Todd, listening to him ask who was giving this woman to be wed, Rita heard Seth say, "I proudly do." She looked up at him and saw tears on his face. Rita tip-toed up a little, just enough to kiss his cheek, and whisper, "Thank you," and Seth returned to his seat.

Handing her small bouquet to Lacy, she turned back and Ron had moved to where Seth had stood. They locked eyes and found strength in each other's closeness.

***

Sarah and Jared sat snugly in the river barge as the vessel transported them down the San Antonio River. Sarah was awed by the beauty of the old buildings and history of this enchanting place. "Jared, this is so beautiful. I can't believe I've never been down here before."

Jared squeezed her hand. "I'm glad I'm the one introducing you to it."

They could hear mariachi music and singing further down the river.

"After we're done with the barge ride we can eat at Biga on the Banks, their food is terrific," Jared suggested.

"That sounds great. Oh, look, it's a wedding," she said, pointing to the little island ahead of the barge.

Jared stared, amazed at what he saw. There, next to the bride, stood Kat, the girl he had stalked some years ago. His jaw dropped as people in the boat began applauding the wedding party, and Kat looked directly at him. He saw recognition in her expression.

***

"Who has the ring?" Pastor Todd asked as he proceeded with the ceremony.

Jake dug into his vest pocket, retrieved the wedding ring, and handed it carefully to Ron.

Ron winked at his brother, took the ring and faced his bride. As the pastor continued, Ron slowly slid the sparkling ring onto her finger.

"Do you, Ronald Albert Davis, take Rita Elyse Crawford, to be your lawfully wedded wife, to love and to cherish, in sickness and in health, till death do you part?"

Ron smiled at Rita through pools of tears. "I do."

Pastor Todd looked at Rita who had accepted the groom's ring from Lacy and was prepared to slip it on Ron's finger. "Do you, Rita Elyse Crawford, take Ronald Albert Davis, to be your lawfully wedded husband, to love and to cherish, in sickness and in health, till death do you part?"

Rita choked back tears. "Yes, of course I do."

"Then by the power invested in me, I now pronounce you husband and wife. Ronald, you may kiss your bride."

Ron didn't need to be told. He pulled Rita close, wrapping her securely in his arms, and kissed her warmly, not wanting to let her go. When finally the guests' applauding had died down, he released his wife and together they waved to their guests as well as to the onlookers from along the Riverwalk and barges.

Pastor Todd put a hand on Ron and Rita's shoulder. "Ladies and Gentlemen, I present to you, Mr. and Mrs. Ronald Davis."

More applause erupted as the others in the wedding party came forward to shake hands and hug the bride and groom.

***

Kat stood apart after giving her congratulatory wishes to the happy couple. Her mind was wandering to what she observed in the barge that had paused next to the island during the ceremony. She recognized Jared Orlov, the one person she never thought she would see again. For a moment or two, the memory of all she went through when he was stalking her rose to the surface, causing her to be distracted during the wedding ceremony. Then, God calmed her thoughts, reminding her that she had forgiven Jared last year, after he became a Christian and came to her for forgiveness. A smile appeared on her face. *Thank You, Lord, for reminding me of Your love and mercy.*

Kat looked over to Rita and Ron and she followed them off the island. She was surprised when she caught the small bouquet of wildflowers Rita tossed in the air. Kat blushed as she made eye contact with Ryan, who was waiting for her with the other special guests.

***

The entire wedding party boarded their reserved river barge for a dinner cruise down the San Antonio River. Once settled around the table and the restaurant brought the first course, Jake rose and proposed a toast. "To the best brother a guy could ever have and to the prettiest sister-in-law in Texas. I wish you both, God's lifelong blessings as you begin your life together." Glasses clinked around the table. Jake resumed his seat next to Annie.

"That was the perfect toast," she whispered.

Ron stood and gazed at his bride. "My toast to the one and only love of my life. I will always be by your side." He raised his glass.

Rita stood and was silent at first. Finding her voice, she declared, "To the man God provided and intended to be my soul mate." She raised her glass and the couple tapped their glasses together as the guests applauded.

Once seated, the barge captain started the engine and set the group in motion.

Kat was seated next to Ryan, who leaned toward her and placed a light kiss on her cheek. "I noticed you caught the bouquet," he whispered.

She gazed over at him. "I wasn't expecting it to fly *straight at me*," she joked.

Ryan laughed. "Sometimes the unexpected is what we value the most."

Kat began eating and pondered his comment. *Ryan entered my life unexpectedly.*

***

"You're awfully quiet since we left the Riverwalk," Sarah said.

Jared couldn't shake the thought of seeing Kat tonight. *What are the odds of my running into her? She looked so pretty and happy. Thank You, God, for helping me let go of my obsession with her.*

"Earth to Jared," Sarah teased, bumping his arm as he drove them through town.

"What? Oh, I'm sorry; I was just recalling the wedding we watched from the barge. It was romantic, don't you think?"

"It was very sweet and they all looked beautiful under the lights and all dressed fancy."

"Is that the kind of wedding you want?" Jared asked.

"I haven't thought about it, but I think I want a traditional church wedding when I marry."

"Really? There's a lot to be said for small intimate weddings. They're cheaper for one thing."

"True, but my parents would be disappointed if I didn't get married in church."

Jared exited downtown and headed to the King William District where Sarah was staying at the Texas Tribute Bed and Breakfast. "So, you're checking out in the morning and heading back to Blanco?"

"Yeah, I need to rest up for work on Monday. I'm going to church with my parents at ten, so I want to leave after breakfast. I've really enjoyed our time together this weekend and I love San Antonio."

"I'm glad you came. We'll catch up with each other next week and make some plans for next month, okay?"

"Sure, maybe you can spend some time in Blanco."

Jared turned and pulled up in front of the bed and breakfast. He got out and went around helping Sarah exit the car. "Want to have coffee early before you leave?"

"Why don't you sleep in? We'll talk on the phone later."

Jared walked her to the entrance and kissed her goodnight. He started back to the car but turned around. "Sarah?"

"Yes?" she said, looking back.

Jared wasn't sure what he wanted to say. His heart felt full, yet words weren't coming to him. "Uh, be careful driving home tomorrow."

Sarah looked a bit puzzled. "I will," she said, staring at him as he got into his car and pulled away. *How strange was that? I wonder what he really wanted to say.*

***

"I am now officially Mrs. Ron Davis," Rita said, as Ron carried her over the threshold of the hotel room.

"Yes, you are," he responded as he carefully set her down. "I guess you realize that when we get back from our honeymoon, I'll be carrying you over the threshold of our home."

Rita wrapped both arms around his neck and stood on her toes to kiss her groom.

Ron held her securely, returning the passionate kiss. "MMM," he said, pulling back and swooping her up into his arms, shoving the door shut with one foot. "I love you, Mrs. Davis."

"I love you more," she whispered, looking directly into his hazel eyes.

Ron carried her to the bed and gently laid her down. "I'll be right back," he said, moving to the desk.

Rita watched as he picked up a "do not disturb" sign and placed it outside the door. Her eyes followed his steps as he removed his cap and kicked off his shoes.

"Now, where were we," he said, grinning as he approached the bed.

Chapter 23

"I can't believe you let me sleep so long," Emily scolded Seth as she followed the aroma of her favorite breakfast casserole into kitchen.

"It's only eleven," Seth chided her, slipping the oven mitt from his hand after placing the dish on the table. He pulled a chair out for her and continued. "Besides, we were up late after the wedding dinner on the barge last night. You needed your rest." He kissed the tip of her nose and then spooned some of the casserole onto her plate. "Now, eat. Our little babe needs nourishment."

Her pretend pout softened when she looked at his boyish grin. She reveled in her love for Seth. *He's such a good husband, Lord. Thank you.*

Emily tasted a bite. "Seth Gardley, this is delicious. You have outdone yourself."

"Thank you, Mrs. Gardley, now dig in."

Emily took another bite. "Mmm, bacon!"

Seth laughed. "My bacon-loving wife, I dared not leave it out. Speaking of food, the dinner last night was great. But you know what my favorite part of the evening was?"

"Tell me," Emily said in between bites.

"I enjoyed hearing what each of our group has planned for the coming months. Did you hear Blanca tell us that Bree is staying home and planning to find a teaching position where she can help medically challenged kids?"

"I did, and Blanca and Rosie will continue working at the Texas Tribute."

"Blanca has a handsome son, I think his name is Roland," Seth mentioned.

"He is, and I think he's taken a liking to Bree," she said, winking at Seth.

"I enjoyed hearing that Betty has more documentaries planned for this year. She wouldn't give details yet, but you know they will be interesting."

Emily nodded. "Yes, and I think I heard her say that the young man, Clay, who was doing the actual filming has decided to move on to other projects."

"That means she'll have to find a replacement. I'm sure God will direct her."

"I forgot the orange juice," Seth said suddenly. "Let me get you some."

"No, I have my tea, I'm fine. Sit down and enjoy your food while it's hot."

"Isn't it exciting that Sheila's quilt shop will open in June?"

Seth smiled. "I love the name she chose. David's Legacy."

"I didn't hear her tell us that. How did I miss it?"

Laughing, Seth was caught in a fib. "She didn't. Lane let it slip to me."

"At least I'm not losing my hearing," Emily said.

"I wonder if Jake and Annie will become engaged. They sure make a nice couple. He seemed to dote on her last night, don't you think, Seth?"

Seth thought for a moment. "If it's in God's plan for them, they will. By the way, I'm calling Jake tomorrow and we'll have a meeting to discuss transferring the bed and breakfast over to him."

Emily finished her meal and set the fork down. "Are you sure this is what you want? You're not having second thoughts about our moving to Essex, are you?"

"Not at all, I want us to be happy. I want you to be happy."

Standing, Emily picked up her plate and placed it in the sink. "I'll miss our friends here," she said.

"It's not like we'll never see them again. I'll have to plan a couple trips a year at least, to check in at the office. After our baby is born and a bit older, we can vacation here so he or she can see Texas and meet everyone."

"When will Rita and Ron get back? Didn't they finally reveal they were going on a vintage train ride out of Arizona?"

"Ron said two weeks," Seth said as he put his dish in the sink. "He mentioned the Grand Canyon National Park."

"They made a beautiful bride and groom, didn't they?

"Yes," but I married the most beautiful bride in the world," Seth bragged, hugging Emily.

"I've changed since then, and I don't think I'm a bride anymore," she said, patting her growing middle.

He placed his hand on her belly. "This only makes you more beautiful, and you'll always be my bride."

Special Recipes from Betty, Rita, and Blanca

Several characters would like to share their recipes with you. Betty hopes you will continue the legacy of Janie's Friendship soup which was given to her when she was going through a hard time. She is also sharing her Snowball Meatloaf Casserole, which her husband, Brian loves.

Rita is very excited to give you her recipe for the King Ranch Chicken (which has no real connection to the real King Ranch in Texas).

Blanca had this author twist her arm to give up the recipe for her Secret Hot Chocolate recipe. They all hope you will try the recipes and pass them along.

Janie's Friendship Soup

(Note: this recipe makes a huge amount on purpose, so you can share with others)

- 1 large onion, chopped
- 2-3 stalks of celery, sliced
- 2 cloves garlic, minced (jarred or granulated is fine)
- 3 carrots, sliced
- 1 link smoked sausage
- 1 ½ pounds lean ground turkey or beef
- 1 carton beef or chicken stock, plus 1 teaspoon of Better than Bullion mixed into 4 cups water
- 2 teaspoons sweet mesquite seasoning from Costco
- 1 - 28 ounce can crushed tomatoes
- 15 ounces fresh or frozen green beans
- 1 - 15-ounce package sweet frozen corn
- 1 - 15-ounce package frozen peas

Note: you could use a 15-ounce bag of mixed frozen vegetables in place of the above 3 veggies.

- 1 - 15 ounce can garbanzo beans
- 1 – 15 ounce can kidney beans
- 1 can cannellini beans (do not drain)
- 6 red potatoes scrubbed and quartered, OR 1 cup wild rice, OR pasta.

Directions:

In a large stock pot, add 1 tablespoon extra-virgin olive oil. Add the onion, celery and garlic and sauté till tender. Add carrots.

In a skillet, brown the link of smoked sausage, poking holes to let some of the fat cook out. Drain, cool and slice.

In the same pan, brown the ground turkey or beef and drain.

Add the meat to the stockpot along with the next ten ingredients. Simmer just until potatoes are tender. Do not overcook.

Note: veggies can be changed around to whatever your family (or the recipient's family) likes. Betty prays over the ingredients, that they might nourish the spirit and soul.

Galatians 6:2, 1 Corinthians 15:8

Betty's Snowball Meatloaf Casserole

Meatloaf:
- 1 pound 90% lean ground beef
- 1 cup dried breadcrumbs
- ½ cup diced yellow onion
- ½ cup milk
- 2 Tablespoons ketchup
- 1 Tablespoon Worcestershire sauce
- ¾ Teaspoon salt
- ½ Teaspoon garlic powder
- ¼ Teaspoon ground black pepper
- Topping:
- ¼ cup ketchup
- 2 Tablespoons light brown sugar
- 1 Tablespoon red wine vinegar
- Preheat oven to 350 degrees

Directions:

In a large bowl, add beef, breadcrumbs, onion, milk, egg 2 tablespoons ketchup, Worcestershire sauce, salt, garlic powder, and pepper. Mix together until well combined. Spread mixture in an 8X8 baking dish. Pat meat down to an even layer.

In a small bowl, add ¼ cup ketchup, the brown sugar, and vinegar. Stir to combine. Pour on top of meatloaf and spread into an even layer.

Bake uncovered for 55 minutes. When done, let it rest 8-10 minutes (while you prepare snowballs).

Snowballs:
- 3 cups mashed potatoes (leftover)

- ¼ cup grated Mozzarella cheese (you could use cheddar but Betty doesn't like the thought of yellow snowballs).
- 1/8 Teaspoon garlic salt
- Olive oil

Directions:

Preheat oven to 400 degrees

Coat muffin tin well with olive oil.

Mix all ingredients together.

Using an ice cream scoop, pack the potatoes tightly into the scoop to form the snowball. Drop a snowball into each muffin well.

Top each with a sprinkle of Mozzarella cheese.

Bake at 400 degrees for 30 minutes or until sides start to brown or crisp up.

Remove from oven and allow to set for at least 10 minutes before removing from pan.

Using a fork, ease them out of the muffin tin, going around the edge and then underneath and gently lift out. Place on top of prepared meatloaf.

Sprinkle with additional Mozzarella cheese and return to oven to melt cheese. Watch it carefully, it only takes a minute or so.

Remove from oven and enjoy!

Note: Betty sometimes layers one can of drained green beans under the meatloaf before baking. (Be sure to drain them well if you choose to do this).

Rita's King Ranch Chicken Casserole

- ¼ cup margarine (1 stick)
- ½ cup chopped yellow onion
- ½ cup chopped green bell pepper
- 2 cups chopped cooked chicken
- 1 (10 ¾-ounce) can cream of chicken soup, undiluted
- 1 (10 3/4)-ounce) can cream of mushroom soup, undiluted
- 1 (10-ounce can) RoTel diced tomatoes and green chiles, undrained
- 12 (6-inch) corn tortillas cut in half
- 2 cups (8-ounces) shredded cheddar cheese, divided

Directions:

Preheat oven to 375 degrees F. Spray a 13 X 9-inch baking dish with cooking spray; set aside

Melt ¼ cup margarine in a large saucepan over medium heat. Add bell pepper and onion; cook and stir about 5 minutes or till tender. Stir in both soups, undrained tomatoes and chicken.

Spread half of the tortillas in the bottom of the baking dish. Spread half the chicken mixture over the tortillas and then sprinkle with half the cheese. Repeat the layers one more time with remaining ingredients, ending with the cheese on top.

Bake uncovered 30 minutes or until hot and bubbly. Serves 6-8

Blanca's Secret Hot Chocolate Recipe

- 4 cups whole (or low-fat) milk
- 1 large cinnamon stick
- 1-1/2 tablets Mexican chocolate (found in the Hispanic foods isle or Mexican market)
- One molinillo (a wooden tool to make the chocolate frothy (or you can use a whisk).

Directions:

Pour milk into a large pot; add the cinnamon stick and the tablets of Mexican chocolate.

Warm the milk over high heat, moving constantly with the molinillo until the tablets are completely dissolved. Watch closely, it will boil quickly.

When the milk and chocolate start boiling, reduce the heat and let it simmer for 3-5 minutes. Let it cool down for 5 minutes.

Whisk until the chocolate gets frothy, and then serve.

<h1 style="text-align:center">Epilogue</h1>

"OWWWW," Emily screamed in the dark, lying beside Seth snuggled close at their manor house in Essex, England.

Seth abruptly sat up, having been sufficiently shocked from his sleep. Emily was writhing, holding her belly. "What's wrong, honey?" He pulled the covers back and found the bed was soaked.

"I think my water broke! I'm having this baby, Seth. Call Ruth to come over, hurry."

Seth scrambled from bed and phoned Ruth, to come immediately. They had decided Emily would have a natural birth at home when the time came. She wanted Ruth to be her midwife and deliver their child.

"Hurry," Seth shouted into the phone. "Her water broke and she's in pain." He hung up and ran back to check on Emily. "She's on her way. Thank God she lives on the grounds. How are you holding up?"

Emily winced, trying not to scare Seth with the pain searing through her back. "I'm handling it," she said in a breathless voice.

"Are you sure you want to do this naturally? I can call the hospital."

"We are doing this just like we planned. Go boil some water."

Seth headed for the stairs when Ruth appeared, meeting him halfway. She carried a small tapestry bag and patted Seth on the arm as she passed him.

"Teddy is in the kitchen making coffee. Go join him, boil some water and I'll holler when we need you."

Seth did as instructed but not without reservations about their plan. He secretly wished he was in a father's waiting room right now, surrounded by doctors and nurses. Not that he didn't trust Ruth; after all, she had delivered many babies throughout her life and never lost a one. It was just that this was his baby and he wanted to be sure Emily and the baby had all the advantages possible.

"Sit down, Seth," Teddy urged. "You'll just be in the way up there."

Seth busied himself putting water on to boil. "How much water does she need?" he asked, filling a quart-size pan and placing it on the stove.

It doesn't matter. That just gives you something to do," he chuckled.

Seth looked puzzled. "What?"

"I'm kidding with you. Don't worry, Ruth and your wife know what they're doing."

Teddy poured them each a cup of coffee and sat at the table. "Come, have some brew. That boy of yours will come into this world in due time."

Seth sat down. My son, Garret Gardley, will soon be here." Seth smiled and took a long drink of his coffee.

***

"This restaurant is so fancy, Ryan," Kat said, looking around at the elegant furnishings, linen tablecloths, and well-dressed servers.

"You deserve to enjoy dining out in a fancy place. I wanted tonight to be special."

Kat looked at Ryan, dressed in a chocolate brown suit that matched his eyes. She felt her heart pumping out of control. "I always feel special when I'm with you."

They had finished their steak dinner and the luscious lava brownie dessert. Ryan moved his coffee cup aside and brought out a small velvet box from his vest pocket. He set it down gently.

"Kat, we haven't known each other too long, but my heart knows love when it happens. I believe you have strong feelings for me too."

Unable to speak, Kat nodded her head. She felt tears pooling and threatening to spill, so she forced herself not to look down at the little package.

"I would feel honored if you would accept this ring," he said, opening the package to reveal an engagement ring. It was 14k gold with a double heart and diamond inlay. "I'm asking you to be my wife."

The tears spilled. She watched as Ryan removed the sparkling ring from the velvet box and held it toward her. She extended her left hand and watched as he slowly slipped it onto her finger.

"I will take that as a yes," Ryan said, smiling broadly.

"Yes, YES!" Kat finally blurted out.

Right there in the middle of the restaurant, Ryan stood and pulled Kat up and wrapped his arms around her. He looked around at the staring patrons. "She said yes!" he called out. Applause and congratulations came from all sections of the room.

Ryan placed his finger under her chin, tipped her face upward, and kissed her gently.

When their kiss ended, Kat looked at the beautiful ring on her finger and held her hand up to show everyone. Applause broke out again as they finally sat down.

The owner of Grey Moss Inn came to their table to congratulate the couple. He handed Ryan a unique gold coin.

"When you get married, come back and present this coin for a free dinner."

Ryan stared at the coin. "We haven't set a date for the wedding yet, but I assure you, we will be back after we're married. Thank you so much."

As the owner left their table, Kat grinned and decided to tease Ryan a bit. "How about next weekend, Ryan?"

He looked at Kat in surprise and his jaw fell. "Next weekend? Uh, I have to work."

Kat broke out laughing. "I'm just teasing. We need to tell our parents first."

"Your dad already knows. I'm a little old-fashion. I asked his permission to marry you, plus, I needed your ring size. How about next spring?"

"Next spring sounds perfect."

***

"Annie," Jake said as they drove toward her home, "I know we've both been preoccupied with our new career moves, but hopefully we can get back to where we were. Now that I've taken ownership of the bed and breakfast, I hired extra employees and have more free time."

"That's great, I'm glad things have worked out for you, Jake. I wish my future was lined out better."

"What's going on?"

The new position is not what I anticipated. I think I jumped into it too quickly. The hospital has had me doing more paperwork than nursing. I want to help people, not get carpel tunnel from typing all day."

"Have you thought about doing private nursing? There's a huge demand."

Annie's head spun to look at Jake, who never took his eyes off the road. "Jake!" she almost shouted. "That's a great idea. Why didn't I think of that?" Annie scooted over as much as possible and put a kiss on Jake's jaw.

"Whoa, I'm driving here," he joked. "And we have arrived," he announced as he pulled his car near the entrance to her apartment.

Annie turned her whole body to face Jake. "We make a good team, don't you think?"

"We do indeed," Jake said, leaning closer to kiss her.

***

Leila locked the diner and walked slowly to her car, keeping the umbrella steady over her head. She missed Tim especially on rainy nights when he would escort her to the car under his big maroon golf umbrella. His heart attack took him six months ago and Leila still couldn't believe he was gone. The bigger shock was when the attorney notified Leila that Tim left everything to her; the diner, his house, car, everything!

She poured herself into running the business and making it a success. Once she had time to think things through, she decided to move from her brother's house, into Tim's. It was close to the diner and the perfect size for her.

She sold Tim's car and put the money into the fund she and Tim had set up to help student employees they hired. Tim would have liked that. Leila enjoyed working in the diner and having the students work around their schedules. She loved hearing about their plans for the future and made herself available when they needed to talk. One student suggested that Leila should take college courses and work toward becoming a counselor. Leila had laughed at the thought then. Who knows, she might give it more consideration.

She folded the umbrella and tossed it in the back seat then slid behind the wheel. Maybe she would stop at the library on her way home and pick up some books about counseling. "Goodnight, Tim," she said as she pulled out of the parking lot.

***

"He's perfect, Emily," Seth whispered as they watched baby Garret sleep in the oak bed Teddy hand made for him.

Emily snuggled close to Seth. "My heart is so full right now."

"Mine too only double." He slipped his arm around his wife as they cuddled together in the recliner. "Earlier I was thinking about Mary and how she would be thrilled to know we married, have this handsome boy, and are living at Summer Bride. The legacy she left will continue on and not just with us."

"I know. I was thinking about Rita and her sister reuniting. Betty mentioned that Lacy was thinking about moving back to the states to be close to her daughter in Arizona and becoming more a part of Rita's life."

"The way things worked out, the estate sale group has grown when you count the people who came into the lives of those who attended the sale. God sure works in ways we can't possibly understand."

"That's the truth!" Emily said, hugging Seth, "That's the truth."

The End

About the Author

June Chapko, a transplanted Texan since 1958, resides in San Antonio with her husband, Nick and Shih Tzu puppy, Chai. She is a mom, grandmother and great-grandmother. She enjoys reading, quilting, and finding teacup treasures for her burgeoning collection.

She is a member of American Christian Fiction Writers and AWSA (Advanced Writers and Speakers Association). June has written several Bible studies, many devotionals, and has been published in Mature Living, Quilt World Magazines and other publications.

June has written two previous novels, The Estate Sale, published in 2018, and Legacy's Path, published in 2019.

In 2020, June co-authored a health and wellness Bible study with Joyce Ainsworth, Count it all Joy: A study in James, and a Devotional for Breast Cancer Survivors: Cancer Courage Christ, in 2021.

June is active in her church women's ministry, teaches a women's Sunday school class, and loves to speak to women's groups. June was diagnosed with stage 2 breast cancer in June of 2020, during a worldwide pandemic, and is an active member of two local breast cancer groups, Metro's Pink Warriors and Overcomers Daughters of the King of Kings.

Contact information:
Email: chapkoj@aol.com
Website/blog: junesteacuptreasures.com
Amazon: amazon.com/author/junechapko
Facebook: teatimewithjune